Coyote Music

Coyote

and other humorous tales

MUSIC

of the

Early West

Grant MacEwan

Rocky
Mountain Books

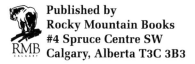 **Published by
Rocky Mountain Books
#4 Spruce Centre SW
Calgary, Alberta T3C 3B3**

The publisher wishes to acknowledge the assistance
of Alberta Culture and Multiculturalism, The Alberta
Foundation for the Arts and the Federal Department
of Communications in the publication of this book.

Fifth printing 2002.

Canadian Cataloguing in Publication Data

MacEwan, Grant, 1902-
　Coyote music, and other humorous tales
of the early West

　Includes bibliographical references.
　ISBN 0-921102-25-9 (bound). -- ISBN
0-921102-26-7 (pbk.)

　1. Canada, Western--History--Anecdotes.
2. Frontier and pioneer life--Canada,
Western--Anecdotes. I. Title.
FC3206.M24 1993　　971.2'0207　C93-091249-7
FC1060.M24 1993

cover design: Rocket Science Design Limited
Text set in Melior 10/12 with heads in Stone Sans
printed in Canada by Friesens

Contents

Oh Great Spirit, whose voice I hear in the winds and whose breath gives life to all the world, hear me.

I come before you as one of your many children. I am small and weak. I need your strength and wisdom.

Let me walk in beauty and make my eyes ever behold the red and purple sunset. Make my hands respect the things You have made, my ears sharp to hear Your voice.

Make me wise, so that I may know the things You have taught my people and the things You have hidden in every rock and leaf.

I seek strength, not to be superior to my brothers, but to fight the enemy within myself.

Make me ever ready to come to You with clean hands and straight eyes, so when life fades as a fading sunset, my spirit may come to You without shame.

— *A prayer often recited by Stoney Chief Walking Buffalo, who died the day after Christmas in 1967, and which was repeated at his funeral by Rev. John Snow.*

Foreword

When watching hockey night in Canada, I am constantly in the grip of the wish that it had a companion program, perhaps Story Night in Canada. Hopefully, it would revive the pioneer interest in making and telling stories, both factual and fictional. The storytelling pastime was at its best in rural Western Canada in the years before radio, television and motion pictures. The stage might be a farm kitchen, a livery stable waiting room or a line fence separating two farms. The performances were not always of a high order but often, where an element of competition existed, there were the marks of creativity, drama and fine speech.

Every district had its star performers and specialists. One person might be an authority on Pat and Mike or Jock and Sandy stories of the hand-me-down kind. With a good teller, these imported yarns made in Aberdeen or Dublin were popular but neither as worthy nor as challenging as the farmspun or factual ones of Canadian origin. Most of the farmspun or homespun originated in the imaginations of men milking cows or driving four-horse plow teams and were tested when their makers met at the livery stable on Saturday afternoons. Many of these stories had a barnyard quality about them but that was not necessarily a defect. Bulls, manure spreaders, constipation and colic cures might figure in a farmspun story but sexy or obscene stories and references, never.

The resource of story wealth in strange and humorous experiences was not overlooked, but poor communication in the pioneer years prevented its best use. Nevertheless, it was unfortunate that a better effort could not have been made to collect and preserve these typically western gems of humour. As it was, they were the editors of local papers who created and preserved the best stockpiles of otherwise unrecorded fun and history. They may not have been fully aware of it at the time but, in bringing the ingredients for laughter to isolated communities where they were needed, they did well. Through the bits and pieces that became columns of "Local News," the editors did better than they realized at the time to bring history and entertainment together.

It is quite obvious that people of the homestead generation, with a simple and unsophisticated fare of entertainment, laughed more than members of the present generation surrounded by radio, television, movies and endless magazines. Perhaps pioneer humour, unblemished by sexiness and obscenities and all-Canadian in content, should be receiving more encouragement today.

And in putting these pages together, I acknowledge my mounting debt to the Glenbow-Alberta Foundation Archives and Library, the *Calgary Herald*, libraries and librarians everywhere and individuals nearby who must suffer the idiosyncrasies of a writer. — GM

Chapter 1

The fur trade years

1

Coyote music

George Simpson's heart was Highland but he travelled far from his native Ross-shire and became the Hudson's Bay Company's strongman in the western fur trade.

For almost forty years he was the Company's Governor in Rupert's Land and, to keep in touch with all parts of his far-flung fur empire, he travelled incessantly in the months when the canoe routes were free of ice. His private canoe, manned by six or eight hand-picked voyageurs, was in motion for 16 to 18 hours per day, making spectators wonder how he escaped labour rebellions.

Notwithstanding constant preoccupation with duties, he liked occasional displays of top hat pomp and, having been born at Loch Broom, he came honestly by his fondness for bagpipe music. And so, when making out an annual requisition for supplies for the following year, said order to be sent to the Company's office in London, he listed the usual pots, pans, flintlock guns, rum and so on, then added: "One Highland Piper, the best obtainable."

Months later, when the York Factory brigade arrived, there were the pots and pans and rum and other things and the Highland piper, Colin Fraser, the best obtainable anywhere. From that moment on, Fraser, carrying his own precious pipes, was Simpson's personal piper, piping the Governor up and down every navigable stream in the country. He was expected to reserve his best wind for the moments when approaching within sight of a post or fort, when the canoemen would be wearing their brightest shirts and the Governor, wearing a plug hat and coattails, would be standing like a soldier at one end of the canoe.

With the canoemen making a special effort, paddling 50 strokes per minute and Fraser blowing something especially stirring, enough to excite even the coldest heart, Simpson would bow gallantly. The native people, hearing the pipes for the first time, called the strains "coyote music" but loved them and one native even offered an armful of beaver skins in exchange for the pipes.

Fraser became a familiar western figure, married a native woman and retired and died at Lac St. Anne. The pipes were passed to a son and finally reappeared in the possession of a great great-grandson at Fort Chipewyan, causing historians and museum directors much excitement. So it was until 1981, when it was announced that Colin Fraser's pipes would rest in a place of highest honour at the Alberta Provincial Museum in Edmonton, for all to see.

The missionary adored cats

It was Paul Kane, the artist, who caught the story of Reverend Robert Rundle's cat and told it in his book, *Wanderings Of An Artist.* Rundle, the first Protestant missionary in the West, was probably also the West's first owner of a domestic cat. He came from Cornwall, England, in 1840 and with the permission of the Hudson's Bay Company, made his home at Fort Edmonton for the next eight years. He was a dedicated churchman and probably without much humour. One of his frivolities was his fondness for cats, especially his own, but no domestic cats had reached Fort Edmonton at the time of Rundle's arrival.

The missionary lost no time in ordering a cat from England and, after the long voyage by way of York Factory, the animal was introduced to its new owner at Fort Edmonton.

Rundle may have been slow in making new friends, but how he loved his cat! Unhappily, there was tragedy ahead and the precious animal was killed by a dog. Rundle mourned but promptly ordered another cat from England. Cat number two was delivered in safety and was enough to warm his ecclesiastical heart.

Often, when Rundle was to make a long trip by canoe, the cat was taken along to ensure against another encounter with a dog. So it was when he had occasion to travel on church work to Fort Carlton, a 300-mile journey each way. The outward part of the expedition was without mishap. But the return to Fort Edmonton had to be made by horse and saddle and the highly impractical Rundle was put to a test. His hope was to carry the cat in a safe, warm and secure pocket made for the purpose inside his greatcoat. To guard against the chance of the cat falling out of Rundle's coat and fleeing to the nearby woods, the clergyman tied one end of a cord around the cat's neck and fastened the other end to the saddle.

John Rowand, the seasoned trader, and Paul Kane were also returning to Fort Edmonton and both offered some advice that the Reverend gentleman failed to take. Consequently, when the three men mounted for the trail, an unscheduled rodeo started. The horses, being fresh and cold and frisky, started with a jump and a fast pace, fast enough to dislodge the clergyman's cat from its cosy nest. Then, in falling, the worried cat did exactly what any falling cat would be expected. It instinctively embedded its claws in the first thing within reach, being the horse's tender skin. Rundle's horse, also reacting instinctively, bucked "high, wide and handsome," trying to shake off the source of pain. The unfortunate cat dangled from the end of the cord tied to the saddle and tried to relieve the pressure on its neck by getting a better claw-hold on the horse's skin. The bucking was renewed and the parson, not a good rider at the best of times, was tossed high and allowed to crash unprofessionally on the frozen ground.

The cat's cord came loose and the frightened thing took off as though heading back to England. It was Fort Carlton's first rodeo display and probably the first anywhere in which an English parson was the principal performer.

The cat was recovered with difficulty and Rundle was glad to accept Rowand's advice to leave it – still the only one in Rupert's Land as far as anybody knew – to be sent forward by canoe to Fort Edmonton as soon as there was opportunity. The three famous personalities, Rowand, Kane and Rundle, then resumed their plan to ride back to the big fort, happy, no doubt, to be without the encumbrance of a cat that had never learned how to ride a horse.

Rowand's bones carried 10 000 miles

John Rowand, who made his mark in the early fur trade and of whom Governor George Simpson said: "The greatest trader of them all," might well be remembered as the "Father of Edmonton." From 1823 until his death 31 years later, he ruled as "the absolute monarch of Fort Edmonton," from which the modern city sprang. Born in Montreal in 1787, the Irish Canadian lad paddled west with a North West Company canoe brigade in 1803 and was never far from the North Saskatchewan River for the next 51 years.

He was largely responsible for making Fort Edmonton the most important inland trading post and expressed his powerful personality in many ways. He liked horses and racing and constructed the first race track in the West on the river flats near the present Mayfair Golf Club. When he built his house at the fort, it was the biggest in Rupert's Land and soon known as "John Rowand's Folly." When he chose a wife, the circumstances were, most naturally, unusual. She was an Indian girl who had seen Rowand ride away to shoot a buffalo for fresh meat and, when his horse came home without him, the girl feared Rowand might have had an accident and rode out to find him.

Sure enough she found him where his horse had thrown him. His leg was broken and he was severely bruised. She succeeded in placing him on her horse and took him to her tepee where she nursed him back to health. While recovering, Rowand realized how much he needed the Indian girl and she became his wife "by the custom of the country."

Everything in Rowand's life was different, it seemed, even what happened after his death in 1854. Being responsible for the supervision of all trading posts in the area, he made a routine trip to Fort Pitt and, while there, became involved in a bitter argument, had a heart attack and died. Dead bodies were never moved far in those years and the great trader was buried right there.

The sad news reached Governor Simpson at Fort Garry who, when he had recovered from the shock, recalled a promise he had made to his old friend that, if Rowand were the first to die, Simpson would see to it that Rowand's bones were taken back to Montreal for burial, close to the late trader's birthplace. Simpson, with customary dispatch, ordered his private canoe and canoemen to proceed to Fort Pitt and have Rowand's body exhumed and the bones placed in a keg with alcoholic preservative for transportation to Montreal. A native woman was hired to make the bones ready for shipment and the canoemen were ready – not very willingly – to take the bones to Simpson. Nobody would feel comfortable travelling with human bones, least of all these highly superstitious native people. But all went well until the big canoe passed from the river to Lake Winnipeg where the danger of sudden squalls was always high.

And sure enough, the men found themselves caught in a wicked lake storm and were worried. "Why did this happen to us," they probably asked. "Who is the 'jinx' in this crew?" If they had been reading the Book of Jonah, they'd recall the similar experience of the boatmen going to Nineveh. On that occasion, the crewmen "cast lots" to identify the source of their bad luck and the "lot fell upon Jonah." They promptly threw him overboard and the storm abated. It was easy for Simpson's crewmen to believe that John Rowand's bones were the cause of their predicament so they decided that, to save themselves, they should throw the keg of bones into the lake. They did and paddled on without them.

The storm ended but at Fort Garry the men faced a different kind of storm when they told Simpson what they had done. "You fellows go right back to the lake and don't come again until you've found the keg of bones," Simpson shouted. The downcast men went back and, miraculously, they found the keg still afloat and delivered it to their boss.

But how, now, to get the bones to Montreal? The cunning Simpson knew that it would be more difficult than ever to get a crew to transport the bones. Instead of inciting more fear, Simpson placed the keg in secluded storage where it would remain until the story of the contents was forgotten. Then, more than a year later, he consigned the unmarked keg to York Factory with instruction to have it rerouted to an officer in the Hudson's Bay Company in London, England. The London office was then notified to ship the keg and its "unknown" contents to Montreal for the attention of one of Simpson's loyal friends. The instructions all along the tortuous course, totalling 10 000 miles or more, were carried out as the "old fox" had planned them and John Rowand's bones were duly buried in Montreal, precisely where and how the great trader had wanted them to come to rest.

Pig war on San Juan

It was a war of bluff and bluster more than pigs and bloodshed, although the issue was real enough. It was a question of the exact position of the Canada-United States boundary in relation to the small and unimportant Island of San Juan, situated in the coastal waters between the city of Victoria and the mainland.

Boundary disputes, throughout history, have been one major reason for wars. Canada's 4000 miles on its southern front and more than another thousand on its Alaska side – all shared with the United States – didn't escape a moderate degree of misunderstanding and trouble, including one war and a few near wars. It took 59 years after the Treaty of Paris in 1783 to gain official acceptance for the first part or eastern end of our International Boundary. Even then, neither side was entirely happy with it.

Not until 1846 was there a very serious effort to draw official geographical limits for the far western part. It was only then agreed that the

International Border would follow the 49th parallel westward across the mountains to the Pacific coast, then bend southward to leave all of Vancouver Island in British territory. In the case of the small island of San Juan, the line would stay with the main channel around it. But it was soon argued that the island had a main channel on each of two sides and San Juan's ownership remained in doubt. Some people contended, philosophically, that it didn't matter because the small island had no value and no future.

Gradually, however, the island attracted settlers, some from British North America and some from the United States. The developing situation was sure to invite a first class international argument about ownership. To hasten the crisis, an American citizen, Lyman Carter, liked gardening and growing potatoes while his neighbour, a red-haired Irishman employed by the Hudson's Bay Company, kept pigs and had one that was particularly fond of potatoes. When the pig became addicted to the neighbour's potatoes, the gardener warned the Irishman to keep his pig at home or face the consequences.

The Irishman replied that San Juan was a free country and no American was entitled to order the restriction of either a perfectly respectable pig or its owner. Next day, the pig returned to the potato patch and the irate American loaded his flintlock and killed it.

The Irishman, doubtlessly in a proper mood to start a war, reported the despicable deed to his Hudson's Bay Company bosses at Victoria and they passed the protest to the local governor. In consequence, a British warship that happened to be at Victoria harbour at the time was ordered to sail to San Juan. When the warship was dropping anchor at the island, the Americans were landing 60 soldiers. An American officer said the soldiers were brought to the island to furnish "protection against northern Indians," but most observers, both British and Americans, knew there was a better reason for the American military presence.

The stage seemed set for war. But, fortunately, nobody pulled a trigger and the very appearance of military strength on opposite sides of the island served like a warning and exerted a restraining influence. By good fortune, both the British and American commanders were sensible and cautious individuals and may have conferred and agreed upon the folly of allowing sparks from the loss of a pig and a few potatoes to blaze into a full-scale war.

For want of a better way of ending the dispute, British and American authorities agreed to refer the entire island issue to Emperor Wilhelm of Germany who had agreed to mediate.

More time was lost but, in 1872, the Emperor reported, giving judgement in favour of the United States, and San Juan became American.

In 1972, exactly 100 years later, island residents marked the anniversary by officially opening the San Juan National Historic Park, which many people in both Canada and United States insisted upon calling "The Pig War Park."

The raft baby of the Peace

Any region that can lay claim to a Twelve-foot-Davis, a Baldy Red, a Peace River Jim, a Ma Brainard and an Emperor of the Peace, can be expected to possess many treasures in local history and an impressive stockpile of frontier tales. One of the strangest stories in the repertoire of Canadian lore concerns the Peace River raft baby that was born to family tragedy in the early 1870s of the last century, a story given to Canadian readers by Reverend Albert Campbell Garrioch in his book, *A Hatchet Mark In Duplicate.*[1]

Garrioch, an Anglican clergyman, born at Kildonan in 1848, went as a missionary-teacher to Fort Vermilion in 1877 and was captivated by what he heard of a chance discovery of a raft with a half-starved baby as sole occupant being swept down river. His research over some years led to one of the most amazing of Canadian stories. It has since been told by other writers with variations but no other has backed his writing with so much investigation.

The story began with Edward Armson, an Englishman whose wife died in England. After placing his only son, then two years old, with his deceased wife's sister, he came to Canada and on to Peace River where he married a native girl – half Blackfoot. Together they tried panning gold on the river and in the autumn of 1871, he wrote to an American friend, Ernest Vining, a real estate dealer, reporting that he and his wife would be paddling down river in their dugout canoe, hoping to find a good location for trapping on the south side of the river.

A few years passed and Parson Garrioch was travelling east on furlough. On a stage coach rolling toward St. Paul, he met Ernest Vining and wife and daughter of ten or eleven years. The company proved most congenial and the American told Garrioch his attractive daughter with black eyes and a dark complexion was an adoption and he and Mrs. Vining were very proud of her. They had obtained the girl from an Edmonton fur trader, a Mr. Nelson, who got her from a band of northern

Indians. It was when the trader's wife died that he found it necessary to part with the girl. She had made the otherwise childless Vining home a very happy one.

When returning from the East in the next year, the clergyman hired a native guide, Jean by name. He had worked for years on the Peace River and, as Garrioch discovered to his satisfaction, it was he who had spotted the raft with its baby passenger and brought it to shore, thereby rescuing it from early starvation. Garrioch wanted to hear more and Jean told him that after taking the little one from the raft, he wondered what he could do to save it; he shot a duck and boiled it, depositing a few drops of the broth on the baby's tongue. The wee one brightened slightly. He then rushed the baby to a nearby camp of Beaver Indians, hoping he'd find there a nursing mother who would be willing to feed a second baby. Sure enough, he found her and the dying orphan revived, miraculously.

The good foster mother was the first to notice and draw attention to a scar or birthmark on the baby's left foot, but it didn't matter; what she was sure about was that the baby had a good face and would become a beautiful woman. What Jean didn't know was what happened to the baby in the years following but, with the information Garrioch was getting, he was beginning to sense a relationship between the raft baby and the pretty Miss Lily. Then, another surprising link was about to be forged in the chain of evidence.

A certain Valentine James, who knew the Beaver Indians and the childless Nelsons in Edmonton and then Calgary, confirmed that, after the Nelsons obtained the raft baby and Mrs. Nelson died suddenly, her trader husband knew he would have to find another home for the girl. By good fortune, the Vinings were looking for a baby and took the orphan. But there were still segments of mystery that remained to be solved.

What happened to Edward Armson and his wife? The guide, Jean, was as anxious as anyone to find the answer because Mrs. Armson was his cousin. Garrioch challenged the pupils in his classes to help. One of them, Sizerman by name and himself a trapper, undertook to comb the bush country south of the big river and he did it well. Although about 15 years had passed, he found deadfalls that were constructed for catching animals in a remote place, then a dugout shelter upon which a huge spruce tree had fallen to completely cut off the entrance. It was indeed, the Armson's home during their last winter. Sizerman dug his way inside and the first objects to catch his eye were two human skeletons, that of Albert Armson on the bed, that of his wife beside the bed. As Sizerman was able to interpret what he saw, the baby had been born there, normal and healthy but facing death by starvation. There was a baby's rattle on the floor and a supply of moss to meet a baby's sanitary needs. It was becoming clear that Armson was the first to die, after an accidental gunshot blew his hand away and infection set in. His wife, by this time, was too weak from starvation to go in search of assistance. Her remaining hope was to save her baby and she resolved to place the child on a small raft of dead wood on the river and ask the Great Spirit to do the rest. Having done that, she returned to die beside her husband.

The centre of interest, however, was Armson's diary, wrapped and in good condition. The items confirmed the fears about the tragic end. It confirmed the little girl's birth on March 31 and recognition of the scar-like mark of a glancing axe blade on the baby's foot, exactly like the one on her mother's foot. It was the scar that Garrioch had seen when visiting the Vining home and the growing Lily got a sliver in her foot and was having Mrs. Vining remove it.

Then, on the date of May 15, Armson wrote: "I am dying – effect of accident – My first wife died in England, leaving a son now five years old. Write to legal firm of Blake and Barstow, London. Wife and baby weak from starvation. The Lord will provide."

The essentials in the story were then almost fully known. But there were still a few unknowns. Lily was informed of the discoveries and the facts of the tragedy from which she had escaped. She took it all like a person of strong character but did not deny herself the solace of tears. She continued to grow in beauty and grace and popularity and, among the good young men who were attracted to the Vining home to be in her presence, were two in particular, both English boys, Herbert Melvin and Gerald Clive, and both sterling lads. The Vining adults couldn't decide which of the two they liked more but Melvin won Lily's favour and they became engaged.

But in the meantime, an enquiry about Armson's son in England was sent by Mr. Vining from Calgary where the family was then living. The reply came with a jolt; Armson's son's surname had been changed to meet the terms of the boy's aunt's will, from Herbert Armson to Herbert Melvin and he was then in Canada. It indicated the shocking fact that the young Englishman to whom Lily planned to be married was her half-brother. Great was the dismay and great was the volume of tears but time was again the healer and, one year later, Lily Vining was married to Gerald Clive, no less an admirable person, and more time proved that both were very happy.

Twelve-foot Davis never locked his door

Call him H. F. Davis in or around Peace River where he became a legend and probably not many people would recognize the name. But call him "Twelve-foot Davis" and everybody would respond to claim him.

He wasn't 12 feet tall and he wasn't a native son but he lived long enough beside the Peace River that he had no interest in living or dying elsewhere. It was an appropriate gesture, a few years after his death at Grouard in 1900, to move his bones to the enchanting hilltop high above the town of Peace River that Davis had wanted for his last resting place. Most visitors ride to the top. Others walk and discover it as a test of stamina. In any case, every visitor should see the site, the gravestone and the view from the top.

It was the magic lure of the gold rush that drew Davis from his home in Vermont to California in 1849 and then to the Fraser River. He was more interested in the adventure than the chance of wealth but at William's Creek in the BC Interior, fortune smiled upon him. Regulations declared that no miner could hold more than 100 feet of frontage in claims. Davis had a hunch that two of the best claims exceeded the maximum and he went out at night to measure them and confirm his suspicion; the claimants were trying to hold 12 feet more than the law allowed. Davis, at once, filed on 12 feet lying between the two offending claims and took about $20 000 in gold from the strip. Hence the name, "Twelve-foot Davis."

But Davis had no wish to be rich. He couldn't read or write but he had a big heart and most of his fortune disappeared in aid to needy friends. With mining in decline, he turned to trading along Peace River, downstream from Dunvegan. His honesty and friendliness made him popular and before long he could command the loyalty of hundreds of trappers and others in the big northern trading area. There he remained for almost 40 years.

It was when returning from one of his annual trips to Edmonton with furs that he became ill at Grouard and died there. There, too, he was buried. But his friend, Jim Cornwell – "Peace River Jim" – did not forget the Davis wish to have the high point of the hill overlooking Peace River as his last resting place. The wish was carried out and the grave was given a distinctive stone cut like a poplar stump, bearing the now famous words:

Pathfinder, Pioneer, Miner and Trader,
He was Every Man's Friend
And never locked his cabin door.

Melfort's premier pioneer and storyteller

Nobody bridged the period between the fur trade and the years of land settlement with greater brilliance than Reginald Beatty, who was remembered by fellow citizens of Melfort for his interest in and support for education, hospital affairs, agriculture and horticulture. An editor at the time of Beatty's death in 1928 identified him as "Melfort's Premier Pioneer."[3] The writer might have added: "and champion storyteller."

Born at Lakefield, Ontario, in 1854, he came west as an 18 year-old and saw Fort Garry for the first time from the weather-deck of the riverboat *International*. Almost at once, he was engaged by the Hudson's Bay Company to work in the fur trade and, during the next 11 years, he served at Fort Garry, Swan River, The Pas, Grande Rapids, Cumberland House and Fort Ellice. Then, in 1883, he left the fur trade and settled on a homestead quarter section beside Stoney Creek, just a couple of miles from where the Town of Melfort would emerge. He started to farm with oxen but soon changed to horses and, to obtain seed for 1886, he drove his team and sleigh over the winter trail to Qu'Appelle – then called Troy – a round trip of over five hundred miles.

He was a popular storyteller, with many tales from his own experience. One that his friends would not forget, began with the day of his arrival at Cumberland House. It was midsummer, about 1876, and local Indians were gathered for a feast. Beatty was invited to accompany the resident fur traders and he gladly accepted the invitation. Indian dances and drum beats left no doubt about the gala nature of the occasion.

When it was time for food, Beatty was confronted by a generous helping of boiled meat. It may have been a mistake on his part but he enquired if the steaming meat was beef and was told: "No, it's dog meat." Beatty winced and instantly lost his appetite. "Thank you," he said, trying to appear grateful, "but I think I won't have any meat."

"Then," said the Indian server, "can I get you some berries?"

"Oh yes, I'd love to have some berries," Beatty answered eagerly. It was the season for saskatoon berries and the offer appeared to present a happy escape from the dog meat.

In a moment or two, the young Indian appeared with a large helping of the native fruit but, instead of whetting Beatty's appetite, the scene before his eyes forced him deeper into dilemma than ever. The berries might have been excellent but, to spoil them utterly, they were being served in a pot of a kind Beatty had seen many times but, always, in a bedroom. By this time, he was wishing he had taken the dog meat and he ate nothing.

There had to be an explanation and Beatty sought it. What he learned from the chief trader at Cumberland House was about a certain Frenchman who was living far back from Cumberland House and had been trading on behalf of the Hudson's Bay Company. When the man in question was about to get married, he requisitioned some special household supplies, including one chamber pot. The item appeared on the requisition as one-twelfth of a dozen. The Company clerk at Cumberland House, thinking to play a joke on Pierre Deschambauly, altered the order to read "one dozen." Then, to make matters worse for the unfortunate newlywed, when the order was forwarded to Fort Garry the number of pots to be delivered to Deschambauly was, by accident or a further prank, raised from one dozen to "one gross."

In due course, the cargo of 144 chamber pots was delivered to Deschambauly and he accepted them without protest. But in the next spring, when he brought his season's trade in furs to Cumberland House, he had a couple of bales of select furs which, he insisted were his personal property and had to be sold and credited to his personal account.

"But," said the factor, "you are in the service of the Company and cannot trade on your own account. You should understand that."

"You're the one who doesn't understand," the Frenchman snapped back. "I get married and order one pot and your Company send me 144 pots and have me pay for them. What am I to do with 144 pots? I tell the Indians that here is the latest kind of table dish and every Indian wants to get one and everybody offers me his best furs and I get rid of all my pots and make big profit. Now, by golly, you can't steal all these good furs from me."

According to Reginald Beatty – for whom the Village of Beatty, west of Melfort was named – the Frenchman had the last laugh.

Searching for Lemon's gold

"Goldrush fever" contracted during the California stampede of 1849 and the rush to the Fraser River a few years later, proved to be an incurable malady presenting some of the same characteristics as drug addiction, inasmuch as there was no known nostrum for relief except another gold rush.

Most of the "sufferers" believed the next rush would be to the streams of the Eastern Slopes of the Rockies. Gold panning on the North Saskatchewan River had given encouragement and, to the south on the same slopes, unscrupulous promoters had succeeded in starting a short-lived rush to

Silver City, near Banff. Some of the exciting news came from the foothills west of Fort Macleod where a cow that grazed there all her life was found, when slaughtered for beef, to have a handful of gold dust and nuggets reposing in her reticulum, which is the stomach compartment serving as the cow's natural catchbasin for heavy objects like nails, bolts and gold watches swallowed accidentally during the animal's lifetime. With luck she might have pointed the way to rich mines and shared fame with Mrs. O'Leary's cow, said to have kicked over a kerosene lantern and started the historic Chicago fire of 1871.

Continuing to excite the most interest among the Eastern Slopes hopefuls was the Lost Lemon Gold Mine legend in which two shady characters, Lemon and Blackjack, were the alleged discoverers of nuggets as big as hens' eggs.

The Lemon Mine mystery remained as tantalizing as ever for 100 years and was no nearer a solution. There were hundreds of searchers, some serious in their hope of finding the gold, some – including this writer – going for no other reason than the novelty of the adventure and the opportunity to boast: "I tramped up the Highwood and into the mountains and found so much of wild Nature that I forgot about Lemon's gold."

Lemon and Blackjack were men of no fixed abode and not likely to inspire confidence. If they had a home base at all, it was Tobacco Plains, in Montana, and at the time of the story they were returning from a summer of panning for gold on the North Saskatchewan River. Apparently, they stumbled upon the mountain gold deposit and then bedded down for the night right beside it. It was then that Lemon had the wicked thought of murdering his partner and having the secret of the fabulous riches all to himself.

As soon as Blackjack was asleep in his blankets, Lemon used his axe to commit the foul deed and then went on his way toward Montana. But, the more he thought about his crime, the more he was haunted by visions of eagles and crows picking flesh from Blackjack's bones and, by the time he arrived at Tobacco Plains, he was totally insane.

The good people at a Montana mission nursed him back to health and, when he felt like a "new man," he told about the gold and confessed to the murder. Residents at the mission then persuaded him to return to the scene of the crime and take them with him to help to bury the body. Lemon was a changed and remorseful man but proximity to the scene of murder brought a return of insanity and Lemon was lost and never saw the gold again.

Other expeditions were organized. A Montana man, McDougall by name, believed he had enough information and went on the hunt alone, never to return. A Stoney Indian was the next to go for the gold and he met death. Lafayette French, well known as a trader and rancher, obtained a map that Lemon was thought to have sketched and was travelling with confidence. His friend, Dan Riley, believed French did make a discovery but when returning to High River, he stopped for a night at Rancher George Emerson's cabin. During the night, the cabin burned to the ground and burns led to French's death.

Stoney Chief Jacob Bearspaw declared the white men should not be trusted with gold and placed a curse on the Lemon discovery. Thereafter, according to the Chief's design, nobody would be able to find the secret location of the gold and live to tell about it. He instructed his own tribesmen to stay away from the place.

The curse, however, did not end the search and Senator Dan Riley was one who believed that Lemon's gold was more than a myth. Both he and George Pocaterra made a number of trips to extend the search. Pocaterra had another theory, that the two mysterious mountain men were the ones who previously robbed a British Columbia mine or bank of $27 000 and then cached the money in a safe hiding place in the mountains before the murder.[2]

Dan Riley appeared serious about the existence of the gold but those who knew the grand old rancher and gentleman suspected that he – like some others – just used the excuse of gold for making many trips back into the hills and mountains to enjoy the magic of Nature's unspoiled wilderness.

Chapter 2

The native people

2

Paul Kane's story of an Indian binge

Paul Kane, the most famous Canadian artist during his years, was born in Ireland and remembered hard times and poverty before his family moved to Canada. Early hardship accentuated his sense of thrift and abhorrence of waste; a good scene, the makings of a good picture or a good story should not be allowed to become lost or wasted.

In 1846, with the approval of George Simpson of the Hudson's Bay Company, he joined a Company canoe brigade going west from Fort William and, in the course of the next year, he travelled and sketched extensively. The search for Indian scenes and Indian faces took him to Fort Garry, Fort Edmonton, the Pacific coast and back to Fort Edmonton where he remained for the winter. In the course of the long tour, he made about 700 sketches, many of which were later developed as paintings.

From the same cross-country journey came Kane's book, *Wanderings Of An Artist,* in which his good sense of humour became obvious. Included was Kane's account of an incident that occurred on the North Saskatchewan River in the previous winter or spring. An inward bound dog sled with its load of freight broke through the river ice and the dogs, sled and freight, including a keg of whisky, were carried under the ice and lost.

No attempt was made to recover the lost articles but a band of Indians fishing and bathing in the summer following came upon the keg and carried it to shore, not knowing what it contained. They quickly convinced themselves, however, that it was fire-water and began to consume it. They were about to have a hilarious time when the Chief intervened and warned that he suspected a white man's plot to poison the tribesmen. He ordered a halt to the drinking until the beverage was tested by the old women of the band. Reluctantly, the men withdrew and the older women, eight of them, were glad to perform the test and fell gleefully upon the booze.

The old ladies became ecstatically happy with no visible ill effects. Again the Chief intervened. Satisfied it was good stuff, he ordered that it was too good to be wasted on the old ladies and they were to have no more. They got no more. From that moment, when the white men were absolved of all suspicion of guilt in poisoning the keg of whisky, the party was for men only and the Hudson's Bay Company was forgiven for all the sins the native people had counted against it.

Maski-Pitoon pointed the way to Indian peace

Buffalo country, in which the native tribes were constantly at war, seemed like the most unlikely place in the world to find a dedicated man of peace like Cree Chief Maski-Pitoon. Incoming church missionaries would have gladly claimed him as a miracle product of their evangelism but Maski-Pitoon hadn't waited to be converted by the new churchmen. He was his own man. His bold decision to adopt an unpopular cause was his own, and he sought only the approval of the Great Spirit.

He was unbelievable but great. Possessing the stuff from which heroes and heroines are made, he should have been introduced long ago to Canadian boys and girls who instead came to believe their best sources of inspiration were in the ranks of comic strip characters, movie actors and actresses and other areas of entertainment.

Birthdates and birthplaces were never considered important in Indian society and nobody can say with certainty where and when Maski-Pitoon was born. The things that counted were courage and success in battle and this young Cree had enough of both to become a great Chief. He was a skilful hunter, warrior, scalper and horse thief. But, inwardly, he had some misgivings. The emphasis on warfare was wrong, he reasoned. He confessed his radical thoughts to his old father and was surprised that there was no rebuke. "Take yourself away to the mountains," the old man advised. "Seek solitude and listen for the voice of the Great Spirit."

The young Chief stole away to fast and pray and await a message from the Great Spirit. And he was not disappointed. He was informed that his reasoning about the folly of war was correct but that it would take no less bravery to win his people to the cause of peace as to win another victory over the Blackfoot people. He tried to convince his Medicine Man without success. But he won over the elders in his tribe and then the young people and then felt ready to take his proposal to his tribe's traditional enemy, the Blackfoot. Many of his own followers thought he would weaken at that point and renounce his ideal of peace. But weaken he did not and the Blackfoot Chief was impressed. It was agreed that a new commitment to peace would last three years, at the end of which time the policy would be reconsidered.

The strictly native compact, without precedent in the Indian country, was launched and working although not without hazards. Circumstances forced tests of good faith on both sides. One supreme test came when a Blackfoot suspected of murdering Maski-Pitoon's father in the course of a raid was captured and brought before the Cree Chief. Doubtless, there were thoughts of revenge in Maski-Pitoon's mind, but instead of ordering the penalty of death the Chief addressed the prisoner, saying: "You killed my father. You killed a better man than you are. Once I would have settled for nothing less than killing you. But I have found a better way and now I ask you to adopt it. Instead of killing you, I'm asking you to join me in making a lasting peace between our two tribes. It would be more important than killing each other."

The accused man was astonished but promised that he would help work for peace.

Maski-Pitoon's reputation was spreading and his strength was growing. Churchmen of all faiths were going out of their way to meet and encourage him. Reverend Edward Ahenakew – a grand nephew of Big Bear and a native Cree who served the Anglican Church in Saskatchewan – knew Maski-Pitoon's story well and confirmed that he was genuinely dedicated to his plans for intertribal peace.

But impulses were sure to arise on both sides and impulses can be dangerous. Moreover, peace treaties have to be renewed and there was tragedy ahead. As Maski-Pitoon was about to travel to the camp of Three Bulls, the Blackfoot Chief with whom he would negotiate the renewal, he invited Reverend John McDougall and his father, Reverend George McDougall, to accompany him. At the Blackfoot camp, the visitors were well received and Three Bulls was conducting himself like a good host.

As Reverend Edward Ahenakew pictured the circumstances: "It was the year before the worst epidemic of smallpox – meaning 1869 – and the negotiations were just getting underway when a misguided young Blackfoot arrived unnoticed and unsuspected. He rode around fast and shot Maski-Pitoon in the back and killed him."

It was the death of a hero. It was the end of a native gentleman who placed the cause of peace ahead of his own safety. It strongly resembled the death later of the Asiatic Indian, Gandhi, who was similarly assassinated when in the practice of his dedication to peace and non-violence.

The tale of an old bonnet

If only the shabby and moth-eaten old war bonnet could tell what it had seen, including western buffalo hunts, Indian wars, scalping horrors and one of the most amazing human friendships since the Old Testament times of David and Jonathan, the history of its proud owner, Sitting Bull, and his Sioux Indians would be much better understood.

Chief Sitting Bull, the most powerful and most feared Indian on the continent, worried the United States cavalry forces for years and when his well-trained warriors were drawn into battle with General George Custer's Seventh Cavalry on the morning of June 25, 1876, the engagement brought victory to the Sioux and left Custer and every man who followed him that day dead on the field. The Indians knew there would be reprisals with the full weight of the United States might behind them.

Sitting Bull knew retreat would become necessary and, burdened by 5 000 men, women and children, retreat would be slow and difficult. He found some comfort in the thought that if his cause became hopeless, he and his people could escape across the "Medicine Line." It came to that and, early in 1877, the main body of the Sioux population – including 1 000 of the best disciplined Indian warriors on the continent – were encamped at Wood Mountain in what is now Southern Saskatchewan.

Settlers recognized two serious threats and were nearly paralysed with fear. They were sure that Sitting Bull would try to persuade Chief Crowfoot of the Blackfoot Confederacy to join with him in an attempt to destroy the white race in the Canadian West and then, if successful, try to do the same in the American West. The second threat was the possibility of the Sioux presence causing an intertribal war on Canadian soil. Either aggression could produce a bloodbath.

As the settlers saw their predicament, their only defence was the numerically slight force of not more than 300 men of the North West Mounted Police. The Mounties lacked nothing in courage but what could they do under the circumstances? It was decided that Superintendent James Morrow Walsh would be appointed liaison officer, giving his full time to the serious task. He was on sick leave in Ontario at the time but he returned promptly when a telegram explained the need.

Late in May, Sitting Bull and the last of his warriors crossed the Border, heading for Wood Mountain. Walsh, with four constables and two interpreters, all mounted, left Fort Walsh to meet the angry Indians at their destination. As the little party of seven came close to Wood Mountain, a minor chief rode out to warn the white men that they would not be welcome. But Walsh, without changing his pace or expression, proceeded on until inside the highly excited camp. Angry glances and the flourishing of guns proved again that every Sioux hated white men, especially white men in uniform.

Having learned where the great Chief's tepee was located, the seven unpopular riders went directly to it. Walsh identified the Chief, dismounted and strode boldly toward him with hand outstretched. The Chief remained ferociously stiff until he seemed to recognize the ridiculousness of the situation and giggled and shook Walsh's hand.

"Chief," said Walsh, "I've come to remind you that you're now in Canada and we have our own laws. You can stay here a while if you behave according to our laws. You must not raid across the Border and expect you can return to this side. And you must not pick quarrels with our Indians. Understand? I'm going to be living near you. I'll see you often."

The Chief understood Walsh's message but he didn't yet understand the man. But his expression was less ferocious. And for Walsh, that first meeting was a triumph.

There were times when the two strong men disagreed and on at least one occasion Walsh kicked the Chief on the appropriate part of his anatomy. But while being firm, Walsh was friendly and mutual confidence grew. The two "opposites" were enjoying each other.

But, after three years, Walsh was being transferred to Fort Qu'Appelle and both men were sad. The Chief wanted to give Walsh a token of gratitude and admiration. He couldn't give money because he didn't have any and there was no point in giving a Mounted Policeman another horse. What, then, would it be? The Chief presented the most precious of his possessions, his old and faded war bonnet that had accompanied him in a hundred battles.

Walsh appreciated the gift and after some years he gave it to Sir William Van Horne, president of the CPR and he, in turn, presented it to the Royal Ontario Museum in Toronto, where it remains to the present time. Doubtless, the old treasure has a good home in Toronto but if the time should come when it needs more intimate attention and expressions of affection, it would probably find them in a museum in the West.

Chief Walking Eagle – Indian weatherman

Whether they had confidence in his long-range prognostications or not, western people liked to know what Chief Walking Eagle of the Stoney Indians thought about "next winter's cold and snow." Many chuckled and said reassuringly that his guesses were as good as any.

Pioneer Canadians were constantly searching for indications of tomorrow's weather. Thousands of times they repeated the old axiom: "Red sky at night, sailors' delight; red sky at morning, sailors take warning." But that wasn't good enough, and people in every community acknowledged a wish for somebody among them with special gifts of weather wisdom or somebody who aspired to become the highest local authority on weather.

Those weather specialists of other years were self-made men. They received no special instruction, no salary and no fringe benefits except, possibly, some added local prestige. Still, to qualify for full acceptance with the rank of weather prophet, a person needed grey hair, a sober mien and a face to match that of an Old Testament patriarch.

As the influence of the national Meteorological Service was extended, the public interest in self-made weather prophets diminished but did not disappear, and Walking Eagle, whose judgements were well publicized by the press at Rocky Mountain House, gained widespread recognition without having to work or ask for it.

"Either he knows more about weather than the rest of us," one of his friends said, "or he's a much better guesser." When challenged to explain the practical basis of his forecasts, however, he refused to comply, saying that he learned the mysteries of weather from his father long ago and if he were to tell them, the white man wouldn't be able to understand them anyway. He'd have to read the signs related to the moon, stars, animals, the mouse's nest and the horse's coat and the white man couldn't do that.

But as if to tantalize his white friends, he told them one day that he would share one source of weather signs with them, namely the spleen of a deer, a sort of a barometer for those who could read it. He admitted that when he had occasion to dress a deer, he never failed to study the spleen. A long and straight spleen in the autumn was a sure sign of a mild winter. And by the same rule, a short and irregular spleen promised a cold winter.

He got along well with his pale-face friends but did not hesitate to criticize them. Visiting Rocky Mountain House in March of the year in which he died, he was louder than usual with condemnation of the white man's use of atomic bombs and power before he understood the possible consequences. Atomic uses, he was sure, were disrupting weather and upsetting his weather calculations. Members of the white race, he said, had themselves to blame for the growing world troubles. "White men are too smart for their own good," a statement that may very well draw more and more support.

He had more invective for "the other race." The Great Spirit doesn't approve of the white man's trips to the clouds and the moon. All humans would be better to stay on the earth. If the white people prayed more and ended their greedy ways, the Great Spirit would become forgiving and give them better weather.

The old chief died at Rocky Mountain House in December, 1965, at the estimated age of 82 years, after 40 years of warning, cheering and counselling people of both races on matters of weather. He probably made his share of weather mistakes but he never disappointed by failure to deliver an answer. He boasted that, in foretelling weather, he was correct in 75 percent of his predictions which, he contended, was a better average than Federal Government meteorologists could claim. In doing his own weather bookkeeping, however, he probably wasn't above giving himself the benefit of a doubt from time to time.

He was quite human and he could be materialistic too. Just a year before he died, he visited Rocky Mountain House full of indignation and anger because, as he told it, some of the federal workers in meteorology came asking him for certain weather information without placing him on the Government payroll. Perhaps he had a twinkle in his eyes when making that complaint. He probably had a sense of humour.

"It would have been wonderful," said the editor of the *Edmonton Journal* at the time of the Chief's death, "to have known Chief Walking Eagle and to have understood the lore that was in his book of tomorrow.... Who can take his place, without appearing a charlatan?"[1]

Dan George – the Chief who captured Hollywood

Canadians looking for storybook characters should not overlook the great achievers among the native people – Maski-Pitoon, for example, Walking Buffalo, Crowfoot, Allen Sapp and Chief Dan George. In their early lives, they were hunters and fighters but, with the passing years, found new purposes and skills that won the admiration of all people.

Born a Coast Salish on the small Burrard Reserve on Vancouver's north shore, Dan George's boyhood years were quite unspectacular. He dropped out of an Indian boarding school to engage in logging with his father and then was, successively, a lumber millhand, a longshoreman on the Vancouver waterfront, a Chief of his small band, a construction worker and, finally, a movie actor.

He rather stumbled into movies. He had never expressed a serious thought about trying for a role in motion pictures although he possessed the characteristics often recognized as assets on the screen or stage. It happened this way: Dan's oldest son had been given a minor part in a production called *Caribou Country*. At the beginning of filming, a non-Indian actor playing the part of an old Indian Chief became suddenly ill and the producer wanted a replacement in a hurry. Dan's son was consulted and to the producer's surprise, the young Indian said: "Yes, I think I could find you a real Chief and he might surprise you. He's my father and he never stood in front of a movie camera in his life but he's a pretty smart old man. If you'd like to see him, I'll go get him."

The producer was sceptical but replied: "Let's see him. Bring him in."

An hour later, Robert George was back and introducing his father to the producer. There was an audition and the old man passed the test with flying colours. The newest and most unlikely actor was a success and his performance led to more screen parts, including a supporting role in Little Big Man that brought surprise and praise in Hollywood in 1970. It also brought the New York Critic's award and an Oscar nomination for Dan George.

Beyond all else, Dan George was a thinker, and how was he to understand a culture in which people not only fought each other but constantly attacked and abused Nature? He had no patience with a concept that was virtuous about sympathetic feeling for fellow humans while showing no concern for other creatures and creations of the Great Spirit's making. Hinting at the source of his ideals, he said: "My mother had a kindness that embraced all life…. My father loved the earth and all its creatures."

Speculating philosophically about the white man's confused sensitivities, he questioned if his palefaced brothers had ever learned to really love. Those brothers, he conceded, did many things very well, but they exercised their love in too selective and superficial a way to be easily understood. They could love anything when it was profitable and turned readily to raiding when exploit proved advantageous. "Man's love must be consistent; he must love all Creation or be an unreliable citizen of Nature's community."

His criticism was kindly but positive and clear. He became a most popular speaker at Brotherhood gatherings and banquets and he travelled extensively. He spoke slowly and his voice was low but he had an unmistakable Biblical quality in his presentations. And like an Old Testament teacher, he had rebukes for his own people as well as for others. He reminded the Indian people that the white man's influence upon their lives was not all bad. He wanted to see his people doing more to improve their own position and he urged them to forget about using force to gain benefit in the new order of things.

The old man of wisdom with the storybook career died at Vancouver in September, 1981, at the age of 82 years, and Canadians and Americans numbering millions mourned the way they would the passing of a close and highly respected friend.

The death of Chief Crowfoot

"General expressions of regret were passed in town when it became known that the great chief of the Blackfoot tribe, Sapoo-Muxima (Crowfoot), had departed this life. The Chief had been ill for some time and, on Tuesday last, Dr. George was summoned and found him suffering from pneumonia…. The scene in the tepee of the dying chief was exceedingly impressive, there being about forty Indians assembled, including the three wives of Crowfoot and the Medicine Men of both camps…. The day before yesterday, Sapoo-Muxima went into a swoon and the relatives, believing him dead, killed his best horse before the tepee for his use in the Happy Hunting Ground. He, however, revived. When the great Chief breathed his last, his death was taken very quietly; he had told the Indians not to mourn for him and to make no noise….

"A few days before his death, a will was drawn up for him and in this document he left his house and one of his medals to his favourite wife, the rest of his medals and his horses to his brother, Three Bulls, who is now Chief of the Tribe…. The Medicine Men received 15 horses as their fee."[2]

Remembering Crowfoot's words of wisdom

"We are getting shut in. The Crees are coming into our country from the North, and the white men from the South and East and they are all destroying our means of living but still, although we plainly see these days coming, we will not join the Sioux against the Whites but will depend upon you to help us."[3]

With the tone of a Churchill: "Though our enemies be strong as the sun, as numerous as the stars, we will defend our lodges."

"Our land is more valuable than your money. It will last forever. It will not perish as long as the sun shines and the water flows, and through all the years it will give life to men and beasts. It was put there by the Great Spirit and we cannot sell it because it does not belong to us."

To Reverend John McDougall: "My brother, your words make me glad. I listened to them not only with my ears but with my heart also. In the coming of the Long Knives with their firewater and quick-shooting guns, we were weak and our people have been woefully slain and impoverished. You say this will be stopped. We want peace. What you tell us about this strong power which will govern with good laws and treat the Indian the same as the white man, makes us glad. My brother, I believe you and am thankful."[4]

A philosophical oration near the end of his life: "A little while and I will be gone from among you. Whither I cannot tell. From nowhere we came;

into nowhere we go. What is life? It is the flash of a firefly in the night. It is the breath of a buffalo in the winter time. It is the little shadow that runs across the grass and loses itself in the sunset."

"The advice given me and my people has proved to be very good. If the police had not come to the country, where would we be now? Bad men and whisky were killing us so fast that very few of us would be left today. The police have protected us as the feathers of the bird protect it from the frosts of winter. I wish them all good, and trust that all our hearts will increase in goodness from this time forward. I am satisfied. I will sign the treaty."[5]

A prayerful plea for conservation, without documentation: "Great Father, take pity on me with regard to my country, with regard to the mountains, the hills and the valleys, with regard to the prairies, the forests and the water, with regard to the animals that inhabit them, and do not take them from my children forever."

That was Crowfoot, called, with good reason, the Chief of Chiefs, the man who would have been distinctive in any race, the Indian orator and thinker, the one without whom settlers and others of the immigrant breeds might have suffered massacre on an awful scale, not just once but twice.

One of those times was in the late '70s and early '80s when the powerful Sioux leader, Chief Sitting Bull, with 5 000 Sioux followers, including a thousand well-trained warriors, was encamped at Wood Mountain, to-day's Saskatchewan. It was no secret that Sitting Bull, whose main hatred was directed at United States cavalrymen, hoped to unite with Crowfoot's Indians and Indian neighbours and – with himself as the supreme leader – deal a totally destroying blow to the troublesome whites. Of course the idea would have had the strongest appeal for western tribesmen, especially the younger ones, and who can say that the Sitting Bull design wouldn't have worked, leaving him to then take the massed force south to settle some old accounts on the American side.

Such an invitation came again in 1885 when Louis Riel urged the western Indians to join with the Metis. It was presented as the last chance for the native people to recover their land and perhaps bring back the buffalo. But Crowfoot, whose support was essential, gave exactly the same answer in both cases: "I promised to keep the peace and work for it. I will never break my promise." It was the same utterance that brought relief to those who were working to find understanding in connection with Blackfoot Treaty Number Seven. "I will sign the Treaty; I will be the first to sign and the last to break the promise." Crowfoot was one who could teach most people a lesson in honest dealing.

An Indian legend of Lake Louise

When the world was young, giants peopled the earth. A certain giant chief, a very famous hunter, was never satisfied with the number of animals and monsters that fell before his arrows or were trapped in his snares. One day he saw a rainbow in the sky. The more he watched it, the more he wanted it, because he believed it could make him a magic bow. Climbing the tallest tree on earth, he tore the rainbow from its place, but when he grasped it, the colours melted. In exasperated anger the giant dashed the rainbow against the nearest rocky peak, and so it fell shattered to the bottom of the lake below and gave its colours to the waters. The god of the elements then made another arch to hold up the sky when it rained, but the colours of the shattered rainbow are still seen spreading through the waters of the wonder lake, which white people now call Lake Louise.[6]

Chapter 3

Sodbusters, plows
and laughter

3

The Mormons carried a plow

As immigrant settlers to the West, Lord Selkirk's weary colonists led the long parade by more than fifty years and they can never be denied that honour and distinction.

But after the passage of the Canada Land Act in 1872, settlers of many races and church connections became part of the great rush inspired by the promise of free land. The Mennonites came by way of the Red River in 1874 and chose Southern Manitoba. The Icelanders came the next year, seeking a location offering farmland and good fishing side by side and finding it on the west side of Lake Winnipeg.

The Ukrainians approached cautiously in 1891 but soon staged their own land rush to John Palliser's "Fertile Belt" or Park Belt. The Toronto people who formed the Temperance Colony Society and planned to live on their South Saskatchewan River reservation, on which the hated John Barleycorn would never be allowed to show his ugly face, followed the trail from Moose Jaw to the site where Saskatoon was to arise – without the Society traditions – in 1884. Hungarians came in 1882 and '86, Germans in 1890 and after, Mormons from Utah in 1887 and Barr Colony Englishmen in 1903.

There was something distinctive about them all but it may be fair to say that no immigrant race or group made a finer record of progress than the Mormons.

Charles Ora Card, son-in-law of Brigham Young, drove north from Salt Lake City with a team of horses and a covered wagon in 1886, searching for a new location for settlement. He knew what he wanted and wouldn't be easy to satisfy. Wiser than most land seekers, he was carrying a walking plow in the wagon. Wherever surface conditions appeared attractive, he would hitch the horses to the plow and turn a few furrows in order to study the soil.

After studying the soil at various locations in British Columbia and Alberta, he found exactly what he wanted at Lee's Creek, where Cardston stands proudly today. A dozen Mormon families came from Utah by covered wagon in 1887 and, in the space of four or five years, the still youthful Cardston had a school, church, store, cheese factory, saw mill, grist mill, a successful irrigation system, a mature social and church life and some of the biggest sheep and cattle ranches in the area.

It wasn't surprising that, when Canada's Governor General Lord Minto and Lady Minto took up residence in Ottawa and a tour of the West was proposed, they expressed a wish to visit a Mormon colony. And thereby hangs a story within a story.

Mounted Police Commissioner Perry and Captain Burton Deane met the viceregal party where it left the railway at Fernie and drove the visitors from there to Lethbridge. From Lethbridge they were scheduled to drive to the Mormon settlement at Magrath to be noontime guests at the home of J. B. Ririe, well known in ranching and agricultural circles for his promotional and breeding work with the finewool breed of French Merinos, the Rambouillet.[1]

There was no reason to believe that the Governor General had any particular interest in sheep but he and his lady were clearly interested in the people and, after the long drive from Lethbridge, they would be understandably interested in good Mormon banquet food too.

But the weather turned unpleasant with heavy rains and wet trails. Police officers had thoughts about cancelling the trip. The Governor General and his lady were consulted and both said "No. Let's go. They'll be expecting us."

The Riries, to be sure, did handsomely in preparing a meal "fit for kings." But the mud was so bad and the rate of travel so slow that the party was soon an hour late, then two hours late and three hours. The Riries were at a loss to know what to do. They had a house full of local guests, all hungry. After waiting for more than two hours, it was concluded that the distinguished visitors had been forced to turn back.

Accordingly, the Riries invited their friends and neighbours to sit in and allay their feelings of starvation. They ate well and practically nothing remained. But then, Horrors! The littlest Ririe girl, playing outside, saw a police wagon and several mounted men driving down the lane toward the house. She drew her own conclusions and, impulsively, burst into the house where neighbours were still sitting around the table, and shouted: "The Lord has come and you've eaten all his dinner." The words were not to be forgotten.

The Riries looked embarrassed but they didn't need to be and the viceregal guests laughed. Everybody laughed and the resourceful Mormon ladies moved at once to put a new meal together, and did it well. Hunger is the best contribution to a good meal and the special guests ate sumptuously, saying they were glad they did not turn back. They decided against inspecting the sheep and the irrigation works and started back over the 28 miles to Lethbridge. Everybody left with happy memories and said so.

The farmer got his loan

William Dunn, manager of the Saskatoon branch of the Royal Bank for many years, told of the local farmer who, in great distress, came to him one morning in August and begged for a loan. The caller wasn't one of the bank's regular customers but the manager listened to the story of his dilemma. His wheat was ripe, ready for cutting, and he needed a loan to enable him to buy the crucial binder twine.

The banker said there should be no difficulty in accommodating the request provided, of course, that the farmer would furnish the customary collateral security. That, however, was the trouble, the farmer said: "everything I own is already 'plastered' with liens." Dunn looked grave and said: "That is unfortunate. Do you mean to tell me that you haven't got even a steer that you could offer as security?"

"That's the way it is," the farmer answered and Bill Dunn shook his head and said: "I'm sorry for you but I suppose there is no point in wasting more of your time and mine." The two men shook hands and parted.

Three hours passed and the man from the country reappeared with a faint trace of a smile on his face. "Have you had some luck in raising money for binder twine?" the banker asked, to which the caller replied: "No, not yet, but I can now offer you a steer as security for the loan I need."

Dunn looked puzzled. "How do you explain that?" he asked. "Just a few hours ago you told me you didn't have a single steer that wasn't already mortgaged."

"Yes, I know," said the farmer, "but I have one now. You see, after I talked with you, I went home to the farm and made a steer out of the purebred Shorthorn bull the Bank of Commerce down the street had a lien on. I'll just have to tell the Commerce people that I don't own a Shorthorn bull any more."

When asked if the farmer got the loan he needed in order to get his binder into operation, Dunn replied: "I'm not sure I did the proper thing but I figured that anybody who was as ingenious as that fellow deserved a break. Yes, he got his loan and when he finished the harvest, he came in and paid us back, every cent."

Jim Speers' roller coaster career

To excel as a storyteller, a person must first of all have something worth telling and then the talent to tell it well. Jim Speers – often called Mr. Racing – had both in double measure. His life in the West was like the proverbial roller coaster and he rode the heights of prosperity and the valleys of bankruptcy as if for fun. In most of his stories, the jokes were on himself and he did more than anyone to bring laughter to homesteading, ranching, and horse raising and racing.

One of the last adventures he told his friends of took place at the fashionable Santa Anita race track in California where Speers had been sitting with some unoccupied seats around him. A stranger asked Speers if he might sit down, to which Speers replied: "I don't mind but this is not my box; my friend who has it invited me to stay and just asked that I keep the bums out. Sit down. I'm Jim Speers from Winnipeg. What's your name?"

The stranger extended his hand, saying: "I've heard of you. My name is Don Amiche."

"Glad to meet you Mr. Meechy," Speers replied. "And what line of business are you in?"

The man was one of Hollywood's biggest names and may have felt deflated but he and Speers became good friends.

Wherever Speers went there was fun. He invited it. When in Toronto to deliver a Thoroughbred mare to Honourable Earl Rowe, Speers found the Minister was out of the city and so asked Rowe's secretary to send a telegram asking what he wanted done with the Speers mare from Winnipeg. Quickly, there was a telegraphic reply: "Give Thoroughbred mare from Winnipeg the best box stall and turn Speers in the back pasture."

Speers' association with the West began at the very beginning of the century. He was 18 years old and didn't see much future in his father's blacksmith shop close to the big Malton Airport of later years. Arriving at Winnipeg, his total assets consisted of one bicycle and four dollars. By the time he reached Saskatoon, he was down to one bicycle and no dollars but he was determined to go to Battleford. Starting early the next morning, he planned to cycle the full distance before nightfall. By midday he figured he was halfway over the course but a bit tired and awfully hungry. Beside the trail he stopped to chat with an immigrant eating his lunch. Speers made no attempt to hide his hunger and the chap, who didn't know much English, pulled out a loaf of black bread from a woollen sock and gave Speers half of it. It wasn't elegant but it tasted good and Speers was thankful. Then he had the local man set him on the proper course to Battleford but the advice wasn't very clear and Speers went on his way with more hope than confidence. When darkness fell that night, the cyclist was thoroughly exhausted but he could see the lights of a prairie town ahead. It would be Battleford, at the end of a 100-mile ride. But it wasn't Battleford; it was Saskatoon, the place he left early in the morning.

Next morning he started again and clung to the proper trail but before reaching Battleford he was so tired he pushed his bicycle through the middle of a small lake rather than face the extra distance by going around. At Battleford he got a job at a mill being built by Senator Prince but poor luck was following him. He fell off a scaffold and broke a shoulder; he went duck hunting with his arm in a sling and fell into the Battle River; when he went driving with a team and democrat, the horses bolted and he was thrown and a wheel passed over his head. It was rough initiation but he proved he could take it.

By 1908, Speers had made a tidy Battleford fortune and lost it. He went to Wilkie and homesteaded. He prospered and made a trip to the Toronto Exhibition, returning in a freight car with the biggest automobile the Wilkie people had seen. Mrs. Speers asked him if he knew how to drive it and he replied: "No, but if I can get it to the middle of the pasture field, I'll learn or I'll teach it to neck-rein."

While still at Wilke, Speers borrowed money to build a couple of grain warehouses and this led to elevators. By 1910 he had 10 country elevators, all full of wheat. That was fine until the price of wheat fell and Speers was ruined again, with his creditors taking the elevators. He turned to horses, always a first love, and was doing well. But in a moment of weakness, as he told it, he accepted the Conservative nomination in the Federal Constituency of Tramping Lake. He conducted a vigorous campaign but, on the morning of the election, he asked his agent, Harry Rudd, how they stood. Rudd's reply was a good example of eloquence and brevity: "You've lost five and a half months of your time; you've spent $10 500 of your own money; you're charged with 1100 gallons of beer for the picnics; three of your workers have been arrested and one is still in jail; you're faced with a $1 200 suit for libel and you have been beaten by 239 votes." Speers then asked if everything else was all right. He added that any man who could analyse a situation so well could be sure of a job "with me" for the rest of his life. Rudd stayed.

When the First World War broke out in 1914, Speers accepted an assignment buying cavalry horses for the Canadian and United States governments and it was when doing that work on February 20, 1916, that a locomotive on an American line ploughed into a sleeping car, killing five of the six people in it. Speers was the survivor and at first it was thought that he, too, was dead. Doctors tried to make a count of the broken bones. For weeks he was in casts and for 13 months in hospital.

When he was in hospital, more notes came due and creditors sold more of his elevators. He left the hospital with a permanent lameness and an eagerness to start again. In 1919, he started a livestock commission business in Winnipeg and then decided to do something about organized horse racing. He knew people loved horses and horse racing and that western racing was being badly conducted. His first attempts at reorganization were encouraging and he boldly built Whittier Park beside the Red River in 1924. Next, he organized the Prairie Thoroughbred Breeders and Racing Association and built Polo Park.

Now, he wanted a farm on which to breed his beloved Thoroughbreds and bought a 900-acre property outside of St. Boniface and called it Whittier. It became the home of many of the best horses of the breed, famous sires like Craigangower, Cudgel, Brooms and Marine. In 1939, Whittier Farm became the first of its kind in Canada to go over the magic million dollar mark in cumulative purse winnings and, in six different years after 1939, Speers won the Canadian title of Leading Breeder of Thoroughbreds in Canada.

And while Speers was gaining international fame, he was becoming ever better known near home as the horseman with the big heart. Money wouldn't buy the stallion, Brooms, the pick of the Kentucky yearling crop in 1926, but Speers would donate him to the University of Saskatchewan, where there was promise of a good home for as long as he lived. Horsemen heard and loved the story of the young Winnipeg man who was coming out to see the Thoroughbreds being trained at very early morning hours.

Nothing was more obvious than the young fellow's desire to own one of them. Speers questioned him and, after being satisfied the fellow was serious, said: "If you can make your choice before the colts reach us, you can have it for the money you have in your pocket." The response was instantaneous: "Do you mean it? I'll take that one, the bay filly." Pockets were turned out and the fellow bought Omar's Gift for exactly 37 cents. That was Jim Speers.

The story behind the McIntosh apple

McIntosh Red apples and the beautiful orchard country of British Columbia seemed to have been fashioned for each other, like shapely ankles and nylon stockings. But how many Canadians know the strange life story of that famous apple variety?

Back of it all, according to legend, was a serious love affair that did not escape some disapproving frowns from the young man's family and may have been the reason for his departure from his home in New York State to settle in Canada. The exact circumstances need not be pursued; the important point is that anything that might have blocked his coming to settle east of Cornwall in Upper Canada in 1796 would have changed the course of fruit growing and deprived Canadian apple production of immeasurable benefits.

The hero of the story was John McIntosh, born to a Scottish family that migrated from Scotland to New York State a short time before the War of Independence. He was 19 years of age when he moved across the border to settle in the district now marked by Dundela, in Eastern Ontario.

Clearing Eastern Canadian land for cultivation was always an extremely heavy task but it was when John McIntosh was so engaged that he recognized some seedling apples growing wild. As a child of Clan McIntosh, he knew that waste should not be allowed and took time to transplant the delicate young trees to his garden area. As plant breeders and orchardists know, apples grown from seed are uncertain things, unlikely to produce fruit like the apples from which the seed came. It is for this reason that apples and other tree fruits of superior quality must be propagated by grafting or budding.

But notwithstanding the great odds against getting an acceptable eating apple from trees produced totally from seed, one of McIntosh's wild seedlings proved to be a winner. The experts could hardly believe it but here was a tree salvaged from the forest that produced a superb quality fruit with excellence in texture, flavour and colour to please the most discriminating judge. At first the tree was seen simply as a local curiosity but gradually its superiority was winning attention in ever more distant parts.

Through most of John McIntosh's remaining years, it was known as the Granny Apple tree but it outlived its discoverer and took the McIntosh name, later McIntosh Red. John McIntosh's son, Allan, recognized the wonder tree's potential and started a nursery on the farm and embarked extensively upon a program of grafting with buds or scions from the parent tree. Thus hundreds of thousands of young apple trees with McIntosh tops were going to apple growing districts in many parts of the continent.

The original tree, no longer well shaped and handsome, lived on to its 112th year and earned the distinction of being the world's most famous apple tree, well deserving the monument raised to it near where it grew. Fifty years later, there was another unveiling, this time of a plaque honouring the discoverer, John McIntosh. Two great grandchildren of John McIntosh participated.

In was appropriate that the monument and plaque should be placed in the area where John McIntosh farmed and made his home but nobody could overlook the fact that British Columbia, especially the Okanagan Valley, had the biggest debt to the discoverer of the famous apple, which had been adopted by B.C. orchardists much as prairie farmers adopted Marquis wheat in the years after 1910.

Sir John – with the dynamics of a firecracker

Sir John Lister Kaye was a pint-sized Englishman with the imagination of a fortune-teller and the dynamics of a firecracker. For almost a decade – or as long as he had plenty of spending money – he kept his rural neighbours thoroughly entertained. Watching him was as much fun as watching a magic lantern show, one of them suggested.

He made his western appearance in 1885 when he was associated with Lord Queensberry in the operation of a 7000- acre farm at Balgonie, east of Regina. But such a farm was not big enough for Sir John and, before the end of 1886, he was making plans for the Canadian Agricultural, Coal and Colonization Co. with British capital and himself as managing director. Almost at once, he was buying 10 spreads of raw land, each 10 000 acres in area and all located along the main line of the C.P.R. between Balgonie on the east and Langdon, near Calgary, on the west. Wasting no time – he was always in a hurry – he prepared for the construction of buildings on each of the 10 big properties.

With the newspaper people, he was a favourite. He was always ready for an interview and could generally offer a new scheme or twist. After a year in the country, his name was like a household term. So good was the liaison with the press that even today – 100 years after his heyday – the ancient news items from papers of his time are still the best references for students.

He told the representative of the *Lethbridge News* that he would soon have stabling on every farm for 50 horses, 400 breeding cows, 5000 sheep and 500 pigs, and the total expenditure for buildings, wire fencing and livestock would be $500 000, with about half of the total outlay going for foundation livestock.[2] It brought a question to some observers: "Did Sir John never learn to count in any other denominations except thousands?"

He bought 7000 cattle branded "76" from the Powder River Ranch Co., formerly of Wyoming, and trailed in 18 000 sheep from Oregon.[3] What figures they were!

When his first grain crop failed because of drought, Sir John was determined to do something about it. Even he couldn't make it rain but, when visiting Winnipeg and noticing street sprinklers in action, he got an idea and acted at once to place an order with Ryan and McArthur, blacksmiths and wagon-makers, for 44 pine water tanks to be mounted on wagons, each tank to be 11 feet four inches long, three feet seven inches wide and two feet high. Each would hold 12 barrels of water. What Sir John didn't realize and nobody told him was that to deliver even one inch of water on a single acre of his dry land would require a hundred tons or more. It just wasn't practical.

But the little man with the big ideas was still "riding high" and when he and Lady Kaye visited Calgary they travelled in their private rail car. Still bubbling over with schemes for extracting wealth from the prairie soil and still convinced that he could employ mixed farming principles in ranching on the Canadian plains, he announced that he was about to convert the wild cattle critters from Wyoming to milk cows and begin dairying on a large scale. The ranch cowboys, of course, were horrified and the wild cows, only a couple of generations removed from Wyoming or Texas Longhorns, were in no mood to submit without a fight to human hands working in their mammary departments and taking milk to which their calves had exclusive claim.

But Sir John built a creamery at Swift Current and offered a silver trophy to the ranch manager who had the most cows contributing milk and cream for the plant "by October." Dairying with ranch cows was not a success, even though Sir John said it was. But he had another "bright idea"; he would enter the retail meat trade at Calgary or Lethbridge or both, thereby controlling the meat product from the moment of the calf's birth on the range to the sales to consumers who came to Sir John's stores looking for steaks and roasts. The Calgary meat store opened with a flourish in November, 1889. Sir John was optimistic but the Canadian Agricultural, Coal and Colonization directors in England were growing impatient and then angry at their long wait for dividends and called for reorganization.

Then, to make matters worse, 1893 brought the "Great Sheep Depression" and both Sir John and the Company were in trouble. Sheep had been the best of Company enterprises and their number reached 65 000 in 1891. Now the sheep too were failing.

Sir John accepted retirement in 1895 and D. H. Andrews – an able and practical man who came to the ranch in the course of the Powder River Ranch cattle deal – was called to England to assist in reorganization and was appointed general manager of the big spread. Much of the fun generated in Sir John's time disappeared with his retirement but the ranch gained new respect as a practical and sensible operation.

Adam MacKenzie and the schoolmam

Adam MacKenzie was at one time the biggest farm operator in Manitoba, not to mention one of the biggest and strongest men in the farming business. He arose early in the mornings, kept long hours and had no patience with anybody who couldn't do the same. When at home on the farm at Arden, he was always the first man up in the mornings and he would then awaken the hired man or men. If the workers failed to get up promptly when called, MacKenzie was likely to administer punishment by pulling the bedclothes away and paddling offenders with the back of a long handled hair brush.

On one occasion, MacKenzie had to drive to Portage La Prairie on business and planned to return the next day. But instead of waiting till the next day, he drove all night and arrived at home at an early morning hour, just in time to awaken his hired man at the customary hour of five o'clock.

But on this particular morning, MacKenzie's call seemed to be wasted. The hired helper didn't respond and MacKenzie was angry. He marched straight into the man's bedroom. The morning was still dark but MacKenzie knew his way around. He jerked the bedclothes from the bed, as he had done a few times before, rolled the poor fellow over and administered a spanking on his bare backside. Thereupon, MacKenzie lit the kerosene lantern and strode through the early dawn to the stable. But the stable held a shock for MacKenzie. There, holding another lantern and starting to perform the morning chores, was the hired man. The boss stood and gazed, without trying to hide his surprise and alarm.

"I thought you were still in bed," he gasped. "Weren't you still in bed when I called you and walloped you just a few minutes ago?"

"No," was the answer. "Mrs. MacKenzie said you weren't coming home until late today. You see, Mrs. MacKenzie had the new schoolmam for supper last night and, when it started to snow, the teacher was afraid to drive home alone so your wife invited her to stay all night. Mrs. MacKenzie then asked me if I would mind sleeping in the hay for the one night and letting the teacher have my bed. I didn't mind at all."

MacKenzie knew he was in trouble, terrible trouble. Instead of waiting to have breakfast with his wife and the new teacher, he reharnessed his team and told the hired man, not very convincingly, that he had to go to Carberry and would have breakfast there.

Peace River Jim

Trader, farmer, musher, miner, legislator and raconteur, Jim Cornwall, or Peace River Jim as he was widely known, became the most influential citizen in the Land of the Peace.

But he wasn't born there; his birth was at Brantford, Ontario, two years after Canadian Confederation and while still in his early teens, he was selling papers on the streets of Buffalo, New York. After that, he was thinking of a life as a sailor and received his initiation by working as a deckhand on a Great Lakes boat. After that, he saw Atlantic service for a few years.

But Jim Cornwall's life demanded challenge and variety and by 1897, when the first rumours of gold were filtering out of the Yukon, Cornwall was already living at Athabasca Landing, right beside the All-Canadian route to the northern gold fields. He started north from there in the gold rush year of '98 but what he saw in the Peace River region convinced him that the area held more "gold" for him than the distant Yukon. He turned to farming in the North, then trading, and was elected to sit as a member of the Alberta Legislature between 1908 and 1912.

Came World War I and he went overseas and returned with the rank of Lieutenant-Colonel and the honour of the Distinguished Service Order. Once home, he vowed he would never again be absent from Peace River for long at a time – and he wasn't. In the years that followed he travelled thousands of miles on mail delivery in the North. It was said that when his sleigh dogs played out, he would put the mail bags on his back and push on. But Cornwall had good dogs with a reputation for taking the mail through on time.

He told stories well and one dog story for which he was remembered and may have been of his own making was about what seemed like a record run on the way to Peace River Crossing. When asked about it, he gave the principal credit to the leader in a tandem team of six dogs. This was a dog of unusual stamina and spirit but, sad to say, the dog got a feed of poisoned fish and died suddenly.

Cornwall was in a bad way because he didn't have a proper replacement. He knew he had several mediocre dogs, especially the one hitched at the rear end of the team, slow and lazy. He had considered giving the dog away but kept him because he was a friendly fellow. But, just as an experiment, he promoted the lazy rearend dog to see what he'd do on the lead and, to his utter surprise, the poor dog that had previously ran immediately behind the one considered the fifth poorest in the team, now displayed fresh interest and new life and, unbelievably, led the team to a new time record.

Jim's neighbours shared his surprise and asked how he could explain it.

"I'm not sure" Cornwall replied, "but when I try to put myself in that lead dog's old position and then in the new position, I'd say his better performance must be due to the change of scenery."

As mentioned earlier, it was Jim Cornwall's idea to move Twelve-foot Davis's bones from Grouard to their hilltop place of honour overlooking Peace River, and it was on Cornwall's instructions and at his expense that the gravestone with the widely known epitaph was placed at that most spectacular gravesite in Alberta.

Peace River Jim Cornwall, DSO, the region's most voluble promoter, died at the age of 86 years in 1955.

Chapter 4

Farm laughing matter

4

Tallyho heard at Lethbridge

Nobody knew exactly how it started but Lethbridge people, in the late 1880s, got the sophisticated urge to indulge in fox hunting as a sport – if it ever justified that term. Apparently, the enthusiasm was brief but the editor of the *Macleod Gazette* enjoyed telling of the madness:

"Lethbridge has gone wild over fox hunting. The first experience of this invigorating sport which the citizens of Lethbridge have enjoyed was on a recent Sunday. A number of the wily doublers [foxes] had been previously captured and on this particular Sunday the town turned out almost en masse to give chase. As many as could get anything in the shape of an animal with four legs went to the meet mounted, while there was also a pretty liberal turnout of single and double drivers.

"Arrived on the spot, the foxes were let out one by one and the pack of hounds [ranging from] fox terriers up to Newfoundlands, let loose. Then the fun began. One prominent Lethbridge citizen, who was driving, was overcome by intense excitement and, entering into the spirit of the thing, threw off his coat and, with a loud whoop, sprang out of the wagon and careened wildly over the prairie in pursuit of the fox. It is not known whether he was in at the death or not.

"Another fox turned townward and arrived, followed by a wild and enthusiastic crowd, both mounted and driving, just as the children were going to Sunday School. The fever seized the latter. The fox darted across the railway tracks and the children joined pell mell in the pursuit. Religiously inclined people felt much shocked and we hear that the matter was reported to the police.

"It is hinted however, that it is not only the ungodly of Lethbridge who take a keen interest in the hunting, even if the meet does take place on a Sunday."[1]

Hatfield the rainmaker

The name, Rainmaker, may have been Charles Mallory Hatfield's invention but it was all he needed to win attention when prairie grain crops were withering on dry soil. For many dryland farmers, 1920 was the third dry year in a row and some of them were leaving their homestead farms. Others were admitting an interest in the American, Hatfield, who, according to his own story, was conducting private research in rainmaking and taking credit for recent rains in California. An American meteorologist declared the man's methods as "absurd" but farmers were in a mood to gamble.

Farm groups at Vulcan, Burdett and Medicine Hat invited Hatfield to consider working for them. But he was playing "hard to get," saying that he was wanted in Australia and South Africa. He did, however, agree to come to Medicine Hat and bring his equipment.

According to the contract that was drawn up, Hatfield could claim credit for half the rain that fell within 100 miles of Medicine Hat between May 1 and August 1 and collect up to $8000 for a maximum of four inches. For rain above that amount, there'd be no charge. The basis of payment was to be $4000 per inch for the rain he could claim.

He arrived at "the Hat" on April 20, 1921, and scores of farmers and others were on hand to gaze at him. On the following day, the United Agricultural Association staged a monster banquet at the Corona Hotel to officially mark the beginning of what people hoped would be a new era in crop production. Walter Huckvale, an early rancher, was mayor of Medicine Hat at the time and was present to join in the celebration.

Hatfield was a good actor and gave the impression of being in command of both physical and chemical resources. For an operations site, he choose Chappice Lake – a close relative to an alkali slough 20 miles north – to which went a string of wagons loaded with mysterious chemicals and equipment. There he mixed his ingredients as farmers watched hopefully. Several even made special trips to town to buy raincoats.

Whatever the explanation, Hatfield's operating towers were scarcely completed before the rains began to fall. Hatfield was at once the Man of the Hour as farmers saw short and pale crops becoming vigorous and green. The rain continued for several days and some farmers came to request Hatfield to "turn it down" until they could complete seeding operations. For the month of May, rainfall totalled 1.3 inches and crops responded well. The whole world was hearing about Medicine Hat. News correspondents crossed the Atlantic to talk to Hatfield and get the story.

But one important point was being overlooked: the fact was other prairie districts far removed from Chappice Lake were getting rains too and, by June, Hatfield was being asked to suspend rainmaking operations so farmers could recover their hay. Then, by the beginning of July, there was another confusing change: the rains ended as if by their own will and refused to come again. Once more, complaints were being heard and sarcasm was proliferating.

Late in July, the United Agricultural Association formally expressed dissatisfaction. The familiar drought conditions had returned. Hatfield's concoctions dispensed from the high towers were not working. He said he would increase the potency but still nothing happened. This was especially embarrassing to the rainmaker because other southern areas were getting rains while Medicine Hat was becoming parched.

Hatfield's seasonal contract ended at the first of August. While he was preparing to leave, officers of the United Agricultural Society repeated complaints about rain failure in the later part of the season when grain should be filling. But the official records for the season showed sufficient increase in rain to warrant the maximum payment even though the crop was only slightly above average. Hatfield did yield to the association's pressure and accepted a settlement reduced by $2500.

In spite of the controversy over the value – if any – of his methods, Hatfield was invited to return in 1922. He gave the impression that he would come back with more effective chemical materials, but he didn't return. In light of the mounting criticism of his methods, his decision to stay away was undoubtedly a wise one.

The doctor had to eat too

One of Weyburn's well-known and greatly loved pioneer doctors answered a farm call where the lady of the home suspected she had appendicitis and satisfied himself that the disorder was a simple case of wind. But, on leaving the sickroom and passing another bedroom with an open door, he recognized the hired girl in her bed. Suspecting, quite naturally, that she too was ill, he entered and proceeded at once to take the girl's temperature and pulse. Failing to detect anything indicating illness, he said to her: "I don't think you're sick; what made you think you were?"

"I know I'm not sick," she answered. "I didn't say I was."

"Then why are you in bed in the middle of the day?" the doctor asked.

"Well, I'll tell you. These people haven't paid me for six months and I decided to stay in bed until they do."

"Ho, ho," said the doctor. "That's not a bad idea. Say, get over and let me in too; they haven't paid me for six years."

Harry's cow wasn't house broken

If there is a thing as rank determined by achievement in the cow world, Harry Hays' Holstein, named Alcartra Gerben, would have been "Number One." In her own way she was like a Charles Lindbergh in flying, a Lionel Conacher in a variety of sports or a Wayne Gretzky in hockey. She was the Holstein cow from an Alberta pasture that became a world champion producer of butterfat.

Luck was with her, of course, when she became the property of Harry Hays, one of the best cattle judges and showmen in the business. Born on the family farm at Carstairs, north of Calgary, on Christmas day, 1909, his career was most distinguished. After breeding and showing many of the best in the Holstein breed, he was drawn into livestock auctioneering, exporting and politics and served as Mayor of Calgary, Minister of Agriculture for Canada in Prime Minister Lester Pearson's government and, finally, a member of the Senate of Canada.

But, first, last and always, Harry Hays was a cattleman with a fine and balanced judgement. He liked buying and selling good animals. And so it was on December 31, 1944, when a herd of purebred Holsteins was being sold at Didsbury, that Hays drove from the family farm, then at Turner Siding on Calgary's south side, to watch the sale. It wasn't a good day to be away from home because the thermometer registered 20 below zero and he had agreed to attend a New Year's Eve party with Mildred, his wife, in Calgary that night. But he had a special interest in one of John Allan's young cows sired by a Hays bull. He had seen her and was much impressed. She had recently freshened and looked magnificent.

The sale was running late and the winter sun was setting before Alcartra Gerben was led into the ring. Hays was worried about being late for the party but he wanted the cow and bid again and again until she was "knocked down" to him. Hurriedly, he wrote a cheque to cover payment, and instructed the sale secretary that he would return to get the cow "tomorrow." He then dashed away to drive back to Calgary, knowing his wife would be waiting. When about as far south as Carstairs, he had a disturbing thought and mumbled to himself: "I wonder if the fellows at Didsbury will know enough to milk that cow out tonight. Gosh, if she's not milked out, her full udder might invite mastitis."

Harry Hays was deep in the quagmire of quandary. To return to attend to his cow would make him late for the party; to continue south might mean the loss of a great cow. He could be in trouble either way but, after a moment of concentration, he turned on the highway and sped back to Didsbury. As he feared, there was nobody left at the stable who was assuming responsibility for the cow and so Harry milked her, fed her, bedded her and started back to Calgary.

Arriving home too late for the party, Harry was unpopular but he felt sure that, if the new cow performed the way he believed she would, his sins of omission would be forgiven or forgotten. Soon after the cow was safely quartered in the Hays barn, brothers Harry, Tom and Jack decided they had a wonder cow and she should be placed on a government-supervised test, fed heavily and milked four times a day for 365 days.

The test began on March 25, 1944, and as Harry said: "We fed her the way you'd feed a threshing machine and everything we gave her, she converted to milk." The world record for butterfat production for 365 days stood at 1402 pounds at that time and was held by an American cow owned by Carnation Milk Co.. Quietly, the Hays boys were wondering if their cow might come close to that figure but nobody else was that optimistic.

Jack Hays, with the help of a trustworthy hired helper, Eugene Okumura, would be responsible for the milking, every six hours around the clock. Through the early months, the milking machine was used but, for the last while, the cow seemed to respond better to hand milking and that became the rule. Late in the 365-day period, when it appeared that a notable record was indicated, members of the Hays family became excited, like kids watching a hockey game with the home team ahead.

When the last milking was weighed and tested at five o'clock on the afternoon of March 24, 1945, and government inspectors and press and radio reporters crowding around the cow, it was announced that Alcartra Gerben's production for exactly one year stood at 27 748 pounds of milk and 1409 pounds of butterfat. She was the first cow of any breed, any age, to reach that level of butterfat. It was the equivalent of 1716 pounds of real butter. The Hays barn rang with shouts and cheers and, certainly, there would have to be a celebration.

Having anticipated something like this, Harry made advance arrangements for a big and elegant banquet at the Palliser Hotel to honour, of course, Alcartra Gerben. There was a guest list of 500 from far parts of Canada and the United States and it was intended that the Dairy Queen, herself, would be present in the ballroom. But an obstacle arose; when the hotel management asked if Alcartra Gerben was "house-broken," Harry had to admit she was not so trained. There were many disappointed guests but there were dozens of pictures of the Queen on the walls and she contributed the second most important beverage for the toasts. The toast to Alcartra was formalized with her own milk.

The name of the famous cow became increasingly well known around the dairy cattle world. Three of her calves sold for $10 000, $8000 and $7000 respectively and the aging lady, herself, and one son sold for $20 000 each in the Hays dispersal sale. Harry Hays said many times that Alcartra Gerben rewarded him most generously for missing the New Year's Eve party on December 31, 1944, and coming to her relief instead.

Shocked but not silenced

A farm wife living east of Vulcan walked light-heartedly to the barnyard to gather a few eggs for supper and, on entering the stable, the first thing she saw was the body of her husband hanging by a rope fastened to a rafter, an obvious case of suicide. She halted in shock but was not silenced for long. She looked again to assure herself that she had seen everything correctly and then gasped: "So that's where my good clothesline went!"

The bugling bull

A Northern Saskatchewan farmer's herd bull was sick and the trouble was thought to be constipation. Having to take a crate of eggs to town and trade them for their equivalent value in groceries, the owner resolved to consult the local veterinarian about his ailing bull. He caught up with the vet at Flett's livery stable where he made his business headquarters.

The veterinarian listened to the farmer's report and said he would gladly drive out to the farm to see the ailing bull but he had quite a few country calls to make and believed that in a case of this kind, where a simple enema was needed, the farmer might as well administer it himself. "I'll tell you how to do it. You should be prepared to give him a big dose, between one and two pails of warm, soapy water. All the equipment you need is a piece of rubber hose and a tin funnel. You shouldn't have any trouble."

The farmer agreed that the instructions sounded simple enough but when he arrived home, he was totally unable to find either a short length of rubber hose or a funnel. But farmers are resourceful people – they have to be – and he was determined to find suitable substitutes for the hose and funnel. Suddenly, he had an idea: his son was playing in the school orchestra and had acquired a brass trumpet with a fine funnel-shaped extremity. It would serve the purpose, he was convinced.

He stabled the bull and tied him in a stall, prepared two pails of warm soapy water and, when no eyes were upon him, he stole into the house and, locating the brass trumpet, took it to the stable. The bull watched with suspicion but the ingenious farmer had no trouble in making the proper connection between the bull and trumpet and pouring the water. But, by the time a full pail of the fluid had been used, the bull was becoming restless. By the time a pail and a half had been poured, the animal was angry and broke loose. With the trumpet still in place, he dashed across the yard and toward the road. The resulting movement of intestinal wind and water produced typical blasts from the trumpet and the harder the frightened bull ran, the louder were the musical sounds. Neighbours rushed out to determine the source of the music and then tried to follow the fleeing bull. The bull's mistake was in crossing the churchyard where he fell into an open grave and broke his neck. The sorrowing neighbours buried the dead bull right there and raised a grave marker over him: "A warning to bulls and men who err in blowing their own horns." *(A western farmspun of about 1911)*

Farm worker wanted urgently

The wartime demands for manpower made it almost impossible for farmers in 1943 to obtain the hired workers they needed. Nothing, it seemed, was too good for a hired man, as this want ad copied by the *Country Guide* from the *Seamans Gazette* made clear: "Farm Hand Wanted. Experience unnecessary but o.k. if you have what it takes. Hours 8 am to 6 pm Half holiday at Saturdays. All operations on the farm by remote control. One day will give necessary experience at the control board. No milking. No stables to clean. Push button horse and cattle feeding. All field equipment remote control. Use of piano. Bring your own guitar. Hired girl has fine soprano voice. No Sunday work and use of car from Saturday to Monday morning with gas found. Wages $150 a month twice a month. Bring your own ration coupon book. Please apply at once as I am in urgent need of a man. Box XYZ, Seamans."2

A war tank on every farm

A Manitoba farm boy, at the end of World War II, wrote to the Minister of Defence in Ottawa, asking: "Please reserve one of them war tanks [for us] when you sell them. With one of them we can do our fall ploughing without fear of being killed by city hunters shooting at ducks."3

Chapter 5

Humorists in ranchland

5

Fred Stimson's alleged visit to Buckingham Palace

Meet Fred Stimson, first manager and part-owner of the North West Cattle Co. ranch west of High River and, by general agreement, the "Prince of Western Raconteurs!"

He was a big man in all dimensions, striking in features and mild mannered until he was made angry and then he could be demonic. They said he was gentle with horses, kindly toward remittance men and unforgiving toward cattle rustlers.

The story of homespun variety for which he was long remembered was told at the Ranchmen's Club in Calgary, which had become a hangout for a little group of English remittance men whose boasting about their "splendid connections at home" was becoming tiresome. When the sitting room had a big audience of Calgarians and two overbearing remittance men, one of Fred's friends asked him to "tell us how you got along in England when you took the last shipment of cattle to market there." It was the opening that Fred wanted.

His voice was clear and he began: "Well, I was lucky. I struck a strong market and my cattle sold well. I decided to take a few days off and visit London. I was there before and I checked in at the Cecil Hotel. Well, I got a surprise. Even before I was settled in my room, I was being paged to take a telephone call and when I took up the receiver a lady's voice asked: 'Is that Mr. Stimson from High River?' I said 'yes' and then, if you please, the lady said: 'This is Queen Victoria speaking. We heard you were in London and my daughter and I are most anxious to meet you, a real cowboy.'

"I was flabbergasted but she kept on talking, said she had a spare bed in the Palace and was sending the royal carriage for me right away. Then before I could say anything, she hung up. What was I to do? I just stuffed my clothes in my grip and went to the hotel door and the Royal coach was there and the coachman, dressed up like the leader of a band, said he'd carry my grip. He did and we drove away to the Palace.

"I tell you, men, I was damned nervous but I didn't need to be. The Queen met us at the palace door and called a couple of servants to take my grip and escort me to my room. And say, what a swanky room! Not much like my room at the ranch. Pretty soon, I was called to supper. Apparently I rated as the guest of honour and sat on the Queen's right. I was worried about what to talk about in the presence of a Queen but I didn't need to worry. She asked questions about life in Alberta, wanted to know how we spent the winter evenings on the ranch. So I told her we played a lot of card games like whist and five hundred. She had never heard of these games and said she would like to learn how to play them. I told her I'd teach her and she said she'd like that but warned that the Palace rules did not permit card games. I told her that would present no problem, that she and the Princess and I could go to a London club on the next evening and play cards.

"'Oh, Mr. Stimson,' she said, 'I think that would be splendid – tomorrow evening.'

"Next evening the Royal coach and four beautiful horses sped away with us to a club of the Queen's choosing and we had dinner and played cards. The Royal Ladies were absolutely delighted and the evening passed too quickly. When the Queen looked at her watch, she gasped: 'My gracious, it's 10 o'clock. I try to be home by this time. I'll go now but you, Mr. Stimson, and the Princess may stay a while longer if you wish. As long as the Princess is with you, Mr. Stimson, I'll have no worries. But be home by 11!'

"The Princess and I had some tea and cakes and then a waltz or two and in no time at all, it was 11 o'clock. The coach was waiting for us and the Princess was worried about her mother being worried.

"We had another worry. The Palace lights were all turned out when we got there and the front door was locked. The Princess discovered she didn't have a key. What were we to do? I suggested that if we could find a window that wasn't bolted, I would lift her inside. She didn't care for that idea. She knocked at the door but there was no response. Well, gentlemen, we had to do something so I took my old revolver from my hip pocket and pounded on the door and, in a few seconds, we heard the window over the door open and a voice say: 'Who's there?' It was the Queen and the Princess answered: 'Oh Mother, it's just Cowboy Fred and me. We're locked out.'

"'Oh you foolish children. You should have been home half an hour ago. But just wait a minute until I put my Crown on my head and I'll be down to let you in.' And so we ended a delightful day."

The Calgary men laughed heartily and the two remittance men moved away quietly and didn't reappear at the Ranchmens' Club.

Eugene Burton – Medicine Hat's man of wit and wisdom

He was a native son of Medicine Hat, one who could never be taken for anything except a cowboy-rancher. Eugene Burton looked like a cowboy, walked like a cowboy, talked like one and was one who saw the old ways of ranching giving place to new ways. Ranches were becoming smaller; kids around the corrals were fewer – they were all away at city schools or university – no more dances or Christmas concerts in the country school; not much time for fun any more.

Burton's V-T ranching enterprise began in a small tent on a half-section property on Bull Creek, 10 miles south of "The Hat" in 1923. The modest beginning followed a three year stint of office work in the Winnipeg Grain Exchange, partly to "test the waters" of business life in a city. The test was a success and the young man was convinced: he was going ranching. For the rest of his life he was a rancher and ranch philosopher.

Prior to his death in 1969, he admitted to some speculation about his arrival at the Pearly Gates and possible conversation with St. Peter. As Chairman of the membership committee in the heavenly realm, St. Peter might be expected to say: "Gene Burton, are you sure you're in the place you want? You probably surmise that most of your old friends are in the other place," to which Gene would reply: "By golly, Peter, you've raised a good question. I don't know much about the living conditions at either place but I want to be with old Tony Day, who took me to the first Calgary Stampede in 1912, and George Lane, who was the Founding Father of Canadian ranching, and Mack Higdon and Walter Huckvale and Charlie Beil and Barney Simpson and the Mitchells and Rosses and Gilchrists and Hargraves. And Hell, yes, old Will Rogers who was the Oklahoma cowboy and great American humorist and movie star. He was one of my heroes and I'd like to be with him too."

It didn't occur to the modest Gene but it did to his friends that he and Will Rogers had something in common and a few people were already calling him: "Our Will Rogers."

He enjoyed telling stories like that of Bill Buller, who was struck again and again by a rattlesnake but had so much alcohol in his blood that the venom had no effect, or Charlie Beil's mule, Judy, a proper celebrity, trained and brought to Canada by Slim Pickens, the well-known rodeo clown. At the end of rodeo season, Pickens presented the mule to Dick Scholten who then presented her to Charlie Beil who took her to spend the winter at Gene Burton's. Judy became the best known quadruped in the country, famous for the problems of her making as much as for her public appearances. When Beil had her at Banff, he often rode her down the main street to the post office for the mail. Banff citizens didn't forget the day Judy, the old trick mule, decided to sit down in the middle of the main street, blocking traffic and bringing the town police on the run. The police ordered: "Get that mule off the street," and Beil answered: "You get her off; you'll need a tow-truck." The crowd grew and the sit-down strike didn't end until Beil made a long-distance call to California, talked to Slim Pickens and got the "combination."

Judy then went to Medicine Hat for the rest of the winter. When asked if he was busy, Gene Burton said: "Yes, I'm baby-sitting Charlie's mule when she isn't baby-sitting me." But Judy seemed born to crises and when Beil came to Medicine Hat for her in the spring he found her fraternizing with a rattlesnake. He, Charlie, was cinching a saddle on the mule when he noticed the fully grown reptile curled up in her manger. Beil rushed to report to Gene who said he didn't have a gun at the house. But Charlie reported that he had one in his luggage. He hurried to get it and then, properly armed, he strode to the stable and some time later emerged with a large snakeskin over his arm, explaining to Gene: "I had to give him three shots; he swallowed the first two."

Gene Burton was a capital storyteller and sharp in repartee. Unfortunately, his friends started too late to adequately collect his gems of humour and his stories but enough survived to illustrate the point. He quoted an Alberta Indian who said the modern institution of "fast time" was just like the crazy white man who would "cut a piece off the bottom of a blanket and sew it on the top to make it longer." The person who asked Gene if he put the words in the Indian's mouth never did get an answer.

His one-liners seemed to be spontaneous and a few that escaped loss can be offered:

Fishing taught Canadians to tell lies for the fun of it and then Income Tax took it from there, saying "cut out the fishy stuff or go to jail."

It was a bad day for Medicine Hat, June 14, 1900; the freight sheds burned down; a Chinese committed suicide and I was born.

There's no cure for short-winded horses or long-winded preachers. You might get rid of one by trading but you're stuck with the other.

A street corner evangelist asked Gene Burton if he wanted to go to Heaven and he replied: "If you can tell me for sure if they'll let me keep a horse and saddle there, it would make your question a lot easier to answer."

There's a right and wrong way to do everything. He's a poor s.o.b. who can't find one of them.

There are no rattlesnakes in Ottawa. A good clean-living rattler could never survive in that habitat.

I don't believe all I read in the newspapers but I wouldn't want to miss any part of it, especially the falsehoods.

"How are you keeping, Gene?" a neighbour asked when they met on the street. Gene replied: "Well, when my feet, my bowels and my banker aren't hurting me, I'm fine and this is one of my good days."

When he wore his aging cowboy hat to a posh theatrical premiere, he responded to a hint of criticism by saying: "It's an honest old hat being worn by one who is trying to be an honest man. It's paid for and I am proud of it. Do you think they can say more for any hat in the house?"

Gene Burton's originality and humour made him ideal company for an evening or a week. But if he could have chosen the area of public influence in which to make a lasting impression, it wouldn't have been in humour. He was so concerned, especially in his later years, about the sharp deterioration of native grasslands, depletion of farm soils, declining populations of native wildlife, losses in forestry, and the greedy raiding of nonrenewable resources, that his strongest pleas would have been in the name of conservation. One who made a Southern Alberta tour with him expressly to inspect certain evidence of neglect and greed could never forget his expressions of sadness when pointing out some of the 23 locations on land he was then grazing where well-meaning settlers had been encouraged by government policy to homestead and make investments before discovering the awful cost of errors in land-use alone.

Michael Oxarart's private horse war of 1884

Michael Oxarart, who gained his first experience with horses in his native Pyrenees Mountains in Southern France and later experience in Texas, became the leading subject of controversy in the Canadian West in 1884. Farmers meeting at the country stores were sure of lively conversation when opening with the question: "What's the latest news about the Oxarart horse wars?"

Citizens who chose to believe that "where there's smoke there's fire," were convinced that Oxarart was guilty of horse stealing or horse smuggling or something related to horses, but were forced to admit that, though he was charged several times and his horses were seized about as many times, he was never convicted and never failed to recover his controversial horses.

The *Edmonton Bulletin's* year-end report of Oxarart's dealings was a fair summary and is presented herewith:

Mr. Oxarart brought in a band of 175 head of horses to Calgary from south of the line for sale in the North West. At Macleod he passed them through the Customs house in due form, paying duty on them [at a valuation] of $35 a head, which was the original cost. He lay at Macleod some time and, while there, purchased a band of a hundred head of horses which had been brought in by I. G. Baker Co. two years previous.

On his arrival at Calgary, where he proposed selling, Mr. Bannerman, customs house officer and postmaster, dropped upon the fact that Mr. Oxarart had more horses in his possession than he had paid duty on and, concluding that the over-plus had been smuggled, made a seizure of the whole band. Captain Cotton, customs officer at Macleod, and D. W. Davis of the I. G. Baker Co., were obliged to come from Macleod to set the matter right and the horses were released. Shortly afterwards, the original Oxarart band was seized again on the charge that [the horses] had been grossly undervalued in passing the customs at Macleod. This claim was also disproved and again the horses were ordered to be released. But, while they were in custody, some 45 head disappeared, presumed to have been stolen and run across the line. For the value of these, Mr. Oxarart held the customs authorities responsible.

During the time the horses were in custody, Oxarart sold some 60 head to Dr. Lauder and on their release he [Dr. Lauder] sold them to the Mount Royal Ranch Company, to which they were delivered. Oxarart then left for Brandon with the remainder of his horses and commenced selling them. But, shortly afterwards, Mr. Bannerman was informed that instead of 60, there were 105 horses at the Mount Royal Ranch with Oxarart's brand on them. As the extra number could only be the stolen animals and as it was impossible to identify the ones that were stolen, Mr. Bannerman caused the whole number to be seized by the police and Mr. Oxarart arrested for stealing the 45 head (of his own horses) from the custody of the Deputy Sheriff. A third trial was held and Mr. Oxarart acquitted.

The Mount Royal Ranch was counted out its 60 horses from the band and the remaining 45 are still with the police, as no one claims them.

Mr. Oxarart has appealed to the United States Government to support his claim for damages in the matter. It is asserted on the one hand that the whole proceedings were instigated by the local ranch companies with horses to sell to prevent Mr. Oxarart from selling out and prevent other parties from bringing in horses in a similar manner, while the other side asserts that the charges against Mr. Oxarart were true and he was really concerned in the thefts.[1]

In presenting the summary a few days before the end of 1884, the editor of the *Edmonton Bulletin* probably believed the episode was at an end. But the end of the Oxarart story was not yet. After Oxarart and Thebo were brought back from Brandon and charged with the theft of the 45 mystery horses – and acquitted – Oxarart departed for Montana to buy more horses, this time to be placed on land of Oxarart's choosing in the Cypress Hills, a location that reminded him of the Pyrenees and which he loved dearly. His ranching operation flourished until he was the biggest horse-breeding operator between Winnipeg and Medicine Hat. High class Thoroughbreds became a specialty. It was fortunate that he was not easily rebuked by customs officers and police. He remained an enthusiastic horseman until 1896 when, for reasons of failing health, he made a trip to France and died en route. His ranch in the Hills became the property of another colourful rancher and horsemen, D. J. "Joe" Wylie.

Dad Gaff needed a bed

To most people who recognized his name, "Dad" Gaff was the rancher who bought a hotel to get a bed for the night. But he was much more than that.

If it had been possible to peer into the recesses of his memory, the searcher might have caught new glimpses of outlaws like Wild Bill Hickock, well known to Gaff, Buffalo Bill Cody, with whom Gaff was a buffalo hunting contemporary on the Kansas and Wyoming plains, pioneer ranching on the south slopes of Cypress Hills and, finally, the unexpected experiences of a hotel owner in Saskatchewan. Altogether, these revelations would have been like viewing a western movie with the best factual origin.

This man, known for so long as Dad Gaff that he all but forgot that he was once J. A. Gaff, had a big frame, a big laugh, a big smile and a good sense of humour. After leaving his home in Indiana, where he was born in 1850, he became a buffalo hunter in Kansas and Wyoming. At first he indulged in the wasteful and unworthy practice of hunting buffalo for their tongues only but then became a hide hunter when buffalo hides found a ready market at two dollars each. Slaughtering for this cash market became a full time occupation.

Gaff liked the life, even though it was dangerous. Hunting on foot presented constant threats of attack from wounded buffalo and, with almost every male adult carrying a six-shooter, unscheduled bullets were ever-present hazards. In the company with which he hunted, he said a man would no more think of leaving home without one or two guns on his belt than going down the street without his pants.

The unrestricted buffalo kill was a shameful business but nobody showed much concern and United States policy makers appeared to encourage it, reasoning that, as long as the native people could hunt for a living, they would not be persuaded to settle on reserves.

In any case, the big kill would not continue for long. Two dollars per hide looked like easy money and hunters boasted about the extent of their slaughter. Buffalo Bill Cody was believed to have had the "best" killing record when he and hired helpers in his camp killed 5000 of the big animals in one year but Dad Gaff claimed a higher number, 5200 in his biggest year. Dad was thus the champion.

But regardless of who counted the biggest kill, the great herds were pursued savagely until only a few animal stragglers remained and the hide hunters were obliged to find other employment. Gaff was attracted to ranching and made a beginning in Wyoming, where he believed he was settled, but, in 1898, with his wife and seven children, two covered wagons and about 30 horses, he was moving to Canada, his goal being the Cypress Hills. They liked what they found and chose a location on Battle Creek, 50 miles south of Maple Creek. Cattle and horse numbers grew spectacularly until the cruel winter of 1906-07. After entering the winter with 1300 cattle, they were able to count fewer than 500 head in the spring. But the Gaffs had no thought of giving up and the herd numbers came back and the family was doing well.

When Dad had money, he didn't try to hide the fact. George Shepherd of Maple Creek told of Dad entering a bar in that town and ordering a 50-cent drink. To pay for it, he produced and flourished a $1000 bill. The bartender was flustered and said he couldn't change it. Fortunately, the proprietor was nearby and upheld the hotel's prestige by withdrawing a roll from his pocket and saying that he could change Dad Gaff's bill. He promptly counted out $999.50 and invited Dad to buy himself another drink.

Dad didn't mind being the centre of attraction and so it was when he and some cronies were engaged in poker in the village of Govenlock. Having had a successful evening at cards, he decided to take a room at the little hotel and thereby spare himself the long drive home. Presenting himself before the hotel owner, who was also the clerk, he asked brusquely for a room and informed no less brusquely that the room rate was $7 per night, payable in advance.

The aging rancher took offence and replied: "What's the matter with you? Seven dollars for a miserable little room? I didn't come to buy your damned hotel."

Said the hotel proprietor: "You make me laugh; you couldn't raise the price of the outdoor two-seater."

Looking the owner straight in the eye, Dad asked: "All right, what's your price?"

The owner named his price and Dad, without a pause, took out his chequebook, wrote a cheque for the full amount and said: "Now, I'll chose my own room. You can stay here tonight but tomorrow you're out. Understand?" Dad chose his room for the night and spent his last years there. A daughter ran the hotel after Dad's passing at the age of 90.

Romance on the range

The two principal characters in this ranchland courtship were not named, nor was the exact locale but the account as presented by the *Macleod Gazette* gave reason to presume that the flirtation was in Southern Alberta. Further identification, however, was not necessary. The following is the account:

> Our western range girls are thoroughbreds when it comes down to any sort of business, courting, marrying, rounding up or being rounded up. One of these prairie pinks who has been visited by a cowboy for nearly a year, became impatient at his failure to declare intentions, and when he next called, she took him gently by the ear, led him to a seat and said:
>
> 'Nobby, you've been foolin' round this claim for mighty near a year an' have never yet shot off yer mouth on the marryin' biz. I've cottoned to yu on the square clean through an' have stood off every galoot that has tried to chip in an' now I want you to come down to bizness or vamoose the ranch. Do the talk act or pull yer freight. If yer on to marryin' an' want a pard that'll stick right to ye till you pass in yer checks an' the good Lord calls yu over the range, just shoot yer wad an' we'll hitch. But if that haint yer game, draw out an' give some other young feller a show for his pile. Now sing yer song or slope.'
>
> He sang.[2]

Horse race down the mountainside

Williams Lake, 325 miles or 540 kilometres northeast of Vancouver, claimed the first rodeo in British Columbia and some of the richest rodeo traditions in Canada. Local enthusiasts told visitors very seriously that the last rodeo – whenever it will be held – will likewise be at Williams Lake.

The first rodeo was in 1920 and, two or three years later, the wild mountainside race was added as an annual feature. It was, without a doubt, the most spectacular and most nearly "vertical" horse race the world has known.

An eastern visitor, seeing it for the first time, asked: "Why don't they use parachutes?" The reply explained that the riders didn't want parachutes because they were more concerned about making speed than making a safe landing.

Horse lovers couldn't be expected to like it but for sheer outdoor roughhouse competition, there was nothing like the Williams Lake mountain race, which started a quarter of a mile high and ended on the flat ground reserved for the fair and rodeo.

Ken Liddell, a well-known writer with the *Calgary Herald* for many years, wrote in October, 1957: "It is a good thing the Highway and a housing development that now parallels the Williams Lake rodeo grounds put an end to the wild west attraction before the Calgary Stampede chuckwagon races, by comparison, got the reputation of being a kids' soap box derby with horses."[3]

Liddell went on to say that: "Considering the vertical track, it is not surprising that cow ponies have streaked the mile in one minute and 29 seconds, a time that would throw rocks aplenty in the face of Citation which did the mile in 1:33 3/5 seconds. A flat mile, that is."

Contestants in the Williams Lake classic took their time getting their saddle horses to the top and were rewarded for their efforts with a perfect "bird's eye view" of town, fairground and endless rugged scenery, unlikely to be equalled except from a plane or balloon.

The race began with a shot from the starter's pistol and at once all was dust, noise and commotion. For the short duration of the race, nobody caught more than fleeting glimpses of the horses and riders as they came into view amid the big trees and disappeared just as suddenly in the mountain forest. But whether seen or unseen, nearly everybody could hear and interpret the sounds of falling rocks, cracking deadfall wood, shrieks from boisterous riders and hoofbeats from galloping, stumbling and leaping horses as they plunged toward the level ground and the finish line within the bounds of the exhibition ground.

Two minutes after the starting gun barked the beginning, the race was over and officials were listing the winners and finishers. Surprising as it seemed, very few horses and riders were ever seriously hurt. It spoke well for the sure-footed and tough cow ponies and equally well for the hardy cowboys and cowgirls.

The winner was an instant hero. Some of the contestants, like Joe Fleigier, became repeat winners and perennial heroes. Nor was it exclusively a man's race. At least one woman, Mrs. Olive Matheson, was among the contestants and finishers in each of three years. An older woman, who remains unnamed, is remembered for having lost her stirrups and her reins but still riding to the finish with hands high as if reaching for clouds and shrieking triumph in tones that drowned out most others.

For a few years after the mountain race was forced to discontinue because of highway and urban development priorities, many visitors to the town asked to be escorted to the spot at which the race contestants emerged from the rock and tree-covered slopes to dash to the finish. Their intention was to climb to the top of the course over which the horsemen and horsewomen had ridden down, just to test the difficulties. Most of them climbed far enough to satisfy themselves that it would be easier and safer to learn the facts of the mountainside from residents of the Capital of the Caribou than attempt the course, either up or down.

Local people said it convincingly that their contest was the fastest horse race in the world, explained satisfactorily by the old law of gravity.

Lionel Brooke – the aristocratic "rawncher"

Lionel Brooke, with monocle in eye, an aristocratic bearing that gave hint of his titled parents in England and no very serious purpose, spent most of his years at Pincher Creek where men in the cattle business fell into one of two categories: they were practical ranchers trying to make a living or they were those with overriding interests in fishing, hunting, travelling and pouring. The latter were the "rawnchers," like Lionel Brooke.

Rather commonly, they were "remittance men," the younger sons of well-to-do English parents, not likely to inherit family fortunes or titles. In failing to find useful purposes for themselves, they were, too often, candidates for bad habits. When their improvident ways brought embarrassment to parents, the young fellows might be sent with promise of a remittance to some place in the Colonies, perhaps Pincher Creek or High River where problem sons would, possibly, become inspired to adopt farming or ranching.

The typical remittance man, as western people came to know him, was a pleasant, well-educated fellow, with "old boy" affiliations at Eton or Oxford, and an entrenched fondness for cigarettes and booze.

Lionel Brooke arrived at Pincher Creek, NWT, in 1882 and found the fishing and hunting ideal. And, unlike most remittance men who remained restless, Brooke formed an instant attachment with Pincher Creek and remained. He did try cattle ranching a time or two but the lure of fishing, hunting, travelling in the mountains with Indian friends and playing polo, which he helped to introduce into Alberta, left little time for the serious business of raising cattle. He even took to landscape painting and did it well. He also volunteered for service in the Boer War. He was a good citizen and a popular gentleman. The man often called "Lord" Brooke, died at Pincher Creek in 1939, at 81 years.

The most famous single escapade of his career began at Seattle. He had visited Hawaii and, having become desperately homesick for his Alberta foothills, returned as far as Seattle before he could no longer stand the delays. With monocle in eye and grip in hand, he stood at the door of his hotel, waved down a passing taxi, and climbed in.

"Where do you want to go," the driver asked and Brooke replied: "Pincher Creek." "Where the hell is that?" was the next question and Brooke said: "Alberta, of course." The driver had to call his boss but he received permission to go and, days later, after a few breakdowns and a few adventures in mud on primitive roads, the taxi arrived at Pincher Creek and Brooke paid the bill with $500 notes and was happy to be at home.

Strayed from the X ranch corral

"From the X Ranch corral, a walleyed Pinto Bronco with a Roman nose and lightning heels. Two broken front teeth got by chewing railroad iron the time the big drought killed all the green fodder.

This bronco has a record of three busters killed outright, one missing, one chawed so he can never ride again, and several who left the country after the first time up. He has never been ridden longer than four seconds.

Also, he has derailed two freight trains, wrecked one sawmill and stampeded three camp meetings. Religious exercises are his long suit.

He has done only one good act in his long and sinful career, but he spoiled it five minutes after. That was the time he kicked the side out of Two-Way Mountain and uncovered a gold pay streak seven feet in. Then he kicked the streak into the setting sun and nobody has ever found it since.

He eats anything from frozen dynamite to live grizzlies.

He will fight anything from gophers to express trains.

When he kicks, the gulch is full of heels.

When he squeals, the sun turns red.

When he departed, he carried with him a section of the X Ranch corral. (Expenses paid for return of corral.)

He was to have been shot next day with a pom-pom from the MP barracks at Calgary. His hide had been contracted for by the Hudson Bay Knitting Co. of Montreal who are making a specialty of tough bronco hides, from which they build their famous 'Pinto Shell Cordovan' Mitts and Gloves.

Reward

Anyone returning said walleyed Pinto to Dan Cashman or the Hudson Bay Knitting Co., will be entitled to all the reward he can get.

The owners positively refuse to provide ambulances or pay doctor's bills.

They reserve the right, however, to bury victims in their private cemetery when relatives insist upon payment of funeral expenses.

Warning

The public are hereby warned from purchasing said Pinto for a pack horse for eggs or dynamite, or a quiet family driver.

Anyone detaining said Pinto after this notice is liable to sudden and painful annihilation.

The safest way to handle him is at a hundred yards behind a rock breastwork, with a 30-30 Winchester, magazine full, muzzle in a true line with the Pinto's head, a good aim and be sure he gets the full seven.

After that, he may keep quiet long enough to get him out of his hide. Anyone returning the hide may keep the rest.

SicTransit – The tail does not go with the hide. He wore it off switching rattlesnakes on the cactus plains in Texas before the cyclone brought him here.

When you think of gloves, think of Dan Cashman. He keeps a real man's store. Has one price and that's Cash. Calgary.

Dan Cashman,
on your way to the CPR Station"[4]

Chapter 6

Livestock chuckles

6

Seven pigs in a canoe

Let today's student of agricultural history suppose that he or she is at York Factory near the mouth of the Nelson River, on Hudson Bay, with seven pigs, weighing a hundred pounds or more each, to be delivered to a point on Red River; with the knowledge that there is no means of transportation for these normally perverse critters except canoes, what would be the chance of success?

It was this problem, exactly, that confronted William Laidlaw who, in 1817, was working for Lord Selkirk, "father" of the idea of an agricultural settlement in the western fur country, where it was highly unwelcome. Laidlaw had been appointed to operate a new experimental farm for the settlement and the Earl advised that, in making the journey from Scotland to Red River, he should take along something useful and needful. The settlers wanted and needed a beginning with pigs and so seven were taken.

There was no problem in transporting the pigs across the Atlantic because such animals were often carried on ships making long voyages. They might be given the freedom of the deck, from which they could not escape, and allowed to grow fat on scraps and food waste from the ship's galley. Then, after a month or more at sea, when all fresh food had been consumed, one or more of the ship's pigs might be slaughtered and dressed.

But regardless of how intently the ship's crewmen gazed upon Laidlaw's pigs and longed for fresh pork, they didn't get it. The pigs, as planned, were unloaded at York Factory where, for Laidlaw, the big troubles were just beginning. The distance from York Factory to the settlement on Red River was slightly more than seven hundred miles. For the young Scotsman, it would be canoe travel all the way except for portages and, with the protesting pigs, it wasn't likely to resemble a canoeing vacation. Moreover, the journey held big risks of failure. The rapids could be a threat to life and the onset of early winter and frozen rivers could bring disaster.

Laidlaw, presumably, obtained a helper to accompany him from York Factory, probably someone with an understanding of canoes. There is no precise information about the size of the canoe or canoes obtained. But canoes they were, and the seven protesting swine were confined to the stern ends while the grain feed brought from Scotland occupied the middle. A quantity of moss was most likely taken along as bedding for the pigs.

Laidlaw also understood the necessity of unloading the pigs every evening and holding them in lightweight corrals overnight. Loading and unloading would be a nuisance but it had to be done and there was no reason to think the pigs – always slow learners when they didn't like an idea – would accept without a fight and squeals unknown in the North up to that time.

As the journey progressed, Laidlaw's troubles grew worse. What he most feared, happened. The weather became wintry and the waterways became so iced over that the canoes had to be abandoned. Now what? The simplest solution would have been to slaughter the pigs and give the natives along the way a taste of pork. But Laidlaw was no less stubborn than his pigs and would not give up – not yet anyway. He made an exchange with the Indians, canoes for toboggans, and prepared to haul seven pigs on two toboggans, himself and helper furnishing the power for the "toboggan party." But the pigs loved the toboggans even less than the canoes, particularly the necessity of being tied down with leather straps and wrapped in buffalo robes to keep them from freezing.

Laidlaw and his helper tried pulling the toboggans but it was too slow. So they obtained two dog teams to furnish the power. Then a new problem arose: the ever-hungry sleigh dogs got the idea that pig meat would be pleasant eating and thereafter had to be muzzled to protect the "guests of honour."

And yet another problem threatened to end the undertaking. The supply of grain feed carried for the pigs came to an end and the pigs would have starved had it not been for the proximity of Lake Winnipeg, a good source of fish. A supply of fish was caught and carried for the pigs and dogs but, having quickly frozen, it was not very satisfactory for the pigs and Laidlaw felt compelled to cook it. The fish were then more acceptable but now there was the danger of bones sticking in pig gullets. It was believed that fish bones caused three pig deaths in those last days of the journey but, fortunately, Laidlaw still managed to arrive at Red River with four healthy pigs, undoubtedly the most famous pig survivors in the history of western agriculture.

The distinguished four should have been given fancy names and entered as the first candidates in a Porcine Hall of Fame. And Laidlaw, too, deserved more honour than he received.

Lady Victorine made hen history

She was only a hen – but what a hen! Her production record was 358 eggs in 365 days and she was the first known hen in the world to make it. Through her performance, she brought more attention to the University of Saskatchewan where she lived and died than enough public relations specialists to make a baseball team could have done. Prof. R. K. Baker and other members of the staff of the Poultry Department could not hide their glee and Dr. Walter Murray, first president of the University, chuckled boyishly each time the purebred Barred Plymouth Rock's name was mentioned and declared 1928 "Year of the Hen in Saskatchewan."

Prof. Baker, who was enjoying the celebration, reported that the question he was being called upon most often to answer was: "How did Lady Victorine use her time in those seven days during which she didn't lay an egg?" He didn't disclose his stock answer.

Prof. Baker's hope was that Lady Victorine, through the genetic resources of her offspring, would raise egg production across the province. But, unfortunately, it was a dream that never came true and it brings no comfort to learn she did not live long after her record year. The notable record was made in the Lady's pullet year and it was intended that she would be used for breeding purposes to the limit of her capacity in the next year.

But there was no "next year" for her and now, more than 60 years later, there are two quite different theories about her demise. The less interesting but possibly the more likely is that she died from some common avian disorder. The other explanation was repeated more often.

There was a tradition in some colleges or faculties of Engineering that members of the freshman class were responsible for furnishing the needed tonnage of dressed chicken for the annual Engineers' Banquet, presumably stolen chickens. In the usual raiding hours, one chicken or hen would look like another and pedigrees would mean nothing after birds were in the roasting ovens. Anyway, as the story was told, the most famous domestic bird in the world at that time just happened to fall into the poacher's pouch.

On teaching cattle to eat fish

The winter of 1960-61 found many farmers in Northern Saskatchewan short of feed for their cattle. The cost of shipping hay from prairie areas was prohibitive and many small herds were liquidated by sale or slaughter for winter beef. But when Honourable Olaf Turnbull, Minister of Co-operatives in the Saskatchewan Government of the time, returned from a tour of northern districts, he reported seeing many examples of northern resourcefulness and told particularly of one farmer who had successfully solved his feed shortage problem.

The farmer's place was at Lac La Ronge, where farming was still at a primitive stage. But the farmer, who had several milk cows flown in from the south, was determined to keep them. He was eating large amounts of fish from local lakes and he resolved to try the fish diet on his cattle.

"I asked him," said the Minister, "if his cows co-operated in adopting the fish diet," and he said "No. They wanted hay."

"Then," asked the Minister, "how do you get a cow to eat fish?"

The farmer, with a twinkle in his eye, answered: "It's not complicated; the first thing you must do is run out of hay."

The government man was both entertained and impressed and might have ended the interview at that point, but he questioned the farmer further and learned that, whether it was needed or not, the cattleman sprinkled the fish with salt and sometimes with crushed grain. As the Minister related, the cattle would at first eat the crushed grain off the fish, then lick the salt and finally, out of sheet hunger, bite the fish and find that it wasn't bad. Ultimately, the farmer was feeding 20 pounds of fish and two pounds of grain per head per day and the cattle were thriving.[1]

Pigs have friends

Winston Churchill liked pigs and didn't mind saying so. What he admired most was the bold way in which they "look you straight in the eye."

Ontario's Peter McArthur, humorist, farm philosopher and writer who lived and died in Middlesex County, liked pigs but admitted in verse that his particular weakness was for little pigs:

With half a squeal and half a howl,
At mealtime Beatrice starts to prowl,
Her family following close at her heels,
Nine little pigs with nine little squeals.

Then the author confesses his prejudice:

> A little pig with a curly tail,
> As soft as satin and pinky pale,
> Is a very different thing by far
> From the lumps of iniquity the big pigs are.[2]

That staunch Irish Canadian author, orator, politician and founder of the *Regina Leader* in 1883, Nicholas Flood Davin, displayed a traditional Irish fondness for pigs, although the following lines leave some doubt if the writer's chief purpose is to condemn tobacco or extol pigs. Anyway, a double play is good baseball:

> The researches of a few immortal benefactors of the pig race have revealed some extraordinary and commendable qualities. For instance, we find that the sense of refinement of pig society does not allow chewing tobacco, nor smoking nor swearing, and a pig's common sense tells him that flooding his intestinal machinery with whisky is not a very praiseworthy occupation.
> We might give innumerable instances to justify the high opinion we have of the moral character of pigs, but the foregoing ought to be sufficient to cause some of the higher class of vertebrates to fling their quids and pipes into the spittoon and hasten to gratefully embrace the first pig they can find.[3]

Beecham Trotter – a great western horseman

He was great because he had a fine sense of sympathy for humans and horses and when he told humorous stories – which was often – the ones carrying uncomplimentary barbs were commonly directed at himself or his business.

By reputation, horse dealers were thought to be sharp and inexperienced customers were warned to exercise caution. When Canada could count more than 3 million horses – all in use on farms and roads and most of them in the West – buying, selling and trading was a leading and hazardous business. Nobody knew that business better than Beecham Trotter of the firm of Trotter and Trotter, which had a big sales stable at Brandon when the city had 23 livery stables. He could say that his firm – meaning his cousin, Alec and himself – had paid $3 million for horses brought to the West.

One of his favourite stories pictured two farm parents who had pinched and saved for years in order to send their son to college, to study for the ministry. But, after a few college terms, the young man announced that he was about to leave the church in favour of another goal.

The sorrowing father shared his disappointment with a friend who enquired what line of work the son was turning to.

"He's going to take up horse trading," the father said with a sigh.

"Oh well," the friend said after a thoughtful pause, "I'm sure he'll bring more people to repentance that way."[4]

A companion story in Mr. Trotter's pleasant book of reminiscences is about Reverend James Moffat Douglas, who served an early Presbyterian congregation at Brandon and later sat as a member of the House of Commons and then the Canadian Senate. He admitted the obvious when, asked if he thought it right for a minister to be driving a fast horse, he explained that for him "it was better to be driving cheerfully behind a race horse than to be thinking swear words all the time behind a slow one."

Horseshoe Smith's big barn

Big barns made first class landmarks in farming communities and, as conversation pieces, unbeatable. And, like the biggest houses in the district and the biggest cars on the road, they did something to satisfy the human infatuation with magnitude.

In many cases, the big showpiece barns were fire hazards and, in almost all cases – except where they were supported by a flourishing dairy operation – they were better ornaments than investments. Nevertheless, the visitor to a rural area could expect his or her attention to be forcibly directed to what had the distinction of being the biggest barn in the municipality, or the province, or the world, regardless of accuracy.

In Saskatchewan, however, the identity of the barn supreme was never in doubt. The idea, from its beginning, belonged to W. T. "Horseshoe" Smith. Neighbours hearing the proposed dimensions – 400 feet long, 128 feet wide and 60 feet high – gazed in awe and speculated over a barn that would occupy a site as big as a football playing field or a market garden or a city block. It didn't make sense but it made conversation aplenty. A neighbour apologized because, as he said, he was unable to find words to fit the barn without "exaggerating or lying."

Although the superstructure disappeared long ago, the foundation, enclosing more than an acre of ground, remains to testify to its great size.

Horseshoe Smith, who was the source of Southwestern Saskatchewan's best entertainment for some years, was a product of Kentucky and, like many of the sons and daughters of the Blue Grass State, he was a well-informed horseman. Before settling to ranch and farm where the Red Deer

River joins the South Saskatchewan, he was dealing in horses in Montana and Manitoba. Selling horses to settlers flocking into the country was good business and it gave Smith the idea of raising horse stock expressly for homestead needs.

The drive to do things on a big scale was ever present. Even in boyhood in Kentucky, he took to raising rabbits and soon had so many that people in the community rebelled. In coming to the North West Territories at the beginning of the century, he fully intended to become the biggest ranch operator on the east side of the Rockies. After securing a tract of land beside the South Saskatchewan River, his first move was to drive 500 horses and mules from Montana to stock it. From that point, his operations grew bigger with every passing year. By 1914 – the year of the barn – he had a 10 000-acre ranch with 2000 acres irrigated by a system of his own design and he believed he was the biggest grower of corn and alfalfa in Saskatchewan. He was experimenting with everything, even with fruits and peanuts. Wheat was still his mainstay and in 1915 – the year of the big crop – he harvested 40 bushels per acre from 2000 acres. As for livestock, he had as many as 1000 sheep, over a thousand pigs and 2000 horses and mules at one time.

He had much confidence in mules and tried to popularize them in Saskatchewan but it wasn't easy. Anyway, with 1000 mules and a string of imported breeding jacks, he probably deserved the title: "Mule King of Canada."

When he started the barn, it took all his time up to 24 hours a day. In the spring of 1914, he drove his mule team and democrat to Maple Creek where he talked to his banker and obtained a loan of $80 000 on the barn account. The money was placed in a bran bag for the trip back to the ranch and Smith proceeded to order lumber and other supplies. He bought 30 000 bags of cement for floor and foundation construction. Then there was the lumber and the need was placed at 875 000 board feet of good quality British Columbia stock which was delivered in 32 carloads. He ordered a carload of nails but the Winnipeg supplier thought there was a mistake and sent the order form back for downward revision. The order was revised; it was raised to a carload and a half.

As the structure took shape, all country roads seemed to lead to Smith's Horseshoe Ranch. Workmen, suppliers and sightseers caused congestion on the roads and at the building site. But Smith, while watching every detail of construction, was enjoying it.

The barn was to be his masterpiece and monument. After the walls, there was the round roof to be covered with 60 000 square feet of corrugated iron – almost an acre and a half of it. Then, when the 100 workmen who had laboured on the building all summer finished their part, the painters moved in and gave the great building two generous coats of white paint. The colour, also, was unusual but that was the way Smith wanted it. And, finally, there was the famous barn-dance to mark the opening. Thousands of invitations were sent and everybody wanted to attend. Two of the best cooks were hired and they worked for days to prepare food for the occasion. Two orchestras furnished the music for dancing, one at each end of the long loft, far enough apart that there was no musical conflict. The dance was a great success. One of the entertainment features of the evening was a 100-yard foot race on the loft floor. It too, worked well.

But Smith was no longer a young man nor a man in good health. He died in 1918 at age 73. It was suspected he was more seriously sick than he admitted during his last two years, which he spent at the ranch. Without his close attention to the fields and stables, the premises fell into disrepair and operations suffered. Horses, mules and sheep used the big barn as an open shelter. It was a sad reversal.

But there was one major contribution yet to come from the barn. As a community attraction, it was a sensation, but as an instrument of utility, it was a failure. It did possess a fairly high salvage value and, in 1921, workers – some of whom worked on its construction seven years earlier – moved in to tear it down. Demolition was only a little less laborious than construction and, with proper care, the lumber – all 875 000 board feet of it – was sound and useful and was bought up by local farmers and homesteaders to be built into hundreds of farm homes, stables and granaries far and near.

Horseshoe Smith didn't plan it that way but he would have been happy to see the good lumber from his barn recycled and put to an even better purpose in farm homes.

Drama at the stockyard

Prince Albert staged an excellent Fat Stock Show at the local stockyard on June 12, 1941, with nearly 300 cattle in competition. The usual sale of show animals by auction followed hard upon the competitive classes and was in the capable hands of auctioneer Fred Taylor from Birch Hills. As was customary at the time, the Grand Champion steer was the first to be offered and sold. There was only one Grand Champion and it was sure to bring a big premium.

There stood the champ, a broad-backed, well-fleshed Hereford weighing 900 pounds, being held in the ring by its owner, a wee lad with the name of Fulton. Bidding started at 10 cents a pound, live weight, and quickly advanced to 20 cents a pound, more slowly to 25 cents a pound and very much more slowly to 29 cents where the price seemed to be stalled. But the auctioneer was not ready to give up. He had a private bet that he could and would get 30 cents for the Champion.

He paused. He knew that one of the best supporters of such sales, James Conn of Safeway Stores, was not present. With obvious disappointment, he said: "Where, oh where, is my friend Jimmy Conn? If he were here we wouldn't be long in getting 30 cents, I'd give a million dollars – if I had that much – to see him climb the stockyard fence at this moment. I've sold him a lot of champions. But we're going to sell this one right now if there is no advance on 29 cents. Do I hear 30 cents? The hammer is up."

At that precise instant, as if it had been carefully rehearsed, Conn, sweating and breathless in his attempt to be present, having just arrived from Melfort, was seen struggling to climb the stockyard fence two pens away. He got the message and knew he had to act fast if he was to get this champion. He shouted to the auctioneer. "Can you hear me? I don't know what your last big is, but whatever it is, I'll give you another cent."

Spectators cheered the congenial Jimmy Conn, who bought another champion while Taylor collected his bet.

Robbed by a hen rustler

It wasn't an ordinary hold-up because the robber didn't know the boy was watching him and, for practical reasons, the boy didn't tell him. It was April, 1915, and I was that 12-1/2 year-old boy, a youthful entrepreneur who had been peddling cucumbers from his garden, mushrooms from a secret dump and eggs from a backyard flock of 10 hens, all in the hope of buying a cow he could call his own. But now, suddenly, the boy was demoted to stowaway in a freight car carrying the MacEwan belongings described as "settler's effects" that in this case included the family's household furniture, a box of tools, two ancient work horses bought for $25 each, the family cow, called Polly, a hand-push lawn mower and my crate of hens.

We were a farm family at Chater, Manitoba, where my father located soon after coming from Ontario in 1889, until 19 years later when the elder MacEwan sold the farm with the object of going to the City of Brandon where he figured he could make money faster and easier. That was fine for a while but when city property dropped in price when it was supposed to rise, the MacEwans tasted the bitter pill of bankruptcy. They were almost totally "broke" and had a sensible urge to get back to the land. They planned to retreat to a farm in Saskatchewan the elder MacEwan had acquired in a "sight unseen" trade for city property.

Apparently the family budget could provide passenger transportation for the mother and younger boy, then 8 years old. The father, as the shipper of the freight was entitled to travel free in the car. But there was still the older boy, the proprietor of the hens, to be provided with transportation and, with the clinging consciousness of bankruptcy, it was natural that somebody would suggest the boy travel in the freight car as a stowaway. He was all for the adventure.

Soon after sundown on the appointed day, the car of settler's effects, with the father officially in command and the hen owner making a bed for himself behind a crate of furniture, moved away toward Dauphin, a divisional point where there would be a two-hour stopover. Just at the moment of departure, a train brakeman opened the car door and climbed inside, presumably for a friendly chat in the light of his kerosene lantern. He was interested in the Guernsey cow and the two old horses and he glanced at the box with the hinged lid, containing the hens. He didn't see the stowaway who was lying perfectly still. Then the brakeman's duties called him away and he disappeared.

The night passed quietly except for the rumble of iron wheels riding the rails. The freight was at Dauphin soon after daylight and the car was set off on a sidetrack to await the way-freight going west. With time to spare, the father told his eldest son to stay in the car while he went to find a store at which he might buy some extra bread and cheese for the days ahead. It was still early when the father walked away and, minutes later, the car door was opened and a man leaped in as if he knew exactly where he was going and why. Clearly, he had been watching the car, expecting to see the man he presumed was the sole human occupant leave to do some shopping. He entered boldly and carried out his planned robbery. The young MacEwan, fortunately, was in his "nest" from which he could see without being seen. He watched the thief unfold a cotton bag, walk directly to the hen crate, lift the lid, catch three of the best Brown Leghorn hens, stuff them roughly into the bag and depart as briskly as he entered.

If the man thought he was undetected, he was wrong. The boy watched intently and was tempted to dash from his hiding place to protect his hens but he recognized the intruder as the trainman who made the unscheduled call on the previous evening and made a quick calculation of the probable cost of screaming an alarm and frightening the man away. He might have avoided the loss of three hens and then been forced to leave the train or buy a regular passenger's ticket. To buy a ticket, he might have to sell the remaining hens. In any case, as he realized quickly, it would be less costly to suffer the theft of the three hens and keep his chance of completing the journey as a stowaway. And the father, when he returned from the grocery store agreed, saying: "You did the right thing."

Years later, when the boy of 1915 met an official of the railroad company at a banquet, he related the adventure and admitted that he was now able to pay for his transportation and was willing to do it. The rail official laughed heartily and replied: "Let's say you paid three hens for the ticket and call it square."

The preacher's pacer won the race

"At Brandon, where horses ranked next to home cooked meals in filling mens' lives, a race could start on Rosser Avenue or any flat surface at any daylight hour. Dealing in heavy horses was a major industry and harness racing was clearly the chief entertainment.

"One of the unscheduled races the local people could not forget took place at a funeral. There were those citizens who considered it disgraceful that a funeral procession would arrive at the graveside in a cloud of dust and feigned a wish to suppress the story. Others, knowing how the deceased farmer loved a horse race, took the view that the manner of conveying the remains to its last resting place was, after all, entirely appropriate. But by whatever moral standard it was judged, it was the most exciting funeral in the history of the rural municipality, with the preacher playing the leading role.

"A certain Brandon livery firm, it should be understood, commonly furnished the horse-drawn hearse for local funerals and one of the partners drove it. A reliable and slow-going team was kept for the purpose but on this occasion the team was not back from a trip to Rapid City. The hearse driver recognized no choice but to hitch a Standard Bred, which had seen some racing, with a young broncho known to be without moral compunction.

"The funeral service was to be conducted at the farm home of the deceased and burial at the country church cemetery another two miles beyond. With the country road to himself, the experienced teamster had no difficulty in handling the obstreperous horses. At the farm, he might have stabled the team until the service had ended but, hoping to eliminate unrest that could result from a strange stable, he decided to keep the horses hitched....

"The service was long, or so it seemed to a man who had cause to be anxious about the behaviour of his horses. With foamy sweat dripping from its overheated belly, the broncho member reared time and again but the driver consoled himself with the thought that, when back on the road, the animals would settle down and show some semblance of respect for the occasion.

"Finally the service ended and with proper solemnity the coffin was placed in the hearse. But the growing stir caused the unhappy horses to become more fractious. Then there was further delay while neighbours hitched to buggies, carts and democrats. The hearse would lead the slow-moving parade and the Presbyterian minister, driving his own horse, would be next in line, then mourners and others.

"The hearse driver felt relief when the minister, with the air of a commanding officer, gave the signal to move. The procession started with dignity befitting the sad moment although the hearse driver was not finding it easy to hold his team to a slow gait; the Standard Bred's instinct was to trot and the broncho's to run. Nobody in the long cavalcade of vehicles was worried however, because the teamster was known to be one of the best.

"But it was too soon for complacent thinking and at the moment the nervous young broncho on the off side turned his head to glance past bridle blinkers and saw the great line of vehicles in pursuit, he reared and lunged forward while the Standard Bred mate showed no disposition to stay behind.

"Despite the driver's best efforts, the hearse was now rolling forward at a disrespectfully fast rate. The minister's pacer, ever ready for a race and forgetting funeral manners, dashed ahead, overcoming any indifferent restraint from the reverend gentleman holding his reins. Those following could see no reason why they should not maintain the pace set by the leaders and the procession quickened all along the line.

"But the forward end was holding the centre of interest. With the minister's horse gaining ground, the task of restraining the hearse team became impossible. The Standard Bred accepted this as a race, pure and simple; the broncho regarded it as a runaway and, either way, the driver was having trouble. The minister's noble pacer, understanding the shame of taking dust from other wheels, forged forward with the best of purpose. Torn between decorum and the urge to race – the latter being the stronger – the churchman made an impressive show of inability to control his horse; but it wasn't very convincing.

"Any way it was seen, there was a horse race and those who were far behind were anxious to advance sufficiently to witness the finish. Buggy whips were taken from holster and applied to slow horses. Nobody wanted to be left behind. At the forward end, where the principal contestants were close together, dust was rising in great clouds and rough places on the road caused the coffin and its contents to bounce and threaten to leave the hearse and come to rest on the trail. The dead homesteader had taken part in many races but never one as closely contested or as eagerly followed as this.

"The hearse team had the centre of the road and was showing no inclination to share it. The preacher's horse had the left ditch, with two wheels on the sod. But it was gaining and the three horses were now abreast, with still a quarter of a mile to the graveside.

"By this time, no spectator could be certain if the spiritual leader was using the reins for restraint or greater speed. But with jaws clamped securely together, lower jaw protruding slightly, his august black beard swaying in the wind, plug hat tilted forward for reasons of security, and one foot braced against the metal foot-rest, he was driving like a master and trying to reveal nothing of what was passing through his mind. It was fairly clear that he was not rehearsing his graveside committal.

"There were now two questions in every mind: who would win the race and could the leading horses be stopped at the cemetery? For answers, nobody would have long to wait. With a 100 yards to go, the wild pace was scarcely slackened and the leaders were still neck and neck. But the experience of some other roadside races in which the ministerial gentleman had taken part was not wasted and he and his pacer were saving something for the last dash. Smoothly and expertly, the minister moved into the lead, made a gentle swing into the graveyard, crossed an imaginary finish line beside the open grave and was the undisputed winner by half a length. From those close enough to see it all came a shout which on such premises at any other time would have suggested nothing less than resurrection morning. It was a cheer for the parson and his pacer.

"There was still the burial. Some of those in attendance seemed to have lost interest. As the mourners and others assembled at the graveside, it was not easy for the minister's admiring friends to contain themselves in silence while the last rites were performed. It was probably no easier for the minister to forget his roadside victory and devote his thoughts to his solemn duties.

"There were those who took a dim view of the day's events but before the drive to farm homes was commenced, the minister's pacer was receiving embraces rather than punishment. The reverend gentleman wisely refused comment but, when a horse trade was suggested to him, he replied: 'No thanks, not even if you throw in the Pearly Gates.'"[5]

Chapter 7

Strength, resourcefulness and daring

7

The Great McKay

The frontier loved men of muscle, men who could hoist two-bushel bags of wheat to their shoulders and walk away or, better still, lift full barrels of water off the ground and place them on wagons "without spilling a splash."

Most areas had their strong men. French Canada was visibly proud of its Louis Cyr whose muscles were said to creak like wheels "turning on dry axles" when he was lifting and whose success in both Quebec and United States contests made him the acknowledged Champion of the World.

Alberta had a worthy superman in the powerful Negro, John Ware, who came out of slavery and arrived in the Canadian foothills in 1882, helping to drive the first big herd of American cattle to the North West Cattle Company. The great black gentleman became recognized as the best broncho rider of his time and strong enough to turn a horse of average size on its back and hold it there while a blacksmith nailed steel shoes to its feet.

Alberta's John Ware and Manitoba's strongman, James McKay, never met and were thus unable to determine who was the stronger. McKay, however, was the bigger and said to weigh between 300 and 350 pounds. His wife weighed about the same, which surely placed a dangerous strain upon the family democrat, family furniture and family bed.

But the McKay weight imposed no apparent limitations on the "Great McKay's" activity and he is remembered as a person of admirable versatility. He was one of the best buffalo hunters, one of the best guides in the West, serving Captain John Palliser in that capacity, a leading farmer and, after being elected to the Manitoba Legislature in the very first election, he served in the first provincial cabinet. He was indeed a showpiece. Somebody said he was built like a battleship but was as gentle and agile as a squirrel. Understandably, the McKay influence upon the Red River community was enormous.

He was born at Fort Edmonton in 1828. His mother was a native woman and his father a Sutherlandshire Scotsman who was in the service of the Hudson's Bay Company. He got some schooling – not much – and, as soon as he was big enough, he hired with the Hudson's Bay Company as a freighter on the 500-mile trail to St. Paul, Minnesota. It was a time when almost all freight moved by ox-drawn Red River carts and the work appealed strongly to the Metis and halfbreed people.

One of the special reasons for remembering McKay was his part in saving the prairie buffalo from extinction. He recovered a small handful of buffalo calves and raised them on his farm. But, while the herd was a small one, it played a big part in furnishing park herds after the wild herds were destroyed. His fondness for animals made his Silver Heights place at St. James look more like a zoological park than a farm. Having concluded that nothing was going to be done to save the wild herd of buffalo, McKay decided to act on his own authority and rescue a remnant of the race for raising in captivity. According to the press of the time, McKay, with the help of Charles Alloway, a freighter, captured five calves and brought them to Silver Heights on Winnipeg's west side in 1876 and, in the next year, they caught three more.[1]

Mr. McKay died in 1879 and, on the last day of that year, his herd of buffalo was offered for sale by auction. The thirteen head sold for $1000 and domestic breeding was perpetuated.

One of the many hand-me-down stories about Strongman McKay depicted another strongman and itinerant prize fighter who drifted into Fort Garry from St. Paul and announced that he was there to challenge Red River's best man to a fighting match for a purse of $40, half to be put up by each side. He was told to see James McKay. The stranger mounted his horse and made his way to McKay's farm and found the owner working in his well-fenced garden. He rode inside and tied his horse to a garden tree, then strolled across to meet and challenge the proprietor. He explained that he would put up $20 against McKay's $20 that he could beat him in a punching or wrestling match. To prove that he was no stranger to punching, he hit McKay moderately hard in the chest area.

McKay, although normally mild in manner, reacted impatiently and promptly hit the fellow back, knocking him to the ground. He then picked the dazed stranger up by his coat and dropped him on the outside of the garden fence. Giving the stranger a minute to recover, McKay smiled and asked: "Is there anything else I can do for you?"

"Yes," answered the stranger, "just throw my horse to this side of the fence and I'll be on my way."

Edouard Beaupré – the Willow Bunch giant

If it had come to a contest between the East of Canada and the West for the tallest man, the West would have won by five and one-half inches.

Angus McAskill of Cape Breton, Nova Scotia, born in 1825 and known as the "Giant McAskill," stood seven feet, nine inches, weighed as much as 425 pounds and had the strength of a Lunenburg ox to match it. He and Edouard Beaupré of Willow Bunch, NWT, never met and may not have even heard of each other.

Edouard Beaupré was a thing of wonder from the time of his birth. He was the eldest of 20 children born to Gaspard and Floristine Beaupré and entered the world with a weight of 14 pounds. He didn't stop growing until he was eight feet, two and one half inches tall and weighed as much as 396 pounds.

That height won admiring attention in any company but produced problems aplenty. Beds were not made for men of his length and finding clothes to fit was almost impossible. It was told that he needed size 15 in boots, which took a lot of leather and had to be made to order. And for a lad with the ambition to become a cowboy and horseman, he quickly became too big in both height and weight for any ordinary horse.

It was inevitable that circus owners would want him as a feature display and, after some negotiations, he left to spend the balance of his all-too-short life in the big top circus tents. He enjoyed the new life but it may have hastened his end and he died at St. Louis while the circus was playing at the Louisiana Purchase Exposition in 1904. He was only twenty-one years of age and problems didn't end with his death. A party that claimed to hold special authorization from Edouard's father accepted the body and proceeded to use it as a side show feature until arrested and charged with unlawfully exhibiting a dead body.[2] Pascal Bonneau, also from Willow Bunch, went south to help in straightening out the family affairs and brought back some of Edouard's personal belongings, including a pair of the giant's shoes that later found use as door stops and as a warning to burglers who would be turned by the possibility of meeting the man whose feet could fill those boots.

A woman's ingenuity

A farmer in southwestern Saskatchewan walked across his field to attend a neighbour's auction sale and bought more items than he intended, mainly because they appeared as bargains. He bought an anvil, a copper boiler, a weanling pig and two hens. He was a muscular fellow but how was he to carry this varied load? He considered carefully and then placed the anvil under one arm, the weanling pig under the other arm, the boiler over his head and held the two hens, one in each hand, and started toward home.

Just as he was starting across the field, however, he was stopped by a woman who enquired how she could reach a certain Sandy Smith's farm.

"Oh," said the farmer, "I know Sandy and I am going the way of his farm. I can point out the location or you can accompany me. I'm going to cut across the field and it won't take long. Come along."

"Oh no, I'd be afraid to cross that field with you. You might try to kiss me."

"But, my dear lady, how could I possibly try to kiss you when I am loaded down as you see me now?"

She thought a moment and answered: "Of course you could do it and I wouldn't trust any man. Why, it would be easy. You could just place the pig on the ground and place the boiler over it so it couldn't run away, then you could place the anvil on the boiler to hold it down – and I could hold the two hens."

That, unfortunately, is the end of the report. *(a rural homespun)*

Sukanen's dream of steamships

Homesteader Tom Sukanen's ambition was to make his own ocean-going steamship and pilot it down the Saskatchewan River and across the broad Atlantic to Finland, the land of his birth. And, with better health, he might have succeeded.

He died in a mental hospital, but neighbours agreed that Old Tom, notwithstanding his eccentric ways, was a genius who, under different circumstances, could have emulated Alexander Graham Bell or Thomas Edison. It made one of the most amazing tales to spring from the Canadian prairies.

The square-faced and muscular fellow with Baltic blue eyes and sandy hair was born in Finland on September 23, 1888, and became part of a large migration to the United States about 1904 or '05. Tom Sukanan, like many of the newcomers, settled in Minnesota where he married and had several children. But Sukanen probably possessed too much self-will and independence to be a good family man and 1911 found him setting out from Minnesota and going to the Saskatchewan homestead country – on foot. People who knew him well were convinced that he walked every step of the way and found good land. In October of that year, he filed on the northeast homestead quarter of Section 14-26-9-W.3, about a two-hour walk west of the Saskatchewan village of Macrorie, close to the South Saskatchewan River. Other Finnish immigrants were located in the district and Tom's brother, Svante, joined them there in 1912. They were hard workers and brought their homestead land into production quickly.

At once, Tom's mechanical skills became evident. He was a first-class carpenter and blacksmith and, drawing mainly upon scrap material, he built his own threshing machine and had it ready for his first crop. From then on, he was creating complex machines regularly and neighbours watched with disbelief. "What will Old Tom invent next?" they asked again and again. He made a violin and learned to play it. He made a sewing machine and then the equipment needed to produce puffed wheat. He constructed his own motor vehicle from the remains of a wrecked one but had trouble getting it registered for use on the road because it didn't carry a manufacturer's name and nobody could be sure if it was a truck or a touring car. In any case, it was further distinguished by a design allowing the motor to be cranked from the inside. It seemed like a first step toward a self-starter operated from the driver's seat.

When Tom's teeth were bothering him, he used his blacksmith shop to fashion a pair of forceps with which he could pull his own offending teeth. It was told that he made a set of false teeth in the same shop but there was no record of how well or how badly they fitted, nor indeed if the blacksmith teeth were really made.

He decided that he needed a bicycle for getting around so made one – every part of it. Those who saw it agreed it was not elegant but strong and serviceable. And when he needed clothes for himself and considered purchase at a local store, the price so angered him he went home and set to work making what he needed. Making a coat from a cow hide wasn't so difficult but then he undertook to make trousers from woven binder twine.

After a few years of cropping – one outstanding which was 1915 and several that were disappointing because of drought and grasshoppers – the attraction of his homeland across the ocean became ever greater. He had a dream about making a seaworthy ship, launching it on the South Saskatchewan near the homestead, and taking it by way of Lake Winnipeg and Hudson's Bay to cross the seas and arrive in triumph at a Finnish port. How lovely was the thought!

Having considered it, this fiercely self-reliant man began collecting materials for a 43 foot seaworthy ship to be constructed right in his farmyard. He must have had a prior knowledge of ships because, although the boat was never launched, informed people who saw his work said emphatically that Sukanen did not make many mistakes. He bought the materials he could not recover from junk piles and ordered enough quarter-inch sheet-iron to completely encase the hull.

He was building the *Dontianen*, as he would call the ship, in three sections: keel, hull and superstructure with cabins. The sheet-iron would be held together by welding and, fortunately, he was already an expert welder.

The three sections were completed at the farm but, with a total weight of 15 tonnes, it was better to move them separately to the river and assemble them there. Together they would be unwieldy and moving each of them over the 27 kilometre trail to the river would be difficult enough. Each was moved with the help of a winch and horse. It was extremely slow work because a winch-post had to be made secure in the ground after each advance of a few feet. At this point the determined fellow quit his farm and lived in a shack beside his work at the river. He could now give his full time to the project and the riverside site became Tom Sukanen's outside blacksmith shop with a furnace or forge. Two of the ship's sections were never delivered the full distance to the river but the hull, boiler and engine were delivered and were taking most of Sukanen's time anyway.

The project was now in progress for more than ten years and Tom's resources were running low. Moreover, he appeared to be too busy to eat regularly and properly. In his latter months at the river he was living almost exclusively on wheat and horse meat and his health was deteriorating.

Exactly who or what prompted it is not known, but, while still working at the river, Tom Sukanen was committed to the mental hospital at Battleford and was forced to abandon the work that meant everything to him. Very soon thereafter, in April, 1943, Tom died at the hospital and was buried there.

The many pieces that might have become a ship on Atlantic water were abandoned. Some were picked up for scrap, some for souvenirs. Interest seemed to have died with the man who shaped them. Some were undoubtedly bulldozed away or buried in the course of preparations for the big Gardiner Dam.

But, fortunately, a few individuals did not forget the homesteader genius. A neighbour collected a few meaningful pieces and, still later, Lawrence Mullin of Lake Valley led a search for parts of the ship and was successful to the point that construction or reconstruction could be undertaken. Hull and keel and most essential parts were assembled at the Pioneer Village and Museum on Moose Jaw's south side. One way or another, the ship with a fairy tale character was resurrected and given a permanent resting place where it will be seen and honoured. At its new home the ship was dedicated reverently on June 19, 1977, and Tom Sukanen's remains were moved from Battleford to rest beside his ship, exactly where he would have wanted.

Please stay – we're going to make ice cream

Many were the examples of pioneer resourcefulness. Numerous families, unable to buy tea and coffee in the years of the Great Depression, discovered substitutes in plants growing near home. Dandelion roots, dried and ground, supplied a beverage that didn't satisfy every taste but probably furnished better nutrition and big economies.

Numerous families that did not enjoy the luxury of matches for starting fires in stoves and heaters knew the necessity of keeping at least one stove fire burning continuously throughout the winter. When the head of a farm family near Neepawa discovered on a January morning in 1879 that his only stove was cold, he might have been further chilled with fear. That, however, would do no good. He acted promptly, instructed the other members of the family to stay in bed until he returned and then, wrapped in his warmest clothes and with an empty metal pail in hand, he set off on foot toward his nearest neighbour, five miles away. There he requested and received half a pail of hot ashes with bits of burning wood in them and strode toward home. And with an extra effort as he plunged through the drifts, he was at home before the ashes he was carrying were incapable of igniting the wood kindling in his own stove.

A story related by the Honourable James Gardiner more than fifty years ago began with a farm family inviting the neighbours to come on a certain afternoon to pick saskatoon berries – and stay for supper. The picking was most rewarding but, by mid afternoon, storm clouds were rolling in angrily. There was a rush to the shelter of the farm house and the berry pickers were no sooner inside than the hail began to fall. The stones were said to be as big as golf balls and it was apparent that the excellent wheat crop that had appeared to promise 40 bushels per acre was being driven into the ground. The storm didn't last many minutes but it didn't need any more time to effect complete devastation.

For the occupants of the farm it was a heartbreaking experience and the neighbours present, in their sympathy, were taking steps to leave at once for their own homes, thereby leaving the owner and his family to ponder in silence. But the lady of the farm, with fortitude in her voice, spoke up, saying: "Don't go. The children are out gathering hailstones and when they come in, we're going to make ice cream. Having no ice, we haven't made it for years. We might as well get something good out of the hailstorm."[3]

The spookiest ride in history

Thanks to the American poet, Henry Wadsworth Longfellow, most people in the English-speaking world have heard of Paul Revere and his famous night ride on horseback at the beginning of the American War of Independence, 1775. But, in the absence of a poet to help to keep it alive, not many people of the present generation would recognize the name of James Mowat, who made a longer and no-less urgent ride from Fort Edmonton to Calgary at the time of the North West Rebellion trouble in 1885. Canadians, of course, have always been slow in identifying and honouring the heroes and heroines of their history.

Paul Revere's ride was to warn citizens of Concord and Lexington and thereabouts of the approach of 800 British soldiers who would strengthen the existing flimsy defence against an expected Indian attack.

The first shots in the North West Rebellion were fired near Duck Lake on March 26, 1885, when Major Crozier and 100 mounted police and volunteers from Prince Albert met Gabriel Dumont and his well-armed following of Metis. The latter were convincing victors and "the fat was in the fire."

One week later hostilities took an ominous turn when Chief Big Bear's Crees fell upon the small number of whites at Frog Lake, northwest of present-day Lloydminster, murdering nine men and taking two women prisoner for no very obvious reason. Citizens across the West were panic-stricken. Many sought shelter at existing forts like Fort Edmonton, where there were rumours of an impending attack by local Indians.

Except for the stockade walls, Fort Edmonton occupants were virtually defenceless and a hastily-called meeting was held at Kelly's saloon to consider strategy. It was noted that Major General Thomas Strange was organizing the Alberta Field Force at Calgary but telegraph lines had been cut. The only remaining means of communication to the south was a long and crooked trail through dangerous Indian country.

"How, oh how are we to get a message to Strange?" Up spoke James Mowat. He wasn't much of an orator but he made himself understood in a few words: "I have a good horse; give me the message; I go." It was then close to midnight and Mowat, when asked how soon he would go, said: "As soon as I can put saddle on my horse." Everybody knew there were many natives along the way to Calgary, any of whom would be glad to help the cause by killing a dispatch rider. And Mowat knew there would be no reward for him, no wages, not even compensation if he lost his horse or had some expenses.

Minutes after midnight, Mowat was riding away from John Walter's stable on the south side of the river and disappearing in the darkness. His horse took fright at something hiding in the bushes and he thought the shadowy outlines in the trees were Indians. But Mowat rode on and by five o'clock in the morning on Wednesday, April 8, he was changing horses at Battle River. He changed again at Hartnett's at Red Deer River, then at Scarlett's, east of today's Carstairs, and arrived in Calgary on Thursday, April 9, exactly 36 hours after leaving Edmonton.

By good fortune, the Lieutenant-Governor of the Territories was in Calgary and Mowat passed the message to him. Having had no sleep and not much food during the trip, Mowat should have been exhausted, but he told his questioners that he "was not very tired." He was asked if he saw many Indians or Metis along the way, and answered that he wasn't sure if the many shadowy figures he had seen were Indians or spooks and didn't stop to find out.

In any case, he had to be admired for his courage and stamina and the toughness of that part of his anatomy that pressed heavily against the saddle. He didn't have to hurry back but, after a few days in Calgary, he was on his way, changing horses in reverse of the order followed on the southward journey and thereby arriving back in Edmonton on the horse with which he started out. He said he wasn't going to hurry on the return but he rode as far as Lone Pine – later Olds – the first day. At that point, he ran into a storm that deposited between a foot and a foot and a half of snow on the countryside making travel much slower.

At Battle River, he heard that the hostiles had burned all the northern bridges and attacked Fort Edmonton, and that he shouldn't go on. He went on and found the report to be false. He arrived at Edmonton on April 20. The troops from the South arrived on the first day of May and Edmonton people rejoiced. They praised Mowat and then forgot. But it's not too late for a good song in honour of one of the heroes of '85.

Constable Peach Davis – like a one-man police force

Daniel Peach Davis was a NWMP constable when the famous force was young and a man about whom stories of unusual skill and daring were popular. One of the oft-told stories was said to be "unconfirmed" although that did not rule out the possibility of its being factual. It was not included in John Peter Turner's standard history of the Force, *The North West Mounted Police, 1873-1893,* although many people were convinced that it was authentic.

It was a difficult time for the native people. The buffalo herds were shrinking and Indians were often hungry. Although the authorities were trying to convince the tribesmen to stay on their reserves, it wasn't easy and many were wandering across the International Border where they were not wanted. As the story was told, a regiment of United States Cavalry rounded up between 200 and 300 Canadian Crees and brought them to the Border, hoping to turn them over to the Canadian Mounted Police.

Police officers at Fort Macleod were notified and asked to assume responsibility for the wayward band. But the message reached the police headquarters at a time when the post was hopelessly short of manpower and, without hiding his frustration, the commanding officer turned to Constable Davis, saying: "Read this. The Americans expect us to send an army to the Boundary. We haven't got the men to handle that situation. Do you think you could handle it alone?"

To the question, Davis replied: "I don't know, sir, but I'll do my best."

Provided with a wagon load of food to accompany him, Davis rode away singlehanded. Waiting at the Border he saw hundreds of Indians and hundreds of U.S. Cavalrymen. Approaching the senior officer, the young Mountie saluted and was immediately asked: "Where is the Canadian force that is to take these Indians off my hands?" to which Davis replied: "I'm it, sir."

"Are you serious?" the American asked and Davis nodded modestly and turned to speak with the Cree chief, Big Bear, saying: "You and your crowd follow me. We'll get along all right. Let's start toward Battleford. We'll stop for breakfast when we get down the road."

The Americans gazed in astonishment as Davis, totally without show of force or arms, took the lead and almost three hundred Crees followed obediently.

But was this the full story or were there two stories arising from separate incidents and Turner relating only the other one? In any case, until this question can be answered with authentication, there is reason for keeping both stories alive.

The Turner story has a slightly later time setting, 1882, and blames the Canadian Indians involved for killing cattle and stealing horses on both sides of the Border. The American force had collected about 1000 of the troublesome natives, mainly Cree, brought them to the Border and looked to the Mounted Police to take them from there.

Commissioner Irvine understood the difficulties and dangers in the big escort operation, especially when he was seriously short of police personnel. The Commissioner looked grave and asked Davis if he would attempt it alone. "You'd have 1000 Indians, you know, and its a long trip to Battleford and the natives are in a mean mood," he warned. But Davis was not one to shrink from a task because it was dangerous and he said he would undertake it but he'd have to be given a big supply of food, enough for 1000 people for a month.

Twenty-five Red River carts were loaded with food but, when Davis was ready to start, the Chiefs refused to move. It was like a modern "sit down strike" but Davis was ready for any test and forthwith ordered the cart drivers with the supplies to follow him as he rode away toward Battleford. The Indians didn't move, not at first, anyway. Davis and the food supplies were on their way and Davis didn't look back. An hour past the next regular mealtime, however, Davis heard the hoofbeats of galloping horses and, looking back, he saw the Crees coming on as fast as their horses could carry them, growing hunger had induced a change of mind and a Chief enquired: "It's dinner time. Why can't we eat?"

Minutes later, the food was laid out and everybody was eating. Temporarily, at least, insurrection was forgotten and the Indians discovering the spirit of Daniel Peach Davis, admired it and didn't make the mistake of letting him and the food wagons get far ahead of them again.[4]

Chapter 8

Life's little tragedies

8

The wrong way to shoot a moose

Having considerable in common with Twelve-foot Davis of an earlier generation, George Robinson of Sexsmith was one of Northern Alberta's most admired pioneers. He was not by any means a remittance man but admitted to a comfortable English background that did not remove the possibility of becoming one. He was smart enough to see how an overplus of luxury and soft living could make a young fellow grow to like idleness and allow himself to be sent away to Canada or Australia with his rich father's promise of a monthly allowance to meet living costs and the price of an occasional drink.

As it was, Robinson rejected all suggestions of "money from home" and became a staunchly independent person. He was, however, no less interested in those who depended upon remittances from the pater. He knew many of the young men, laughed at the stories told about them and tried to help them to adjust. His own classical story about the remittance man who was anxious to shoot a moose must be related later in this sketch; but, first, more about the pioneer, this strikingly progressive individual who clung tenaciously to the old-fashioned values and pastimes in which he had faith.

It made him sad to see time-honoured diversions like high-grade conversation and good reading suffering serious deterioration in a single generation, due mainly to lack of practice. As for himself, he made it a rule that he would never be too busy for either conversation or good reading.

For many years he was a supervisor for the federal government program known as Prairie Farm Assistance. He performed well and it was admitted that he could have risen much higher in the government service if he had been willing to move but he answered that there was no position at Ottawa, not even that of prime minister, that would induce him to leave Peace River and the way of life he had grown to love.

"I believe in mixed farming," he once said, "but I reserve the right to choose the ingredients for the mix." A visitor seeing his premises would get the point; there were the marks of diversity and intensity, his big greenhouse, called "my funhouse," his private museum, his fine library, his geological collection that won international attention and a home rich with collectibles from many world tours. His garden was one of his joys and his apples one year were the best that Peace River had grown "since Adam was the gardener at Eden." But a paralytic stroke at the age of 84 years, which left his entire right side crippled, was enough to break the stoutest spirit. There'd be no more world travel and he would be in a wheelchair for the rest of his life, it was thought. But the 84 year-old sensed a ray of hope; he ordered a typewriter and taught himself to use it with his awkward left hand and then embarked upon the writing of his autobiography and finished it.

Yes, there was his story of the remittance man's moose hunt in the Sexsmith area. The fellow had come to visit an English farmer from the same part of the Old Country and wanted, more than anything, to shoot a moose. But his host was otherwise engaged for a few days and the remittance man couldn't wait.

"I'm sorry," said the farmer, "that I can't go at present but you can hitch our Thoroughbred mare to the democrat and take my rifle and drive north about three or four miles and you'll be in good moose habitat. There is a good combination of forests and swampland and, when you see country that looks likely, tie the mare to a tree and give her some hay. But before you walk away with the rifle, be sure you are straight on your directions and will be able to find your way back. If you got lost you would be in terrible trouble."

The visitor assured his friend that he had a good sense of direction. "I won't get lost," he said confidently. "But what will I do if I shoot a moose?"

"Oh," answered the farmer, "if you get your moose and can't get what you want of it on the democrat, just mark the place and we'll go back later with a team and wagon."

The young hunter drove away in high confidence and, after an hour's driving, came to swampland and tied the mare to a poplar tree and walked away, rifle in hand. He walked for an hour and didn't see a moose, then walked for another hour without seeing what he wanted. Tired and discouraged, he decided to make his way back to the democrat but he had gone only a few steps when, through a narrow opening in the trees, he saw what he was looking for and quickly manoeuvred to get an unobstructed line of vision, then aimed and fired. His aim was perfect and the moose fell with a thud that proved the animal was a big one. He rushed to inspect his prey, proud of his success – until close enough to see to his horror that the lifeless form was not a moose at all but, rather, his friend's Thoroughbred mare, dead in her harness.

The unhappy fellow had indeed become lost and walked in a circle. How the poor chap explained to his friend, the farmer, that he hadn't shot a moose but his friend's beautiful Thoroughbred mare isn't known but a fine English friendship ended abruptly.

Button! button! who swallowed the button?

When a neighbour's darling won first prize at the Baby Show held in conjunction with the Summer Fair, the judge asked the father how he accounted for the fine state of nutrition his infant displayed and received the answer: "He eats all the buttons, coins and hardware he can get in his mouth and lacks nothing in iron and other minerals."

But all babies swallowed buttons, coins and other foreign objects of convenient size and mothers worried as though it had never happened before. Pioneers in Northern Saskatchewan remembered a year when there appeared to be an epidemic of reckless ingestion of indigestibles by babies. The country storytellers certainly made the most of it and, if the babies themselves were not ready for a competition to determine the biggest intestinal obstruction, the storytellers were ready for anything.

They reported a baby that, in the course of a Sunday service at the local church, chose to swallow the 25-cent coin its mother intended to place on the collection plate. Everybody in the church became conscious of the crisis and the Presbyterian minister, with a special interest in the silver coin, dismissed the congregation and escorted the mother and babe to the manse where the wee one was treated to a double dose of castor oil from the presbytery reserves.

The mother and baby then horse-and-buggied home to wait and see. The next morning, she was able to ring the minister's number on the party-line and, with everybody listening, thank all her friends for their good wishes and report that: "Baby has passed its first financial crisis." The minister added: "Glory be, the Church can use every 25-cent piece it can get."

It was at a country picnic that another mother found reason to be alarmed that her baby had pulled the tiny tin bell from the neck of its stuffed toy lamb and swallowed it. She sent an urgent message to her husband who was elsewhere at the picnic, engaged in a game of horseshoes. Just like a man, he answered his wife's message by telling her to "shake the baby well and listen" and, if she could hear a tingle, she should take the baby home and give it a big dose of castor oil, the standard remedy. Shake the baby she did and believing she detected a "tingle" she acted at once to furnish the castor oil. At the last report, things had returned to normal and both the baby and the bell were in good order. There was no report about the winners of the horseshoe game.

Of course, it was an area in which the makers and tellers of homespun stories could excel themselves and they responded with embellishment to the account of a farm tot who swallowed a .22 calibre rifle bullet that under no circumstances should have been within the child's reach. Instinctively, the mother – whether she was aware of the grave dangers of lead poisoning or not – was frightened and ordered her husband to hitch the horse and buggy for a fast trip to the town where they could confer with a medical doctor.

The doctor admitted that an unspent bullet with a lead missile in the baby's stomach was something he had never before had to deal with. But he could think of nothing better than the "old reliable" castor oil and said he was going to administer a double dose. The special circumstances called for some special instructions for the parents and the doctor, speaking in terms of solemnity, said: "You must now take your baby home with all possible speed and don't aim him at anybody along the way."

A duty-free outdoor toilet

Property damage and losses resulting from the Red River flood of 1950 exceeded $50 million. Both the Canadian and Manitoba governments contributed generously to the repair or replacement of buildings that were victims of the water and appointed a Red River Valley Board to assess damages and attempt to make equitable assistance payments. Rural and urban citizens from the flood area were expected to make application to the Board and assist the Board's inspectors sent out to make systematic appraisals.

A certain farmer from the district of Morris duly listed the buildings that literally floated away. He was hoping, of course, to obtain assistance in replacing them. One of the buildings carried away by the high water was, as he described it, "a two-seater outdoor biffy." His statement of losses was confirmed and his claim was being processed for payment when he arrived at the Winnipeg office of the Board, asking that the two-seater outdoor biffy be deleted from his original claim.

Knowing that if the man's biffy had floated away, it would certainly not float back, a member of the Board asked why the change was being requested. The refreshingly honest fellow explained that the flood water that carried away his two-seater, perhaps as far as Lake Winnipeg, had carried in a North Dakota three-seater and deposited it on his property where it wasn't recognized until the flood waters had completely subsided.

"I'm satisfied with the exchange," he said, "but tell me if I'll have to pay customs duty or income tax on that extra hole."

A farm boy's frustration

George MacEwan was a farm boy growing up on the homeplace at Melfort, Saskatchewan. As with other members of his family, cattle and horses kept him busy and cattle and horses kept him interested. Already he was an annual exhibitor in livestock in children's classes at the local summer fair. But he was thinking of bigger things and his mind was set upon fitting a steer for the Brandon Winter Fair, where competition was interprovincial and tough, and perhaps winning a grand championship.

By the autumn of 1920, when the lad was 14 years of age, the best pen in the farm stable was occupied by a carefully selected and well-shaped crossbred steer that, as the family owners chose to believe, held the potential for high showring honours. Already pampered, the steer was being groomed daily and given just the right amount of exercise. And, in formulating a fattening and conditioning ration, nothing in the line of feed was considered too good for the steer.

From reading the *Nor'West Farmer*, the boy learned about a new molasses feed for cattle, said to be highly palatable and nutritious. It was being sold under the trade name Cane Mola and most feed stores were supposed to stock it.

At a breakfast table conference it was agreed that the special steer, already eating well, should be treated to Cane Mola. George and his older brother could raise the five dollars for the proposed investment in molasses. The brother would do the farm chores on the next day and George would drive by horse and buggy to the town and see if the particular brand of molasses was available at Code's Feed Store.

But, before reaching the town's only feed store, the boy was confronted by many advertising signs, some of them entirely strange to him, and he became confused. At Code's feed store, the clerk asked him what he wanted and he replied: "Five dollars worth of Coca Cola." The surprised clerk said: "Sorry, we don't handle Coca Cola. You can buy it at Graham's Confectionary, across the street."

Dutifully, the boy crossed the street and, just as mystified as ever, addressed the clerk with the request: "I want to buy five dollars worth of Cane Mola." The clerk was no less puzzled than the first one and said: "Sorry, we don't handle that; it's cattle feed and you'll have to get it at Code's."

The confused boy returned to Codes and said: "You told me you didn't sell Coca Cola and I went to Graham's and they said I had to go back to you, that you're the only one who sells it. Why won't you sell me five dollars worth of it?"

The Code's clerk, growing impatient, said emphatically: "I told you we do not sell Coca Cola. Now don't come back."

George returned home without the molasses and trying desperately to solve the puzzle. At home he reported his wasted day and added that neither Code's nor Graham's acted as if they had ever heard of Cane Mola. When in town a few days later, George's father took it upon himself to stop at Code's to complain: "I see you're advertising Cane Mola, yet when my boy tried to buy some a couple of days back, you told him you didn't keep it. What was the matter?"

The clerk thought a moment and then recalled the boy and his question and sensed the reason for misunderstanding: "It was because he asked for Coca Cola," he explained.

The special steer didn't get the Cane Mola and didn't get to the Brandon Winter Fair but it became a winner nearer home and brought a handsome price premium from the local butcher.

It didn't look like caragana

Joe Griffiths, director of physical training at the University of Saskatchewan for many years, was one of the most popular people on the campus. He wasn't above playing practical jokes on his friends and expected to be the victim of jokers in return.

He wanted a caragana hedge on two sides of his Saskatoon home property but, wishing to avoid the expense of buying the large number of seedlings, he resolved to gather seed at a city park and plant it. The seed was duly collected and placed in a glass container in the family cupboard. Come spring, the perpetually cheerful Joe planted two rows of seed on two sides of the lot. "Every seed appeared to have germinated," he reported, "and the hedge was away to a great start." The baby plants were watered faithfully and were making record growth.

But there was something odd about the appearance of these plants. Joe's brother called and agreed they didn't look typical. "They look more like cabbages than caraganas."

Joe was increasingly puzzled and invited a horticulturist to examine the crop. "I planted caragana seed," said Joe, "but what the heck have I got?"

The expert glanced and smiled, saying: "You've got the best crop of turnips I've seen this year." Joe looked angry and then laughed and asked the horticulturist to help him pull the plants up. "Things have come to a bad state when you can't even trust the seed that falls from the caragana bushes; but I suppose one of my friends knows all about this." One of his friends did, indeed, know all about it.

Toothache 1000 miles from a dentist

What was a person living at Fort Edmonton to do about a defective tooth, causing constant aching, when the nearest dentist was 1000 miles away, at Fort Garry? That's what Reverend John McDougall, who came to the Northwest in 1862, asked himself and then proceeded to seek and test possible answers.

After months of sheer misery, he could report burning the offending tooth with a red-hot iron, poulticing it gently and practising both kindness and cruelty but nothing brought relief. And, as there was not a pair of forceps in the country, he could not have it pulled. "All this time," he said, "my tooth was getting worse."

But, when searching for forceps, somebody discovered a pair of blacksmith's pincers and, with the help of "the carpenter," McDougall filed them into the shape of forceps. Then, "with this improved instrument," the carpenter set to work to extract the tooth but, "after five fruitless efforts, he broke the tooth off square with the gums, and then it ached worse than ever."

"I owe it to dental history," wrote McDougall, "to record that nine years later, after paying my first visit to Ottawa, I sat down in cold blood and told the dentist to dig out those roots; for verily there was deep rooted in me the desire for revenge on that tooth. He did dig it out and I was pleased and satisfied to part with my old enemy."[1]

One way to deflate a public speaker

Members of the Montana Bankers' Association admitted an addiction to golf and it was the reputation of the golf greens at Banff for outdoor enchantment that resulted in a decision to hold the 1982 annual meeting of the Association at the Banff Springs Hotel. Late in August, well-nourished bankers, well-groomed bankers' wives and well-polished V-8 cars with Montana licenses and trunks loaded with golfing gear converged upon the holiday capital of the Canadian Rockies.

The bankers were in high spirits. With a widely known Western Canadian figure, Mr. Mhic Eoghain, as the special speaker, lots of time for golf, plenty of Canadian whisky and complete separation from bad cheques, second mortgages and farm bankruptcies for a few days, delegates and spouses were assured of a glorious holiday.

The special speaker arrived by car from Calgary a couple of hours in advance of his two o'clock speaking appointment so that he might mingle with the Montana visitors and get to know some of them. He was well received by the Americans who insisted that they were looking forward to hearing his talk, entitled: "The Romance of the Long Border." Some added that they would not miss this part of the program for anything and it was a principal reason for their decision to attend.

Most of the delegates with whom he chatted added, naturally, that they were bitterly disappointed in the weather, meaning the unceasing fall of rain that was cheating them of the anticipated hours of golf.

The speaker had been instructed to be at the Mount Stephen Room at least a quarter of an hour before the speaking time of two o'clock. He presented himself at the time instructed, ready to deliver, hopefully, a talk that would do something for understanding between people residing on either side of the border. But, after glancing around the big hall and seeing only one person, the Association secretary, he wondered if he had made a mistake and come to the wrong room.

He advanced to the table at which the secretary was seated and was warmly greeted by the lady who reassured him; he was in the right room and he could expect it to fill in the next few minutes. She had asked the hotel to place 200 chairs in the hall and she was positive every one would be in use because the delegates had said again and again that they were sure the talk would be good.

But, when two o'clock came, the secretary and the speaker were still the only ones in the hall. A few minutes later, two press reporters arrived and, after a few more minutes, two of the delegates came and felt it necessary to explain that they considered themselves the only two bankers in

Montana who were not golfers. There were then a total of six people in the hall and the secretary, looking ever more gloomy, jumped to her feet, saying: "There's something wrong and I think I know what it is." She dashed from the hall and some minutes later returned, shaking her head and wiping tears from her eyes. "I was afraid this might happen," she said. "The rain stopped and the sun came out about half past one and you can guess the rest; every Montana banker except the two who are with us now, rushed to change his clothes and grab his bag of clubs and head for the links. I arranged this program and I'm terribly upset."

The intended speaker might have felt angry but he recognized humour in the eventuality and laughed, saying it must be good for speakers who are accustomed to receiving a good deal of praise and could be candidates for arrogance, to be adequately deflated now and again. The secretary, who was not to blame for what happened, felt relieved and she laughed too.

Plucking chickens

Johnnie was late for school, which was most uncommon, even where the kids had to walk up to two or three miles. He arrived at the country school at half past nine when he was supposed to be there at half past eight. "How do you explain this?" asked the teacher with anger in her voice.

"Ma said to tell you we're sorry," Johnnie replied, "but we had troubles and I'll tell you about it. Ma wakened from a noise in the hen house about the middle of the night and she wakened Pa. She told him to get up fast and see what's wrong. Well, Pa got up in a hurry for sure and he grabbed his loaded shotgun as he was leaving the house and strode toward the hen house. You know, Teacher, Pa doesn't wear a nightgown or pyjamas when he goes to bed and he didn't wait to put anything on. So just when he got inside the henhouse door, with his finger on the trigger, our old hound dog, who has the coldest nose in the world, walked up behind Pa and when his cold nose touched Pa's bare behind the shock made Pa pull the trigger and, Teacher, we've been plucking chickens since four o'clock this morning."
(a farmspun story)

Chapter 9

And bigger tragedies

9

The heartbreak decade

"I could hear a crashing sound like the collapse of tall buildings," said a Saskatchewan Wheat Pool man at Saskatoon. "But it wasn't from falling buildings at all; it was the economic earthquake of October, 1929, and the aftershocks were rumbling around the world for almost a decade."

Prairie farmers had excellent grain crops in 1928, exceeding the production total of half a billion bushels for the first time ever and everyone sent a big mail order to Eaton's in Winnipeg. But it may have conveyed a false sense of security because the same people waited long for the next big crop and, before it came, they saw thousands of fellow settlers abandoning their farms.

The heartbreak decade began with the events of "Black Friday," October 18, 1929. It marked the onset of depression and then, to compound the disaster, drought and eroding winds seemed to join forces with the rebellious economy to destroy the still-youthful West. What followed in the next 10 years wrote the "blackest" chapter – short of war – in Canadian history. It was the chapter of the notorious '30s.

The optimists – capable of being more dangerous than the pessimists – repeated monotonously that "returning prosperity is just around the corner." It wasn't. The rains failed; the wind blew harder than ever and the price of wheat kept falling until December 16, 1932, when it reached the lowest international level in 300 years and traded at 39-3/8 cents a bushel for No. 1 Northern grade at Fort William.

Farmers knew that when such a price was translated to farm returns on the prairies, after freight and handling charges were deducted, the net returns would be little more than 20 cents a bushel. The farm price at distant Peace River fell to as low as 10 cents a bushel for wheat and, for barley, eight cents. Other farm products fell in like manner, butcher cattle to as low as three dollars per 100 pounds at Winnipeg and pigs to two dollars per 100. Eggs fell to three cents a dozen.

While many commodities were trading at their lowest prices in history, the yields of crops were doing no better. Even the rankest pessimists were surprised when the wheat yield for Saskatchewan plunged to two and a half bushels per acre in 1937 and oats to five bushels.

What was left to laugh about? Not much but somehow the '30s produced a few philosophers and many more who discovered strength in laughter. When asked how much crop he expected to recover in 1936, a Bassano farmer replied: "If I can lower my binder to cut two inches below the ground surface, I think I can get my seed back."

An Estevan farmer reported that everything was so dry he had to soak his only remaining sow in an irrigation ditch before she would hold slop.

When a collector called to repossess a combine for which no payment had been made for five years, the farm wife told him her husband was in the field trying to recover some retarded crop with a broom and dustpan but she was sure the machine company could take the combine if the representative could find it under the sand dunes and dig it out.

R. I. McNamee of Cayley longed for chewing tobacco and hoped to buy a 50-cent plug. He didn't have the 50 cents but gathered 12 dozen eggs and took them to town. The merchant would give him four cents a dozen. He was still unable to pay for the plug of tobacco but went down to the livery stable and borrowed two cents.[1]

At Rosetown a traveller heard about four-year-old frogs that hadn't learned to swim.

Innisfail citizens saw a farmer take a load of good wheat to the elevator and display anger when offered only 18 cents a bushel. Instead of selling, he drove out onto the street, loosened the endgate and spread the grain for blocks as he drove toward home. But the town policeman objected and issued a summons to appear in court and the farmer was fined five dollars for littering.

Leonard Nesbitt, in *Tides in the West*, related a story that became a classic. A farmer's barley was low in quality and badly smutted but he hauled a big load to the village elevator where it was weighed, sampled and unloaded. The appropriate deductions were made for weeds, smut and chaff. The deductions reduced the net worth until the farmer owed the elevator man a dollar for handling. The crestfallen farmer didn't have a dollar. "Oh well," said the agent, "don't worry. Next time you come to town, bring me a dressed turkey and we'll call it payment." Days later the farmer appeared at the elevator carrying two dressed turkeys and handed them to the agent. "You've made a mistake," said the agent, "I asked you for one as settlement".

"I know," said the farmer, "but I've brought you another load of barley."

Sour fruits of the depression

In the carefree days of 1928, a Saskatchewan farmer – from Melfort, according to the narrator – mortgaged his farm in order to buy a pair of diamond earrings for his wife on her birthday. That was fine until a year later when, with the depression setting in and agricultural markets collapsing, the farm wife found it necessary to take in washing to pay the interest on the said mortgage. But, in the very first washings, she lost one of the diamonds and, when she failed to find it, tried to hang herself in the barn. It was a time, however, when nothing seemed to work as planned and the rope broke, the farm wife falling on the back of a purebred Jersey cow valued at $500 and fracturing the animal's spine.

When the farmer came home and found his cow suffering from a broken back, he resolved to end her misery by shooting her. But that, too, was a failure because the gunbarrel burst and blinded him. The unhappy wife then ran away with the bill collector who had come to the farm to repossess the self-propelled combine. At last report, the diamond has not been found and the mortgage was still on the farm. *(a farmspun story)*

The black blizzards

Drought and ruinous prices were bad enough. If anything was more depressing in the ugly '30s, it was the perpetual wind and blowing soil, the "black blizzards" that reduced visibility, made midday resemble twilight, sent fine soil sifting through microscopic cracks around windows to settle on clothes, furniture and dinner dishes, and left farm fields in various states of desolation.

Too much constant cropping and not enough attention to losses in organic matter or humus in the soil left fields increasingly vulnerable to the forces of erosion. He was a foolish farmer who wasn't frightened about the growing menace of wind erosion. One of the serious aspects of drifting soil and black blizzards was that much of the best soil was being removed and wouldn't be coming back. In some cases, the departing soil included everything – except stones – to full plow-depth. The badly eroded fields might still have been cultivated and made to appear useful but they were positively poorer and might need 100 years to fully recover.

The people most affected tried to halt the destruction and, win or fail, many of them were determined that they were not going to forget how to laugh. A farmer at Climax, speaking of the concentration of soil in the wind over his fields, told of looking up and seeing a gopher digging a summer home in it, 10 feet above the ground.

A man with a poetic flare sat down after a day of serious soil blowing and wrote words for the song: "Oh Where Is My Wandering Soil Tonight?"

A fieldman for the Provincial Department of Agriculture at Saskatoon reported that everything seemed to have blown away except "the mortgages and the farmers' sense of humour."

A Maple Creek farmer admitted that he was on better terms with snow storms than with dust storms because: "When a man comes in from a winter blizzard and he is covered with snow, at least his wife will still allow him to come to bed without taking a bath."

The whole story was painted on a wagon being driven north in 1938:

1930 – Frozen out
1932 – Hailed out
1936 – Rusted out
1937 – Dried out
1938 – Moving the hell out

The oil well that went berserk

Canadian Atlantic Well No. 3 tormented oil workers in the new Leduc field southwest of Edmonton for six long months in 1948 and died rather than submitting. Defying modern technology, it was completely out of control for that time and crudely belched up an estimated 1.25 million barrels of oil and 24 billion cubic feet of natural gas, thus temporarily paralysing the famous field. Some $50 000 worth of oil and gas were escaping from the ground daily. When a spark turned the well and its surroundings into a never-to-be-forgotten holocaust, flames and smoke could be seen for 40 miles. Edmonton newsmen called it "Hell's Well" and sent stories and pictures around the world.

This, the wildest oil well in Canadian history, was less than a mile from the Imperial Oil Company's Leduc No. 1, the discovery well that drew part of its fame from being the most costly; it came after its persevering owner drilled 133 consecutive dry holes before the 134th attempt turned out to be the good one that signalled the drilling rush to Leduc.

But oil wells, like people in the oil business, were born with widely different dispositions. Some were gentle and easy to get along with; some were rambunctious. Atlantic No. 3 brought cheers from spectators when it spouted its first oil and mud but headaches followed when the surging oil began making new channels for itself and bubbling out of the ground at unpredictable points around the wellhead. Geysers of oil reached heights of 20 feet to mark it a "blowout" well, one threatening "the heart of the Edmonton field."[2]

The flow had to be halted, but how? One hundred tons of mud were pumped into the drillhole almost at once but it was soon apparent that the mud was escaping from the hole by way of a fault in the rock formation. Workmen turned to drilling relief wells at an angle on two sides, hoping to strike the main hole about a mile down and give new entry for plugging materials. Through these, unbelievable amounts of water and stranger stuff were pumped in the hope of choking off the flow of oil and gas. Ten thousand bags of cement, tons of cottonseed hulls, more tons of sawdust, hen feathers, wheat and even golf balls were forced down. A local farmer said he had never fed "golf balls" to his cattle but he advised feeding the underground with "something more constipating than wheat."

The nagging fear was that a wayward spark would ignite the gas and sea of oil. John Rebus who farmed the land, ploughed a heavy fireguard around his buildings and signs were posted on the trails: "Extinguish all cigarettes, pipes, etc. here." But there is always somebody who chooses to treat rules lightly. It was such a workman, so it was told, who fled to the outdoor biffy to enjoy a cigarette. He locked himself into the retreat and proceeded to light up. But the lighter never reached the cigarette; there was an explosion that shattered the four-by-four structure and blew the workman through the air. He was properly frightened and when reprimanded, he said in most contrite tones: "I promise I'll never do anything in a biffy again – I mean smoke."

The well fire may have come from an unexplained spark a short time later and thousands of tons of water were hauled from the river and forced down the relief holes before the flames appeared to be subsiding noticeably.

The firefighters were still hopeful but, as if mustering their combustible resources for one last blast, the flames returned to their worst form and the Edmonton press of September 7, 1948, reported:

> Wild, uncontrollable fire wrote a raging climax to the worst week-end in the six-month long rampage of Atlantic No. 3 oil well when it broke out at 6:15 pm. Monday. [But] fire that turned 40 acres into an inferno of flames which boiled 600 feet into the air and could be seen for 40 miles was definitely localized Tuesday... Nobody was injured in the fiery outbreak which came 17-1/2 hours after the 140-foot derrick suddenly toppled and fell into the badly-cratered hole. By Tuesday the fire seemed destined to rage on for days or until the rogue well of Edmonton's $500 million oilfields could be flooded into submission... It was hoped 30 000 barrels of water could be injected Tuesday.[3]

The desired water was injected and the *Edmonton Journal* of September 9th announced in supersize headline type "Wild Well Flooded Into Submission" and the story that followed added: "Wild Atlantic No. 3 oil well is dead. But the burial – the complete plugging of the undermined well – will be a long, costly and difficult task."[4]

Chapter 10

Wit and wisdom from the pioneer editors

10

News and views from the pioneer press

Publishing a small-town paper in pioneer years was not a highly lucrative occupation. Often the editor's pantry bore an unfortunate resemblance to Mother Hubbard's cupboard. But the need for a local paper was as obvious as that for a barroom bouncer. To the editor fell the duty of informing, inspiring, entertaining, generating laughter and reporting the goodness of area soil in such a way that it sounded like the truth.

The following selected items appear with no particular arrangement or order, just as they might have been presented in the columns of the *Muskeg Mirror* or the *Jackrabbit Junction Journal*.

What a tiresome old world this would be without the musical notes of merry laughter. [*Rocky Mountain Echo*, May 6, 1911]

The police have found a large quantity of liquor packed up as pork – eleven barrels – each barrel containing 144 bottles of very fair liquor destroying it seems to us to be a great mistake. Spilling it on the ground is waste. Let it be confiscated and sold and the proceeds given to the Editors of the North West papers. [*Regina Leader*, January 17, 1884]

A man who has some horses to sell wrote to a friend in Ottawa, asking if they could be sold in that city. The friend replied: 'The people of Ottawa ride bicycles; the wagons are pulled by mules; the street cars are run by electricity and the government is run by jackasses, so there is no demand for horses here.' [*Lethbridge News*, June 15, 1898]

Mr. Allan Adamson lost a valuable horse from bellyache a few days ago. [*Manitoba Mountaineer*, September 6, 1884]

Astronomers have discovered a comet coming toward the earth at the rate of sixteen million miles a day. It may strike about May 11. [*Garberry Express*, February 27, 1896]

The comet which was to have played smash with our terrestrial sphere on Wednesday last has now changed its course and will not touch the earth. We can now breathe freely for a little while longer. [*Macleod Gazette*, March 13, 1896]

Two tramps struck Wawanesa last week and meandered around town until Tuesday evening when they were locked up in a cattle car. [*Wawanesa Enterprise*, June 22, 1894]

Mr. D. S. Macdonald of this town owns a very faithful dog with answers to the name of Cuff. Yesterday morning Mr. Macdonald left on the train for the Portage. Cuff had been shut up in the store but by some means escaped just as the train was leaving. He traced his master to the depot and followed the train out of town. He made a good stern chase for a couple of miles when Conductor Brownless took pity on the faithful brute and made a halt to allow him to be taken on board. [*Minnedosa Tribune*, April 18, 1884]

The old fashioned balloon as a means of navigation is no longer talked of…inventors are now working on a different scheme, that of the aeroplane. By setting the planes at an angle to the currents of air, the machine is expected to balance itself as a bird floats poised upon its wings. Then the aeroplane will be driven through the air by a steam engine. It should be easy enough to make an airship go if some way could be devised to hold it up in the air while it is being driven forward. [*Lethbridge News*, August 26, 1891]

What with murder trials, suicides, amputated legs, bear hunts, stray dogs, conventions, politics and other matters of interest too numerous to mention, our town is stepping quickly into the limelight of notoriety and no one can find fault at the dullness of life just now anyway. [*Red Deer News*, August 29, 1905]

A man in St. Louis who had been drunk for twenty years, died within a few hours of sobering up. What a terrible lesson for those who are thinking of sobering up! [*Regina Leader*, March 1, 1883]

Lost, strayed or stolen, eaten by coyotes, killed for pork or fallen into the river, one spotted black and white sow, two years old, fit to kill, weight about 200 pounds net. Any person who will return the sow, or the thief, or the butcher, or the villain who cut the hole in the ice, or the scalp of the coyote that did the bloody deed, will be looked upon by this subscriber as a humanitarian, a philanthropist and a brick and will be otherwise liberally rewarded. – J. M. Glass [*Edmonton Bulletin*, January 10, 1881]

Winston Churchill who lectured in Winnipeg recently on his [war] experiences in South Africa, says Winnipeg is destined to become the centre of gravity in British North American. [*Nor'West Farmer*, Winnipeg, February 20, 1901]

This has been a pretty good winter at Pincher Creek, Alberta, but recently it snowed 14 feet of snow in 24 hours. A rancher coming into town tied his horse to a telegraph pole in front of Garnett Brothers and went inside. A warm chinook came along and a thaw set in which fairly sucked the snow up. When the rancher came out of the store he found his horse hanging by its neck from the pole. Its hind feet were four feet from the ground. [*Western Winks*, Winnipeg, January 1, 1894]

We begin the publication of the Roccay Mountain Cyclone with some phew diphphiculties in the way. The type phounder phrom whom we bought our outphit phor this printing ophphice phaled to supply us with any 'ephs' or 'cays', and it will be phour or phive weeks bephore we can get any. The mistaque was not phound out till a day or two ago. We have ordered the missing letters, and will have to get along without till they come. We don't lique the loox ov this variety ov spelling any better than our readers, but mistax will happen in the best regulated phamilies and iph the ph's and c's and x's and q's hold out we will ceep (sound the c hard) the Cyclone whirling aphter a phashion till the sorts arrive. It's no joque to us; it's a dam serious aphair. [Believed to have originated with the editor of the *Rocky Mountain Cyclone* of uncertain date]

The age of scientific inventions has reached its climax. A St. Louis man has discovered the means of solidifying whisky so that it may be carried around in the pocket like chewing tobacco and when a man feels dry he has only to produce the plug and bite according to the extent of his dryness. The only practical advantage we can see in the invention is the great benefit it will be to orators and temperance lecturers. [*Weekly Tribune and Marquette Review*, Portage la Prairie, November 23, 1884]

Strayed onto the premises of the undersigned, March 9, about 9:15 pm, a horse and cutter containing a lady and two children. Owner may receive further particulars by applying to William Hasselbush. [*Manitou Mercury*, March 13, 1885]

Whitefish, ten for a dollar. [*Saskatchewan Herald*, Battleford, January 4, 1886]

Milk is now brought into Winnipeg from the country and sold on the streets by the bag – ordinary grain bag. It may be necessary to remind those who are not accustomed to this sort of thing that the milk is previously frozen. [*Daily Free Press,* November 30, 1874]

Citizens of Winnipeg are hereby cautioned to lock all doors carefully at night. The politicians are all in town. [*Western Winks*, Winnipeg, January 13, 1894]

Joe Schwartz, a wealthy farmer near Rochester, Alberta, is now collecting his mail in a wheelbarrow, all because he asked the mayor of Edmonton to get him a wife. [*Alberta Homesteader*, September 12, 1913]

The rule of good writing is this: Write in the fewest possible words and, when you have written it, stop and don't try to say it over again… The editorials in Eastern Canadian newspapers are far too long, making for irksome reading out of otherwise readable stuff. Our western editors have the right idea as to length, though it is no virtue on their part. Their habit of terseness and coming quickly to the point is due to an unwillingness to allow too great a period of time to elapse between drinks. [*Calgary Eye Opener*, August 12, 1911]

Lethbridge climate is of the invigorating kind. An Egyptian mummy would take on new life after six months residence in this town. [*Lethbridge Herald*, November 8, 1905]

Police Court, Winnipeg. His worship dispensed lots of justice this morning. A number of people had got hold of next year's almanac and thought yesterday was Dominion Day. The irrepressible police court habitus, Sarah Larocque, was up again for a relapse of her old complaint – too much rum; and as Sarah felt the prevailing stringency too much to fork over $1 and costs, she went up for a week. Kako-ush was a big Indian, and he got a big drunk, and went to jail for a big week, in order to give him a chance to get a big sober. Frank Dishant was just out of jail, and had celebrated the resumption of his liberty to such an extent that he got in again, for another week. Jane Cochrane, an old offender, although not a very old person, had been drunk again, and was ordered to stay outside the city limits, which she will probably do till she feels dry again. Antoine Pillon had been very tired, and he was given one week's sweet rest in the police shanty. [*Daily Free Press*, Winnipeg, July 3, 1875]

Western Winks did not appear last week because the editor met some friends from Morden... From what we can learn, we were arrested while trying to convince an electric light pole that Grover Cleveland was a Conservative. Anyhow, when we were bailed out, it was too late to go to press. [*Western Winks*, Winnipeg, December 2, 1893]

How far the bicycle will supersede the horse, it is hard to say but there is no doubt that it is obtaining a hold in our West that is astonishing. Clergymen make their parish calls on the steed that tires not, neither does it consume oats; doctors make sick calls; creditors make the oft repeated visit and young men and maidens tell the old, old story during the exhilarating spin in the gloaming on the whirling wheel. The West needs the bicycle. The bicycle was built for the West. The only hinderance to its general adoption has been its first cost. [*Moose Jaw Times*, June 7, 1895]

The cayuse [seminative or Indian pony] has done a good day's work in this country. His wants were few and his services many and various. If speed, courage and sure footedness were required as in a buffalo hunter, he filled the bill; where strength and endurance were needed, he was the freighter's stand-by. But though the days of buffalo hunting are past and the days of freighting are likewise numbered, let us not forget an old friend of our need. [*Regina Leader*, October 8, 1885]

The Bulletin never bets but there are men who will hazard a small sum about the size of the [Calgary] *Herald*'s pile that although Calgary has had the railroad for over two years and Edmonton has not had it at all – nor is it likely to have it for some time – Edmonton can show more farms occupied and under cultivation than Calgary can within an equal area. Also that there is more land under crop, that the crops will yield more bushels to the acre, that the grain will be better and the harvest will be earlier at Edmonton than at Calgary. Calgary has the railroad but Edmonton has the soil to produce crops that will eventually bring settlers who will in turn bring the railroad. It is an error that many editors fall into that people farm on a railroad. They don't. Soil and climate are the first necessities for successful farming, while the railroad comes a good second. [*Edmonton Bulletin*, August 1, 1885]

This town requires either a police patrol at night or a reduction in the number of whisky permits. [*Edmonton Bulletin*, September 22, 1888]

The idea of establishing a temperance colony [Saskatoon] into which no liquor will be permitted to enter is a good one and commends itself to everybody. A company has been formed and applied for 2 million acres which they are more than likely to get. [But] in what way will they succeed in keeping the whisky out? There is no use building a wall around a colony for you could never get it so high, so close and so thick that sooner or later there would be decided smell of whisky on the inside. [*The Sun*, Winnipeg, December 15, 1881]

The sheep arrived. Mr. Kerfoot of the British American Ranche Co. arrived with his band of sheep at the Elbow River on Monday evening. On Tuesday morning, they swam across and the novelty of the operation caused a flutter of excitement among the onlookers. The band which is composed of Merinos and Shropshires and a cross of the two breeds, numbers about 8000. They have averaged about six miles per day and came through with scarcely any loss and are as fat as butter. Until Mosquito Creek was reached, not one was footsore but, having encountered a storm there, a few of them became lame. They will reach Big Hill [Cochrane] this week. We are persuaded that the sheep interest which is just budding, will in a few years be the biggest in the Territories. [*Calgary Herald,* September 24, 1884]

J. R. Matheson is at home now – can be found at any time at his place on Sturgeon River. Now is your time. Bark now, ye sneaking curs that have so much to say behind his back or shut your mouths before he has to shut them for you. [a paid ad, *Edmonton Bulletin*, January 24, 1881]

Citizens of Winnipeg are hereby cautioned to lock all doors carefully at night. The politicians are all in town. [*Western Winks*, Winnipeg, August 2, 1883]

Marrying a deceased wife's sister is not an infraction of divine law but it is, nevertheless, an attempt to dodge the responsibilities of two marriages by having but one mother-in-law. [*Regina Leader*, August 2, 1883]

… And speaking of subscriptions, the *Guide* gets some great letters with its renewals. Take this as one of them:

See here, gents. I hereby this day of our lord do insert in the wee envelope one-quarter of a buck in order to keep peace in the family. Not that ye can learn me anything of value about the country. The country is jake but the scum that is at the tits is sciming the milk for the farmer. In fact tha are biting the hand that feeds them. I never did vote for Willie Aberhart but if tha can jugle the markets to give the preachers the gout and let the producer live on cold beans for supper and not a drop of whisky in the house to cool his tong it makes a man feel like breaking open the bounds of reson and voting for CcF or social Credit. Its enough to drive a man to drink if home brew could be hid from mortal view and I have a strong suspision that the shiners and legons will come to our assistants if the venders don't stop reducing their giggle soups. Now don't get me rong becas I never let in enemy No. 1 to steale away me brane in fact I am opposed to all strong drink that is raging. I aint even bread up in the pirple of english enuf to cry for tea . will ye never wake up to your sens of dutie and cast your vote on the winning side lest a wors thing come upon yeas. So go long with yis. if this letter is to deep fer yer comprehenson let it go in one eare but dont let it out the other. Old Jack. ["Straight from the Grass Roots," The Country Guide (Winnipeg), June, 1944]

Balaam's ass

The *Calgary Herald*, still in its first year of publication, was unimpressed by the two candidates, J. D. Geddes and J. K. Oswald, who contested the election for a seat in the Legislative Assembly of the North West Territories in 1884 and told it very clearly. Following the election in which Geddes was the winner, the editor humorously expressed the wish that Calgary citizens had nominated a third candidate, a certain bronco horse that had distinguished itself, bringing great advantage to the district by bucking at the right moment and unseating its rider, Deputy Minister A. M. Burgess from the Department of the Interior, Ottawa.

Nursing a broken shoulder and a lot of bruises, the unfortunate fellow was obliged to remain at Calgary for a couple of weeks and make himself available to homesteaders and settlers who needed answers to land questions. The same cayuse earned another credit not yet confirmed but one that would bring joy a short time later.

It was like this: Burgess was riding to make an official inspection of crown land near Fish Creek when the bronco took offence at something and went into a bucking fit, dumped the Ottawa man to nurse his fractures and pride and galloped away. Then, as if the drama had been rehearsed, along came Col. James Walker who, after retiring from the North West Mounted Police, came to Calgary and settled to farm beside the Bow River, right on Calgary's outskirts. He was driving a team and wagon and probably daydreaming about Calgary's first fair, of which he would be president. He was hoping the infant Agricultural Society would obtain a block of land that would become a permanent home for a fair.

When close to Fish Creek, Walker saw a man lying on the prairie and turned toward him to see if he was in trouble. He was and, without asking any questions, Walker helped him into the wagon and took him home to recuperate. Since he did not know the injured man, Walker could not have had ulterior motives. But, after playing the role of "the good Samaritan," Walker discovered that his new friend was a man of much influence in the disposal and administration of crown lands. It was to be expected, then, that Walker would guide the conversation to a certain piece of choice parkland beside the Elbow River. Yes, it would make an excellent home for an agricultural fair and the injured guest was in no position to argue.

Instead of resisting, the Deputy Minister promised he would see what could be done when he returned to Ottawa. It didn't happen at once but it happened and the 94 acres that became the permanent home of the Calgary Exhibition and then the Exhibition and Stampede was acquired from the Federal Government at a price of $2.50 per acre or a total cost of $235. The credit in getting the best of all sites for a fair ground was, by common consent, divided evenly between Col. Walker and the bucking horse.

With good humour, the *Herald* editor explained further why the said horse should have been nominated to represent Calgary in the Legislature. The editorial, titled "Balaam's Ass," was obviously written by one who was familiar with the Book of Numbers in the Old Testament and, so, the following is from the editor's pen:

We were unable, for reasons that are perfectly understood, to take sides in the recent contest for a seat in the North-West Council. But now that the contest is over we may, without any disrespect to Messrs. Geddes and Oswald, express our regret that no-one thought of nominating a third candidate who has probably done as much for the country as any man in it. We refer to the cayuse to whose prompt and energetic action lately on the banks of Fish Creek we owe it that the Deputy Minister of the Interior has thought fit to prolong his stay among us. The lengthened stay of the Deputy in this part of the country at the present time, when lease holders, squatters and miners are alike anxious to have their various systems of tenure brought prominently before the notice of the Ottawa government, cannot but be fruitful of good. Deputations and individuals have quickly availed themselves of the opportunity of gaining the private ear of Mr. Burgess, and the result of this interchange of views will, in all probability, lead to such representations to the Minister of the Interior, as may make themselves felt in future Orders-in-Council. We think accordingly, that the Fish Creek cayuse chose his opportunity and his man with a wise and statesman-like instinct that reflects the highest credit on his Indian blood. He is worth six North-West councillors to us, not only for what he has done in the past but for what he may do in the future.

What he has done, we know. He has presented the defects of the mining regulations to Mr. Burgess with a vigour not equalled by the combined efforts of fifty delegations; he has upheld the rights of the squatters with sustained vim not surpassed by a Fourth of July oration; and he has assailed the landlord privileges of our paternal government at Ottawa like another Parnell. What he may do surpasses the boldest dreams to imagine.

This autumn will probably see the Minister of the Interior, the leader of the Opposition and the president of the British Royal

Society in our midst. The influence of these three gentlemen for good or evil is considerable... All evils, we may hope, will be redressed, a land made smiling and happy for a decade and restrictions removed from the settlers, till the foothills of the Rockies, under their nursing hands, be made to bloom like a garden.

This is what the cayuse may do for us if, as we said before, this autumn sees him in anything like his usual good health and spirits. We will pray the pastoral deities to be kind to him. If they will supply the hour, we will undertaken that Fish Creek will supply the cayuse – a cayuse that will shed eternal lustre upon Fish Creek and stamp his equine mark upon the pages of history.[1]

Wit of the world

Charles Walter Peterson, an immigrant from Denmark in 1887, became an oxpower homesteader, rancher, deputy commissioner of agriculture for the North West Territories, secretary for the Board of Trade in Calgary, manager of the Calgary Exhibition and editor of the *Farm and Ranch Review*. Obviously, he was a superman for his community and ever an agriculturist at heart. One of his goals was to encourage more farm reading, partly as a means of making better farmers and partly to generate more humour and laughter. Working with a partner, he launched the *Farm and Ranch Review* in 1905 and in 1918, when he was still the editor, announced an important innovation for the magazine, a new section to be known as "The Wit Of The World."

He introduced the new section on February 5, 1918, saying: "You know the old saying about 'a little humour now and then...' is true, so if you like this page, help make it better. We'll offer two cash prizes each issue, the first $1 and the second 50 cents for the two brightest anecdotes forwarded..."[2]

It was Peterson's hope that the contest entries would have a distinct originality but he knew it wouldn't always be possible to separate the genuine farmspun entries from the imported and secondhand yarns that were sure to be submitted and might even win prizes. In any case, he was making an effort to create more interest in humour and more laughter among rural readers who, even then, were isolated from conventional entertainment.

The first entries appeared in the *Review* of February 20, 1918; one of the winners portrayed dinner with guests at a farm table. The host, when carving and serving a pork cut, held aloft a pig rib and said: "Ladies, you know it was from this, a rib, that the first of your sex was made."

"Yes, it was," one of the ladies replied calmly, "and from very much the same kind of a critter."

From the same issue came the account of a rancher who, after suffering an attack of appendicitis, was rushed to the local hospital for surgery. Following the operation, he was being returned to his bed in the general ward and was heard to mutter: "Thank Goodness, that's over," to which the man in the next bed answered: "Don't be too sure it's over; they left a sponge inside me and had to open me up again to get it."

Then the man on the other side spoke up, reporting his own bad experience: "they had to do a second operation on me to recover a pair of forceps."

At that moment, the main door to the ward was opened and the doctor who had performed the operations looked in and asked in a loud voice: "Has anybody seen my hat?"

Many of the contest stories won widespread attention. Of these, one was submitted by a lady member of a well-known pioneer family in the foothills, Bertha Standish of Priddis, Alberta. It is presented herewith:

> The family had not had its telephone very long and everybody took a deep and abiding interest in it. On the outside of the directory they noticed the words: 'Trouble, Call No. 4217.' It had been a hard morning and everything had gone wrong. Finally, the lady of the house, in desperation, turned to her telephone and called: 4217.
>
> 'This is the trouble department,' the operator answered sweetly.
> 'Is this where you report your troubles?' asked the lady.
> 'Yes, Mam.'
> 'Well, I only want to report that our cat got drowned in the cistern this morning; the baby is cutting a new tooth and the cook left without warning; we are out of sugar and starch; the stove fell down; the bread won't rise; my oldest child is coming down with the measles; the plumbing in the cellar leaks; we have only enough coal to last us through tomorrow; the paint gave out when I got only half way over the dining-room floor; the mainspring of the clock is broken; my three sisters-in-law are coming to visit tomorrow; our dog has the mange; the looking glass fell off the wall and broke to pieces, and I think my husband is taking considerable notice of a widow lady that lives next door. That's all for today but if anything happens later, I'll call you and tell you about it...'[3]

Chapter 11

When the old century was fading

11

Preacher John at Fort Whoop-Up

Wild and mysterious were the stories told about Fort Whoop-Up, built by Montana whisky interests at the junction of the St. Mary and Belly rivers, just a nice stroll from the spot at which Lethbridge would be built. The first trading post at the location was known as Fort Hamilton and built by Healy and Hamilton in 1867. But, while it was lost in a fire before it was more than two or three years old, Fort Hamilton confirmed the high suitability of the location and the Montana owners lost no time in rebuilding. The new structure was Whoop-Up, much bigger than its predecessor and recognized as the Capital of the whisky business as carried on from Fort Benton, Montana.

Indians wishing to deal for "firewater" were free to camp nearby and could approach the outer wicket but were not allowed to enter the fort. The traders made their own laws and ruled on the inside. Some of those who entered, never departed alive. Most wayfarers had no wish to see the inside. Reverend John McDougall who, with his father, Reverend George McDougall, saw Fort Edmonton in 1862 and built a house and mission at Victoria, northeast of Fort Edmonton, displayed more curiosity and courage than most travellers and was at Whoop-Up on at least two occasions in the heyday of the whisky trade.

When approaching Whoop-Up on the first occasion, he was over-taken by a heavily-armed and flamboyant frontiersman who shouted his question: "Be you Reverend John from the North? Well, I'm damned glad to catch you. I want the help of an honest preacher down at my shack. Yes I do. My woman and me have been together some time. We have three kids, damned fine ones they are. Say, Elder, I want you to come to my shack and splice Betsy and me and pour some water on the kids' heads. I want all this done sure and strong and no fooling. Can you canter down and do this job?"[1]

The Canadian House of Commons passed the North West Mounted Police Act in May, 1873, and it was the prime minister's wish – a wise one – that the western Indians who had been the principal victims of the illicit whisky trade should be informed by a special emissary. In consequence, John McDougall, who had established residence with the Stoney Indians at Morley, was asked to prepare for an extended tour of the Southwest to explain the reasons for the incoming police and the Government's determination that the new force would bring an end to the evil whisky trade and ensure justice for all, meaning Indians and non-Indians alike. Wisely, McDougall invited Chief Bearspaw of the Stoney to accompany him; the Chief was highly regarded by all the Indians and he proved a source of strength. One of the first contacts was with the great Crowfoot and ended when he seized McDougall's hand, saying: "My brother, your words make me glad."

The churchman should have known that he would do no good at Whoop-Up, but he went that way regardless. The big gate opened and McDougall's party entered. There the visitors saw a huge accumulation of buffalo hides, wolf and fox and other skins shortly to be taken to Fort Benton and there McDougall realized the skins had all been bought with whisky. He also learned that within a few miles of Whoop-Up, in that winter of 1873-74, no less than 42 Indians had been slain in drunken brawls. "There was no law but might."

McDougall was met by the powerful J. J. Healy, one of the proprietors, and the meeting was congenial. But, when Healy learned of the incoming police, he hastened to tell McDougall that it would be a big mistake. The police weren't needed, he said. The traders had everything under fine control. There had been people who came in and tried to change things but he and his friends attended to them; one of them was buried at Standoff, one at Freezeout, more at Slideout and here at Whoop-Up. "No, no," Healy assured McDougall, "these bad men could not live here. No, Parson John, we did not let any really bad men stay in this Whoop-Up region."[2] He repeated that there was no need for Government action.

D. W. Davis, another Montana strongman, one who managed the Canadian trade for I. G. Baker Co. and later represented the District of Alberta in the House of Commons, came upon the scene and tried to enlighten McDougall. "If you're looking for the police," said he, "I can tell you, Parson John, you won't see them this year [1874]. We will flood this country with whisky for [at least] one more year."

Neither McDougall nor Davis knew it but the new force of Mounted police was at that moment on its way and was to reach the place where Fort Macleod would be built, on October 13, 1874, striking the first devastating blow at the whisky trade almost forthwith.

Splitting the blanket

"One of the cowboys and his lady this morning agreed to disagree and the old-time ceremony of splitting the blanket was gone through with. It reminds one of the good old whisky times when law and other things were a little loose."[3]

Splitting the blanket was a handy device used quite often in years of the fur trade when marriage unions, such as they existed, were to be dissolved. The procedure was simple, fast and economical and served the two parties concerned about as well as the complex and high priced divorce measures demanded by a sophisticated society of later years would have done.

It took three people and not more than three minutes to carry out the act of dissolution; the man and woman seeking freedom from the union held adjacent corners of a family blanket and the third party, with no needless words of wisdom beyond the instruction to "hold it tight," simply used a sharp knife to split the article of bedding down the middle. When the blanket was severed, so was the union, the theory being, it seemed, that a marriage could not survive under half a blanket.

There being no documents requiring signatures, the two principals in the ceremony simply walked away, in opposite directions, and the officiating third party was free to collect the damaged blanket as his reward.

House rules at Harry Taylor's Hotel Fort Macleod

Harry "Kamoose" Taylor joined the gold rush to the Fraser River and then crossed to the prairie side of the mountains, hoping to make the fortune he didn't make at the mines. He tried his hand at whisky trading with the Indians but the coming of the Mounted Police induced him to reform and, a short time later, he was building Hotel Fort Macleod. The house rules for the hotel – said to have been the most unique in the world – were about as follows:

1. Guests will be provided with breakfast and dinner but must rustle their own lunch.
2. Spiked boots and spurs must be removed at night before retiring.
3. Towels changed weekly. Insect powder for sale at the bar.
4. Crap, chuck luck, stud poker and Black Jack games are run by the management.
5. Every known fluid – water excepted – for sale at the bar.
6. Two or more persons must sleep in one bed when so requested by the proprietor.

7. Baths furnished free at the river but bathers must furnish their own soap and towels.
8. No kicking regarding quality or quantity of meals. Those who do not like the provender will get out or be put out.
9. Assaults on the cook are strictly prohibited
10. Quarrelsome persons and those who, without provocation, shoot off guns or other explosive weapons, and all boarders who get killed will not be allowed to remain in house.
11. When guests find themselves or baggage thrown over the fence, they may consider that they have received notice to quit.
12. Jewellery and other valuables will not be locked in the safe. This hotel has no such ornament as a safe.
13. In case of fire, the guests are requested to escape without unnecessary delay.
14. The bar in the annex will be open day and night.
15. Guests without baggage must sleep in the vacant lot and board elsewhere till baggage arrives.
16. No cheques cashed for anybody. All guests are requested to rise at 6 am. This is imperative as the sheets are needed for tablecloths.
17. Meals served in rooms will not be guaranteed. Our waiters are hungry and not above temptation.
18. Board and lodging $50 a month with bench to sleep on, $60 a month with bed.[4]

Hotel Macleod's new Ten Commandments

1. When thirsty, thou shalt come to my house and drink.
2. Thou shalt always keep my name in memory, and forget all others in the same business.
3. Thou shalt honour me and my bartender, so thou shalt live long in the land, and continue to drink at my house forever.
4. Thou shalt honour me and mine, that thou mayest live long and see us again.
5. Thou shalt not break or destroy anything on my premises, else thou shalt pay for it double its value.
6. No singing; thou shalt not raise thy voice in song, or they feet in gaiety.
7. Thou shalt not dare to pay thy bills in bad money.

8. Thou shalt not steal from me, as I need all I have and more too.
9. Thou shalt not expect over-large glasses, as the landlord must live on the profits.
10. After eating and drinking at my house, thou shalt pay me promptly, for the landlord never likes to 'chalk,' especially to poor customers.
   — Harry Taylor, Macleod, Alberta."[5]

A famous iron lady settled in Winnipeg

Who is she? You are invited to guess while a few clues are presented. She is an aristocrat, as her name will show, but not a stuffy one. From her age, you'll agree that she is, indeed, a senior, yet she looks about as fresh as she did 40 years ago. At that time, she was a striking brunette and she is still a striking brunette. But that's of small account because if she were a blonde, her friends would doubtless love her just the same. The old view that blondes and brunettes have different dispositions has been declared false by a prominent resident of Regina who conducted a 10 year study under ideal experimental conditions: his wife was a brunette for five of those years and a blonde for the other five.

There could be no doubt; the aging lady was quite a gal in her youthful years. Men stared in admiration. She was certainly a terrific gadabout and at a time when very few ladies smoked, she was an incessant smoker. But she smokes no more and she gads no more.

Clearly she has lost some of the glamour of youth but not without compensation in added character and every year, on October 9th, she marks another anniversary of her arrival on Western Canadian soil. Too often, unfortunately, she celebrates alone.

Who is ready to identify her? Yes, she is the Countess of Dufferin, the grand old "lady" locomotive, the first of her kind in the West, that stood for many years after her retirement in a little park on the south side of the CPR depot in Winnipeg and was then given a nearby location on the east side of Main Street.

It was on October 9, 1877, that the locomotive and six flatcars and a supply of steel rails were delivered by barge on the Red River. They were unloaded on the St. Boniface side and practically told to get to work. The West, until that date, didn't have a single rail in place anywhere. But, with the promise of help from the Countess, a rail line to be known as the Pembina Branch of the CPR, was soon to be constructed southward to Emerson and the boundary where it would permit the new West a connection with an American line.

The task of delivering this new "iron lady" to Manitoba had been assigned to Joseph Whitehead who, significantly, had been the engineer on one of George Stephenson's pioneer locomotives that had startled English viewers.[6] In delivering his charge to the land of its adoption, Whitehead moved it under its own power from St. Paul, Minnesota, to Fargo, North Dakota. At Fargo, the engine and its six flatcars were placed on the river barge to be pulled to St. Boniface by James J. Hill's riverboat, *The Selkirk*. Hill, of railroad fame in the United States, was living in Winnipeg at that time.

Lord Dufferin, Governor General of Canada, and Lady Dufferin, were visiting in the West that season and being royally received wherever they went. It was expected that the locomotive would be delivered before the vice regal party started back to the East, making the first part of the journey by stage coach. The plan would have allowed Lady Dufferin to perform the naming and christening of the engine at St. Boniface or Winnipeg. But the riverboat was delayed and plans had to be changed. It was arranged that the stage coach and the riverboat would reach Fisher's Landing about the same time to allow Lady Dufferin to come on board and formally name the locomotive Countess of Dufferin.

As the iron Countess rode the current down the Red River, residents along the way crowded to the water's edge to gaze and cheer and, for the short approach to Winnipeg and St. Boniface, Joe Whitehead saw to it that the little locomotive, of which he was very proud, was generously draped with flags, ribbons and flowers. He made sure, too, that the locomotive's boiler had enough steam pressure to maintain an unbroken blast from the whistle so that no settlers for miles around would fail to get the message, that for Manitoba and the West, a new day was dawning. Fort Garry replied with cannon fire.

Many of the spectators who were born in the West, had never before seen a locomotive. Some were puzzled. One man, while gazing intently, enquired: "How many horses you need to pull zat?" The mystery deepened more when he was told: "That is the horse." The questioner had another question: "You say zat is the horse? Can you put saddle on an' ride him?"

The riverboat paddled on past Fort Douglas to a point where rails could be laid to the water's edge for unloading. Winnipeg residents were visibly annoyed by the realization that their rival community of St. Boniface was getting the spotlight attention. And St. Boniface made the most of the circumstances; the mayor and members of the St. Boniface council were present in morning coats and top hats to further diminish the Winnipeg image. But there was enough self-esteem and no need for more.

The Countess was unloaded and put to work. The Pembina line on which construction began officially on September 19, 1874, reached completion on December 5, 1878, when the press reported; "The last rail is laid; the last spike is driven." The Countess had performed well and, without delay, was shifted to mainline construction. Not until the aging engine was overshadowed by bigger and more powerful locomotives was there any thought of retirement and then a sale was made to a lumber company at Golden, BC. The price was said to be $1000, perhaps enough for an engine to shift cars of logs and lumber. Then, after a few more years, the Countess was admitted as a candidate for the junk pile.

Still, it wasn't the end. Mercifully, Winnipeg's Mayor R. D. Waugh, with a flare for history, heard about the indignity of sending the Countess away for eventual scrap. He asked for a report and then appealed to President Thomas Shaughnessy of the CPR. It was 1910 and almost at once the old thing the Blackfoot Indians called "the iron horse" was bought and presented to the City of Winnipeg. After a repair and refurbishing job, the Countess was moved into a place of highest honour, just a few rods from the spot at which she was unloaded from the river barge 33 years earlier. There and on her later stand near Main Street, the grand old lady of western transportation heard the click of more cameras, perchance, than any other object between the Ottawa Peace Tower and the Pacific coast totem poles. And with loving care, she should still be there 1000 years from now.

News from Fort Macleod

A Chinook
"The morning was cold and I stepped outside to see... I hadn't been out more than two minutes when puff, puff came the [chinook] wind from the southwest, just like a fellow's best girl throwing red-hot kisses at him through a stovepipe, and in less than five minutes – jewhillaken – down she came, a regular howling, snorting ringtailer from away back, blowing like sixty. Well, sir, I hadn't time to get off that platform before my feet were wet and in two hours... our snow had entirely disappeared. The whole country was dry by noon and we had a prairie fire that same evening."[7] [It sounds like Harry "Kamoose" Taylor of Hotel Fort Macleod or Fred Stimson of the North West Cattle Company but no names were given.]

Quick justice for mule thieves
"A short time ago, two men named Counestie and McDonald – the latter an ex-policeman – stole the NWC & N Co. mules [North West Coal and Navigation Co. at Lethbridge] and ran them across the line. The Company

advertises its brand in the *Gazette* which has a considerable circulation in Northern Montana and their stock was recognized. Joe Kipp arrested the thieves and was on his way with them to Benton when he was met by a party of cowboys and relieved of his charges. Very few preliminaries were bothered with. The thieves were taken to the nearest tree and very quickly paid the penalty for their roguery with their lives. Montana is an unhealthy retreat for such characters."[8]

A sure preventive for Klondike gold rush fever
"To cure the Klondike [gold rush] fever, go into a ploughed field some cold morning before breakfast this winter and with pick [and shovel] dig a hole 16 feet deep; come back to the house in the evening about dark and eat a small piece of stewed buffalo robe and go to sleep in the woodshed. Repeat the treatment if necessary."[9]

A rare collection of marine monstrosities

At a time when all incorporated communities were becoming anxious to attract tourists and tourist dollars, urban promoters considered their chances of finding or adopting attractions in the form of sea serpents or hairy monsters that weren't likely to become aggressive.

Tourists never demanded factual statistics about monsters but loved the opportunity for speculation about them and the tall tales that usually accompanied. It may be that every town or city with water resources greater than a creek or slough should have a monster of tantalizing size and shape and a modicum of mystery about its appetite and hiding place.

Scotland did well with its Loch Ness Monster, now an international pioneer that has defied all attempts to disprove its existence and, still secure in its hiding place in deep water, gets as much journalistic attention as ever. Canada, at the same time, has accumulated a wide variety of marine old timers and some have won headlines now and then by allegedly stealing a lakeside or riverside farmer's horses or cows and dragging them to deep-water hideaways.

If a complete inventory could be made, it would show the West with scores of the strange, attention-getting critters, all of them different. Vancouver Island's Caddy, residing in Victoria's Cadboro Bay, was one of the pioneers and won more recognition than if it had been captured or proven by a highly qualified scientific commission to be a fake.

The same would have been true of Manipogo, the Lake Winnipeg monster that was said to be six times as long as a tall man and have a face like an English bulldog.

For long time survival and reappearances, the famous Okanagan Lake monster known as Ogopogo was a winner. There was constant controversy over his size and disposition and the numerous people who watched for him never lost interest. When a television crew was sent from Los Angeles with the hope of capturing the strange fellow on film, the members of the party were not themselves hopeful that they would encounter him but, as if the vain fellow was eager to be photographed, he appeared almost immediately and posed for three minutes, or so the cameramen said. There have been lots of pictures taken but they have never agreed.

Indians displayed more confidence in the existence of the lake and sea monsters than their paleface friends and reported seeing Ogopogo and other mystery creatures more often. They were said to have seen him lying in the reeds at the Okanagan lakeshore in 1933 and talked to him. And the well-known Indian weather prophet, Chief Walking Eagle, saw and gave the best account of a huge creature that might have been adopted by Rocky Mountain House. He and his family were fording the North Saskatchewan River above Rocky Mountain House when this big creature took after them. The Chief, having seen circus elephants, believed it was a water elephant but, when he was shown a book with many pictures of other big animals, his eyes fell upon a picture of a hippopotamus and he said: "That's it; that's what I saw in the North Saskatchewan River."

There was doubt concerning what the Chief encountered in the river but people believed the popular Chief when he said he tried to be honest and didn't drink and what he saw was big enough to be an elephant; it had horns and was ferocious. Although he was not easily frightened, he admitted he would not return for a further inspection.

Calgary, too, had its unique experience with water creatures. A river monster was reported in the Bow River, making his home under Bow Marsh bridge. It was never given a name except some unprintable ones used by worried drunks who were obliged to cross the bridge late at night.

But, before long, the Bow River monster seemed to have departed and there was speculation about him swimming far up the Elbow River and remaining there until Glenmore Lake was created, at which time the serpent travelled back down stream to make his home in the lake. A resident of the city district of Haysboro reported privately of seeing the serpent following his sailboat on the lake on a summer evening. The fearsome thing, he said, was "as long as a cowboy's lariat and frightened me half out of my wits." He admitted to having a few drinks earlier that evening.

But Calgary seemed to lose interest in the sea monsters, possibly due to an early report that mermaids had been seen in Qu'Appelle Lake in Saskatchewan, and a much later one that the same race of beauties had been spotted at nearby Chestermere Lake. With mermaids making their appearance, the other water creatures didn't have a chance.

Old Doc Pill's frontier medicine

Sure, frontier folk fell victim to illness like other people but they were loathe to discuss it. In the absence of a doctor or nurse, they were likely to treat themselves with a tested high-alcohol colic-cure found in all the best horse stables or resort to one of the common home remedies handed down from experienced mothers. The most common of the home remedies was, of course, Epsom salts, the sure-fire cathartic kept in every pioneer medicine chest or beside the sugar and salt containers on the breakfast table – like the bottles of vitamin pills that followed years later.

They were terrible to take. Kids hated them and some were known to quietly dump the contents of the salts jar and refill it with sugar. The same kids were warned that if they told lies or stole marbles they could expect to end up working in Satan's furnace-room where Epsom salts were the only beverage served, replacing both milk and water.

Everybody knew how the salts worked but at a time when constipation was accepted as the universal punishment for man's misconduct in the Garden of Eden no mature person had a bad word for them. In addition to being a mysterious medicinal panacea, the salts product was thought to possess an equally mysterious nutritional value. Some farmers bought their salts supply to serve both the house and stable in 100-pound bags. Others knew the gravity of the message when the farm wife said: "Pa, you'll have to go to town tomorrow; we're out of salts."

The father of a big and robust son was asked if there was a dietary explanation and he replied: "Yes, oatmeal and Epsom salts, lots of both."

And a farm lady who gained a favourable reputation for her successes in a neighbourhood role of medical adviser admitted her secret: "For disorders above the belt, order a mustard plaster; for trouble below the belt, a double dose of Epsom salts."

Some new districts could count a farm wife who had been a nurse before coming to the homestead and she quickly became the most overworked person in the region. There being no telephones, buggies and wagons began calling at her cabin night and day with urgent pleas: "Will you come at once?" Of course, she went without any mention of payment. A day or two later she returned, richer only by a pail of potatoes, a pound of butter or the dressed carcass of a farm rooster that had achieved a record age. She might have been returning, also, with a satisfaction not likely to be duplicated in later generations.

Another frontier district might find that it had a self-educated medical authority who became known as "Doc." The one best known to this writer was Doc Pill and many local citizens didn't know him by any other name. He was gruff and not overly clean but he made friends. It was whispered that he obtained his only medical training at the Ontario Veterinary College when it was located at Toronto.

He conducted his part-time practice from a room in his farm house and, notwithstanding his medical monopoly in the district, he showed no ambition to become rich. He'd accept payment for services in anything from silver money to firewood, and took in more firewood than silver. He was not very professional but his neighbours knew what to expect.

"Put your tongue out," he'd say gruffly. Then after studying the thing the way a modern doctor would study an X ray, he'd report: "You're sick," and begin at once to mix medicine, drawing mainly from one or all of six big bottles on his shelf. The exact contents of the bottles were never disclosed but, from long observations, neighbours concluded that at least two of the bottles – and perhaps all six – contained varying concentrations of Epsom salts, carrying different colours. In any case, the medicines always appeared to work and patients generally recovered – as they probably would have done anyway.

Finally, the thoughtful Doc Pill, for good measure, offered each customer a candy bonus "to serve an important purpose." He was convinced that everybody was harbouring parasites in the form of intestinal worms and should be treated with a vermifuge. His goodies were simply candies made in his farm kitchen, with enough of an ingredient that would deal death to the horrid little parasites trying to make an easy living on the inside.

As a person qualified to practice medicine in the modern world, the old Doc wouldn't score very high or wouldn't even get on the scoreboard but in performing what he believed to be a service, and doing it with dedication, he may have earned praise.

That he had a good sense of humour was in itself praiseworthy. He told of a testimonial that came in the mail from a local lady: "A month ago I didn't have the strength to spank my baby but after two bottles of your red medicine, I've been able to pound hell out of my husband, something that was long overdue."

Chapter 12

When the 20th century was young

12

The day the Governor General came to lunch

It was May 13, 1938, a day that residents of Maple Creek and district would never forget. As if one reason was not enough, there were two – both good ones. First, the day brought Canada's Governor General, Lord Tweedsmuir, to the Maple Creek area and high up the planned side-trips was a drive to the ranch home of William and Mrs. Martin who ran about 5000 sheep and almost 1000 cattle on the Great Sandhills grass, about 40 miles north. Mrs. Martin was ready with lunch and the visit was one the Governor General was particularly anxious to make.

The other force that promised to make the day memorable was weather. Just when many people believed the "dirty thirties," which featured drought and blowing soil, were moderating, along came the 13th of May with the worst dust storm in many memories. George Spence, who had homesteaded and farmed at the base of the Palliser Triangle, said it was the blackest "black blizzard" he had ever seen. And what a day for it!

Public servants in charge of the vice regal tour advised cancellation of the trip to the sheep ranch. To take the Governor General over the trail on such a day was too hazardous. The recommendation was taken to the distinguished guest and he said: "No, positively no. When I met Will Martin at the Royal Winter Fair, and found that we grew up in nearby parts of Scotland, I told him I was coming to see his ranch at the first opportunity and that's today. Besides, Mrs. Martin has arranged a party at her house."

That was final. Those who were afraid of the day, could stay back but the Governor General was going. Visibility was practically nil but drivers were instructed to drive very slowly and keep the car lights on. The cavalcade was reduced to six cars and it moved away from Maple Creek at a snail's pace.

Mrs. Martin, in the meantime, had indeed prepared a handsome spread of food, meats, cakes, pies, everything, and neighbour ladies had responded to help her. Bill Martin looked at the handsome table and said it was, indeed, fit for a king. "But," he added, "did you no cook any scones for the Governor?"

"Scones for the Governor General? Indeed I did not. I'd no insult him with scones."

Bill added, "You'd better have a few. If you're not proud of them, you can hide them behind the flowers." And, strangely enough, the lady of the aging ranch house did cook a few of the lowly bits of Scottish cookery and placed them on the table where they would be inconspicuous.

It took almost four hours to drive the 40 miles to the ranch but the party arrived with everybody in it carrying a layer of dust. Tweedsmuir entered wearing a smile of delight that showed clearly through the crust of dust and held the two Martins in his arms, confirming that he was really pleased that they had not cancelled the tour. He then glanced at the big table, loaded with fine foods and repeated: "Another reason why there should have been no talk of cancellation!" At that moment his roving eye fell upon the humble scones and his eyes beamed. "Scones!" he shouted. "I love scones and cheese. Please place them where I can reach them."

The storm hadn't diminish their appetites and everybody ate well. The Governor didn't sample all the various pies and cakes but he ate every scone and Bill Martin chuckled.

George Spence, who gave general leadership to the tour, said that, in his opinion, the adventure in the dust storm and the visit at the Martin home were together the highlight of the prairie junket for Lord Tweedsmuir and the highlight of the year for the Martins.

Willie W. enjoyed the storm

Winter blizzards that caught country residents some miles from home could be cruel and sometimes fatal. But even in the Arctic blasts there were touches of humour as the comportment of a farm boy, Willie W., who regularly walked three miles to school and the same back, would show. At noonhour on a February day, the temperature was as amiable as a salesman who thought he was winning a purchaser for a steam engine. But both the weather and the manner of a salesman can change quickly; pleasant weather can give place to a storm and a sales specialist, seeing his prospects failing, can turn rude and leave the farm without saying "farewell" or "thanks for lunch," and without closing the gate. And so the mood of the February weather was suddenly nasty.

At 3 o'clock pm, a cold northwesterly wind loaded with snow brought shivers of cold and fear and the wise teacher dismissed her pupils in the eight grades and advised them to start home and hurry. Willie W. was at once facing the angry blast. But he persevered until he reached the MacEwan gate where he turned in. He was still almost a mile from his farm home and he intended to stay at the neighbouring place just long enough to get warm.

There being no telephone, there was no way by which Willie's family could be notified of his whereabouts. But Mother MacEwan quickly prepared hot chocolate and bread and butter and jam and invited Willie to stay all night. Willie was at once deep in thought and after proper hesitation, he expressed thanks and added: "My mother will be worried but maybe she'll guess I'm here. I'll do my homework."

Willie was told where he could sleep and he took his pencil and paper from his pocket. But the boy was strangely quiet for an hour and when Mother MacEwan looked for him, she couldn't find him. At the supper hour, he was still missing and there was at once a new worry and a proposal to go out into the storm to search for him. That, of course, would introduce a new hazard but, happily, about 7 o'clock, Willie staggered in from the storm and, when asked where he had been, replied cheerfully: "I went home to get my nightgown and ask mum and pa if I can stay here all night. They said I can."

Willie reported later that he had enjoyed the storm and added: "I hope there'll be another pretty soon."

How to get a haircut in a small prairie town

"My hair was beginning to cover my collar and curl lovingly about my ears, so I cast around for an itinerant barber. Noticing a guy sitting on the sidewalk with a brand new haircut, I asked him, after engaging in a little banter, where he got the 'chopping off' done."

"'Well,' he volunteered, 'you'll have to walk a mile and a half from here and more than likely you'll have to milk the cows if you arrive between five and seven in the afternoon. Then you may have to separate the milk or hold the baby while the barber does the separating. Then, if you don't mind keeping the kids amused while the barber fixes up a batch of bread, she will probably cut your hair before she puts the kids to bed.' All this I found true but it was fun and well worth the time spent."[1]

The church that vanished

Horses and cattle were favourite objects with rustlers and lifters in earlier times but thieves could be versatile too and were known to turn to strange prizes. A Saskatchewan farm family had its telephone stolen from the wall while members slept, and workers at the University of Saskatchewan reported a daring daylight robbery that entailed two hives of disapproving bees.

Even farm buildings were known to vanish, as a newspaper advertisement of early date gave testimony; August Nilson of the Moose Jaw area was offering a reward of $10 for the detection of the party or parties who "removed a log house from his farm."[2] There was no indication that Mr. Nilson had a further complaint by being in the house at the time of the theft.

Surpassing all these unusual larcenies, however, was the loss of the Anglican church at Donald, a small place on the CPR between Revelstoke and Lake Louise. The town was one of the first along the new railway line to have a church, thanks mainly to the zeal of Reverend Henry Irwin, widely known in the intermountain country as Father Pat. It wasn't a big church but it captured the affection of church supporters in England and became the recipient of some fine gifts, including a handsome quarter-of-a-ton church bell from Baroness Burdett-Coutts. As further evidence of overseas feeling for the little church, a prominent bishop made the trip from England to dedicate it in 1889.

Then, with the usual rise and fall in fortune of new railway towns and villages, Revelstoke was moving ahead faster than its neighbours and certain railroad workers and buildings were being moved from Donald to Revelstoke. A proposal from the latter place called for the moving of Father Pat's church and its conversion to an addition for the church at Revelstoke. The Anglican Synod approved but, when the church movers came to relocate the Donald church, they couldn't find it. It had vanished like a stolen horse. Only the foundation remained and it was telling no secrets. But anything as visible as a church could not be kept in hiding indefinitely and, in time, the Donald church was recognized at Windermere. The Synod, displaying the appropriate Anglican disapproval, ordered the return of the stolen property but nobody was in a hurry to act and Windermere simply kept the church.

But how did the church get to Windermere? There was more interest in the church's recent past than in its immediate future. Was it a case of theft? Who was the artisan?

Most stories mentioned the names of Mr. and Mrs. Kimpton, loyal friends of Father Pat and highly respected citizens of Donald. They were unhappy about the impending movement of Father Pat's church with its loss of identity and incorporation into an existing church. To give it a new location but keep it unchanged in structure seemed like the lesser sin. The Kimptons, as it happened, were moving to Windermere; nobody had a better sentimental claim to the church than they. Why should they not quietly take it along like a beloved member of the family? They dismantled it more or less, piled the pieces on a flatcar and sent them to Golden where they were transferred to a river barge and hauled south to Windermere.

The relocation went well except, while the church was on the barge, somebody stole the precious bell. The bell was traced to Golden and those responsible for lifting it were invited to return it. But they never did. Nor was the church ever returned to Donald. At Windermere it had a good home and most Anglicans seemed satisfied that Father Pat's church should remain where it could be loved for its own sake and serve with its own complete personality.

After more years, the little Father Pat church was still hearing the question: "Is this the church that was stolen?" but was hearing the answer: "No, this is the church that was rescued."

Pegleg Paul and the Hot Stove League

Pegleg Paul was one of the most faithful winter members of the Fleet Livery Stable's Hot Stove Liars' League and author of most of the wooden leg mirth. He reported to his friends that he was once engaged to a girl with a wooden leg – until he "broke it off," and, philosophically, he declared that wooden legs are not inherited, "which is more than can be said for wooden heads."

Paul's wooden leg was several inches shorter than his natural limb and he explained it this way: "I was living in the rattlesnake country on the sunny side of Cypress Hills. It wasn't uncommon for a traveller on the trails to step accidentally on a rattler's tail and then feel a quick strike somewhere near ground level. Everybody knew that if the victim was going to survive, his toe or foot or whatever part was struck had to be amputated before the venom moved into other parts of his body. It was sure urgent but we had a neighbour who was an expert at chopping-block surgery. I was on foot the day the snake aimed at me and he struck on my wooden leg side, struck hard too. A hurry-up message went to my handyman neighbour and he came on the run. He took one long look at my wooden leg and says: 'Yes, by golly, it's swelling. We gotta act fast.'"

"He pulled off his coat and told me to stretch out on the kitchen table. I did as I was told and the neighbour rushed to get my bucksaw from the woodpile and, in less time than it takes to tell it, he cut the lower five inches off that hickory leg. He did a nice job; I didn't even feel it and he saved my life." *(a farmspun tale)*

Sam McGee was not from Tennessee

Canadians took to the poetry of Robert Service the way cats take to cream. He was the young man from Preston, England, who migrated to Canada at the age of twenty years in 1894 and after accepting work with the Canadian Bank of Commerce, was posted to service at Whitehorse and Dawson City where he quickly captured the spirit of the North and translated it into poetry. He saw his first book of poems published in 1907. His verses, with the rhythm and force of ocean swells, were exactly what the North needed and Service became the unchallenged Poet of the Yukon.

Ask a representative Western Canadian if he is familiar with the poetry of Robert Service and there is a good chance he will say "Yes" and proceed to prove it by reciting some favourite verses from "The Cremation of Sam McGee." The lines chosen for evidence will likely be drawn from the following:

> The Northern Lights have seen queer sights,
> But the Queerest they ever did see
> Was the night on the marge of Lake Lebarge
> I cremated Sam McGee.
> Now Sam McGee was from Tennessee, where the cotton blooms and blows.
> Why he left his home in the South to roam round the Pole, God only knows.
> He was always cold, but the land of gold seemed to grip him like a spell

But, to confuse the interested onlookers, there were two Sam McGees in the Yukon, the one in the poem and one in the flesh whose birthplace was in doubt, either Ireland or Ontario. In any case, it was believed that he was born in 1867 or 1868 and left home to make his way to California at the age of 15. When news of the big gold strikes in the Yukon reached him, he joined the rush and went in over the Chilkoot Pass in '98. At Dawson, he dug tirelessly but the big discovery of which he dreamed eluded him and he turned to building bridges, cabins and dance halls. He was doing very well until 1902 when he heard of his mother's serious illness at Lindsay, Ontario, and left the Yukon to be with her. His mother died but Sam met and married an English girl with pioneer spirit and they returned to Dawson City where Sam resumed work in construction.

It was then that Sam McGee met the newcomer, Robert Service, and almost at once they were friends. Sam took the poet on a canoe trip on the Yukon River and it may have been then that Service revealed his outline for a poem that needed a good name. He had made up his mind that the name should be "The Cremation of Sam McGee" and he asked for his friend's permission to use the name.

Sam agreed and, of course, read the completed poem with added interest. He was fascinated by the story of the other Sam's misfortune and then his sad end. Mushing over the Yukon Trail, he was being made ever weaker by the severe cold and gradually dying. But, before death overtook him, the mythical Sam extracted a solemn promise from his travelling partner that if and when death came his companion would see that Sam's body was cremated. It wasn't that the dying Sam McGee had any fear of death but he made no secret of his dread "of an icy grave."

Sam's partner didn't like the idea of cremating an old friend but after the sick man's death and the corpse had been carried for days on the sled, the dogteam outfit came to an abandoned furnace "on the marge of Lake Lebarge" and the unhappy survivor discharged his obligation, loathsome though it was. He went on his way, but haunted by what he had done, he turned back to look once more into the blazing furnace and was surprised at what he saw; there sat his old partner looking happy and the last verse of the poem explained it:

> And there sat Sam, looking cool and calm, in the heart of the furnace road,
> And he wore a smile you could see a mile and said: 'Please close that door.
> It's fine in here but I greatly fear you'll let in the cold and storm,
> Since I left Plumtree in Tennessee, it's the first time I've been warm.'

Confusion after the death of the McGee from Tennessee was instantly intense. Then adding to that confusion was the later sale of cremation ashes, allegedly from the Sam McGee of the poem, with many people buying the souvenir packages. One of the first to buy a package was Sam McGee who was still breathing and boasting that he was the first human in history to purchase ashes from his own bones.

The surviving Sam remained in the Yukon for nine years and then made successive moves to a small fruit farm in British Columbia, a forest project in Northern Alberta, a construction business at Edmonton and Great Falls,

Montana. The time for retirement was approaching and in 1938, when 70 years old and nursing a nagging desire to make one more prospecting trip into the North, a friend with a plane arranged it. It was a sentimental journey but still without the big strike of which he dreamed. On his return he went to make his home with his daughter and son-in-law, Ethel and Emil Gramms, on their farm about 10 miles east of Beiseker, Alberta. Life became peaceful for the Old Man of the North – except when he came under attack from a bad-tempered Holstein bull on the Gramms farm. But, with the help of his son-in-law and a hayfork that happened to be in McGee's hands at the time, he escaped without injury.

Later in the same year, 1940, the Sam McGee who wasn't cremated died and was buried in the little church cemetery close to the Gramms farm where his grandson, Lorne Gramms, lives today.[4]

Jake's spreader was a great success

Constipation was a universal villain in the lives of farm livestock and humans alike. Epsom salts appeared as the rescuer and hero. Together, they did as much as prairie weather to sustain conversation.

Sex in those years of farmspun humour was not a topic with which storytellers and individuals engaging in conversation took liberties and to tell a sexy story in public was unthinkable. It is a sad commentary on the state of modern humour when, in many Canadian circles, a story is no longer considered funny or worth telling unless there is something indecent about it.

Farm discussions of matters essential to animal breeding and management were quite different. Rural people, long ago, agreed that terms like nutrition, ventilation, barnyard manure, digestion, constipation and Epsom salts should be used without restraint or blushing. Constipation was a legitimate term for a commonplace disorder; a manure spreader was a manure spreader and there was no other name for it. Most rural people who would shun the uncalled-for use of sex terms would have no compunction about using proper barnyard terms in conversation at any time.

Often did the farm wife's instructions reverberate across the kitchen or barnyard in words like these: "Pa, ye've gotta go to town tomorrow because we'll be clean outa salts by noon." Or it might be one neighbour greeting another this way: "Mornin' neighbour. It's a right fine day. And tell me, how's the state of your bowels?" In making reply, the one questioned was expected to tell all. Why not? Individuals who discovered "sure cures" for intestinal cussedness were always ready to share their "secrets." Most secrets probably produced nothing more than laughter but there were people on the frontier who believed very seriously that, in regulating intestines, there was no better cure-all than laughter.

A cowboy remedy for constipation, propounded by a well-known range character, called for catching "the biggest grasshopper you can find and swallowing it head first. He'll kick you out of your trouble in 20 minutes."

A Manitoba farmer was said to have called the veterinarian to consult him about a sick animal on the farm. "How old is the ailing critter," the veterinarian asked and was told "about a year and a half." Constipation was the most obvious symptom and the vet said: "I'm too busy to go out today but you can give the animal a pound and a half of salts as a drench and call me in a day or two and let me know how you're getting along." A day or two later the farmer called and heard the vet ask: "How's the calf?"

The farmer answered: "I haven't got a calf. I had a sick cat. You misunderstood me."

"Oh my gosh," gasped the veterinarian. "Don't tell me you drenched your cat with a pound and a half of salts. That's the dose for a cow."

"Yes, I made him take it. He didn't like it but the trouble has passed. But, I can tell you, the cat was sure busy for a few days and had four other cats digging holes for him."

When the manure spreaders appeared, one of the manufacturers announced that he would personally stand "behind every machine we make – except our manure spreader."

Farmers gathering at Burroughs' Livery Stable at Melfort about that time heard that Old Jake, one of the best storytellers, had just bought a manure spreader and it had passed its first test. Jake piled a big load on the spreader, hitched his team of bronco horses to it and headed for the field. In going to the field, he had to drive down a country road for a quarter of a mile before turning in.

Suddenly, Jake became aware of a new Ford touring car with a factory-fresh shine following him. When it came within a few feet of the spreader, he could see four occupants, all young and well dressed. When the car was just the length of a fork handle from the manure spreader, the tactless driver sounded a loud honk of the car's horn, a blunt invitation to get off the road to let the well-dressed townspeople pass. Jake's team took fright and tried to run away and Jake's Irish temper came to a boiling point. Instead of turning off the road, he moved the gear handle by which the spreader mechanism was engaged.

Instantly, there was an outpouring of barnyard effluence, falling into the laps of the discourteous strangers like cloudburst rain. When Jake left the road to turn into his field, he looked back and concluded that the touring car was carrying more of the barnyard product than remained in the spreader. He said he was well pleased with the result of the manure spreader's first test of performance.

Future Prime Ministers got their bumps too

"R. B. Bennett, MLA and owner of a new automobile, was out for a ride in it last night with Mr. Edgar of the Hudson's Bay Company. Their outing was tinged with incident. Mr. Bennett, who was acting as his own chauffeur, had been spinning along Stephen Avenue and had turned down Centre Street. A youth on a wheel loomed up immediately in front and was in some danger of being overtaken and injured. Mr. Bennett both thought and acted quickly. He steered the automobile to one side. He mounted the pavement and bumped with violence into the wall of the [Imperial] Bank. The Bank and the bicycle were both uninjured but the machine itself is at present out of repair."[3]

The molasses won satisfied customers

If every farmer in the Saskatchewan dry belt didn't recognize the name of Alex Slaney early in the '30s, they certainly did before the end of the decade. The affable Irish-Canadian, raised in Ontario, had been in Saskatchewan government service for a few years and, when it became obvious in the dry years that thousands of farmers were being forced through lack of feed to sell their livestock at give-away prices, governments adopted "feed and fodder" policies, meaning feed relief, and needed men like Slaney.

Farming people, generally, were not asking for the amounts of feed needed to support big herds but they knew and governments knew the importance of maintaining a certain small number of animals, including one or two family milk cows, a team of all-purpose horses and a few pigs that were satisfied to live on potato peelings and other kitchen waste and then contribute their carcasses to keep the family in meat for the winter.

Into this unhappy situation, Alex Slaney was projected as relief feed co-ordinator. Acquaintances noted that he was being given a different assignment. But those who knew him best said he was the man for the job because nobody could better him in "priming the pump" to get laughter.

His experience with a carload of molasses illustrated the point. A Montreal business firm sent a telegram to Honourable M. A. MacPerson, Attorney General for Saskatchewan at the time, offering as a donation a carload of molasses in barrels. The shipment was at Montreal at the time and was probably a West Indies product. Slaney was consulted. He was not enthusiastic. He knew the molasses was capable of making otherwise low-grade feeds more palatable but it would be extremely difficult to distribute across Saskatchewan and when farmers knew it was available they would all want it. He told the minister it would create problems beyond its worth.

But, in spite of the advice, the government was loathe to refuse a gift of this magnitude and the molasses in steel drums and wooden hogshead's arrived at Moose Jaw a few days later. It was placed in storage on the second floor of a building, the first floor of which was being used to house unemployed men. Fortunately, the farm people of the area didn't hear about it for some time and Slaney didn't tell them, or there would have been a stampede. While weather remained cool, all was well but with warmer days the molasses expanded and began to ooze from the big wooden containers. It spread out on the floor and then leaked through to the floor below. The lower floor residents were being sprayed with molasses and the attorney general was deluged with protests. He called Slaney. "What are you going to do with that molasses? It's making trouble for us. Can't you sell it?" Slaney shook his head. "Your department, Mr. Minister, is in no position to retail that stuff. We might be able to give it away to people on relief in this city but they couldn't pay for it. I wish it was in Hell or back in Montreal. If you want to get rid of it at no further cost to your Government, however, just let me know. I should tell you, of course, that it is stock molasses for cattle feeding. It doesn't have the quality of table molasses but if those people were feeling hungry, they might eat it with no harm."

The minister said: "Do as you like with it but move it."

The news about free molasses travelled fast. To most citizens, molasses was molasses and the words "stock molasses" didn't frighten them. Men, women and children with pails and pans lined up to get supplies and the popularity of the product surpassed all expectations. Slaney smiled in silence as the molasses disappeared but, two or three years later, he had several visitors, one of whom mentioned he had been living with the unemployed when the molasses business became so brisk. "There was something funny about that."

"Yes," said Slaney. "Something funny about it. I doubt if even the Attorney General knows the full story. And you, you son of a gun, you know it too. Now be honest."

The visitor nodded. He did know it and said: "That molasses whisky was great stuff; I know because I drank too much of it."

Slaney grinned broadly and said: "I know, every gallon from that carload went to make home brew and you reliefers celebrated for three months. They called it 'Moose Jaw Five Star' and I have no reason to think it was anything but the best. What I wrote in my report to the Government didn't disclose everything I knew but I told the truth, that not one pound of the Montreal molasses was wasted and we didn't spend even a nickel for advertising and distribution."[5]

An innocent travelling with a Mounty

A certain lieutenant-governor of Alberta received an invitation to be the luncheon speaker at Western Fairs Association meetings being held at Anaheim, California, in 1972. The American organization would pay the travelling expenses and the Canadian agreed to go. It would be a pleasant experience and probably justifiable inasmuch as the proposed luncheon was billed as a Canada Day gesture.

When Edmonton friends learned of the Anaheim date, they responded with thoughtful suggestions, uppermost among them that the LG should take an aide in a fine uniform. "You know how the Americans love the Canadian Mounted Police; why don't you take a Mounty?" they asked him. He thought well of the idea and so it was arranged that the aging fellow would have one of the most handsome and dashing members of the force stationed at Edmonton to accompany him.

On the appointed morning, the two Albertans – the old man looking like an old man and the young one looking like the answer to a potential mother-in-law's prayer – flew out of Edmonton to set down and change planes in Vancouver. At the latter place, the travellers were met and whisked to the Mounted Police headquarters to lunch at the Officers' Mess, then back to the airport to await the southbound flight.

They were admitted to the flight departure lounge where they could sit comfortably until the departure was announced. Sitting immediately opposite the two Edmonton men and facing them were two dear old ladies, probably Americans returning home after their first visit to Canada. Both were obviously deaf and they had to speak loudly to make each other hear and consequently everybody in the waiting room was able to enjoy their observations and remarks.

After staring intently at the Mounted Policeman, one of the ladies said to the other: "Look at that Canadian Mounted Policeman; isn't he handsome! And what a uniform! Did you ever see anything more stunning than that! They can't beat that at Hollywood."

"Yes, I confess I can't take my eyes off him," the other said. "You've heard said, I'm sure, that the Canadian Mounted Police always gets his man. But that old fellow he's got today wouldn't be hard to catch. Poor old fellow! I feel sorry for him. He's being deported, no doubt. I wonder what crime he has committed."

"I suppose we'll never know, perhaps bank robbery, maybe he's a rapist."

"No, no, not at his age, surely. More likely to be shoplifting in his case."

"Well I don't know about that but after studying his face, I don't recognize it as the typical face of a criminal. I wonder if the court might have made a mistake in his case."

To this, the other took strong exception. "Don't fret yourself. I've been studying men's faces a while too and that old scoundrel has the typical face of a criminal, if ever I saw one. I'd feel a lot more comfortable if the Mounted Policeman would keep the old man handcuffed."

At that point in the discussion, the flight south was called and the Mounty, performing like a professional movie actor and, while suppressing a chuckle, took the LG by the arm and led or escorted him to the plane. The two ladies were a few paces ahead and one looked back to confirm her views about the old man being a seasoned criminal and could be heard to say: "Still no handcuffs! I'm sure that is a mistake."

The final remark heard from the ladies was from the other member of the pair: "At least, what we've seen today should be a good lesson for every young man, 'Crime doesn't pay.'"

The Mounty enjoyed the show. The LG felt slightly uneasy but said he enjoyed it too, which must have been true because he told it many times.

Uncle Dan wanted a shallow grave

Every community needed an "Uncle Dan," a jovial old timer with an unfailing sense of humour and the ability to relate entertainingly with everything of consequence in the pioneer years. The subject of this sketch, Uncle Dan Hays of Carstairs, was on good terms with everybody in the town and far beyond and had a fierce loyalty to every local operation, right down to the beer parlour; but Dan objected, saying: "No! Don't say it that way; don't say 'down to the beer parlour'; say 'up to the beer parlour!'"

Uncle Dan was born in Missouri, the state that produced Mark Twain – if that explains anything. Dan and brother, Mr. Thomas Hays, went to Carstairs, north of Calgary, in September, 1905, to farm. But they saw opportunities on every hand and as Dan told it: "We started the firm of Hays Brothers, Real Estate, the day after we arrived and had fair success." It might have been more accurate to say the business flourished.

Almost at once, members of the Hays family were embarking upon dairying and herd building and did not relax until they had one of the premier Holstein herds in Canada. Harry Hays, second oldest child in Dr. Hays' family, was born at Carstairs on Christmas Day, 1909, and became eminently successful as a cattle breeder and showman, an auctioneer of pedigreed livestock with an international clientele, a Mayor of Calgary from 1959, Member of Parliament from 1963 and Canada's Minister of Agriculture for several years, after which he was named to the Canadian Senate.

With his uncle's flare for humour, the Honourable Harry was as popular in the East as he was in the West. When asked at a Calgary gathering how he was getting along with Prime Minister Lester Pearson, Harry answered: "We're getting along fine. He's teaching me to talk French. I'm teaching him a lot of words from the cattleman's vocabulary he never heard before and he's learning. With what I'm teaching him from stockyard and barnyard language, he's going to be trilingual long before I'm bilingual."

Although the Honourable Harry became a national and international figure, Uncle Dan repeated that he'd have to be "a better man than I am to tear me away from my little town where I know every human, horse and dog it in." He would not exchange Carstairs for Calgary or Edmonton, even if they had twice as many oil millionaires and better football and hockey teams.

Nevertheless, Carstairs as at its best, he asserted, in the earlier years when potent drinks were served at the hotel bar for 10 cents each and a five dollar meal ticket was good for 21 meals. "Why be poor," he wrote, "when 20 cents invested at Mellon's bar would give you a feeling of prosperity."[6]

Honourable Harry Hays was a staunch fan of Uncle Dan and delighted to relate the latter's expressions of wit and wisdom. Dan, Harry said, made a fortune and then adopted the policy – right or wrong – of contributing it gradually over the years to the local beer parlour. Daily, he kept a date with his old friend, Joe King. But Joe died and Dan was told that his long-time pal had asked to be buried eight feet deep at the local cemetery.

Said Uncle Dan thoughtfully: "Well, if that's the way Joe wanted it, that's the way it must be. But I'm telling you now, I don't want to be planted that deep. Please remember that, when my time comes, I want to be buried just two feet deep and I'll have the laugh on Joe. That way, when Resurrection Morning comes, I'll be first up and I'll be clear down to the beer parlour before old Joe is out of his hole."

A lousy story by Frank McGill

Frank McGill homesteaded and farmed near Elbow and, when circumstances demanded a bigger railroad town, he drove northeast to Davidson or southwest to Morse. He soon became known as a talented stockman, a popular writer and a capital storyteller. In an article that appeared in the magazine section of the *Western Producer*, he related a prize story concerning a neighbour who had been a schoolteacher and then a professional wrestler before turning to homesteading as McGill's neighbour. In the story, he remained nameless.

He had occasion to drive over the long trail to Davidson and hoped to obtain a room for the night at the Great West Hotel. But, as at most times, the hotel was full and the manager reported: "Sorry, but I have nothing to offer unless you're prepared to share a double bed with a stranger."

McGill's neighbour was unhappy about the prospect of sleeping with a man he had never seen before but even that seemed preferable to sleeping without blankets under a tree. Not being one whose life was complicated by nightgowns or pyjamas, he quickly removed everything, including his heavy woollen underwear.

As those who have worn heavy woollen underthings will understand, removal at night was always followed by itching and scratching. The scratching was intense and the man to whom the room had been assigned originally blurted out a question: "Hey fellow, are you lousy by any chance?" The homesteader recognized a chance to improve his bedroom position and answered: "I'm sorry to say it but I guess I am," and kept on scratching. Without further conversation, the questioner began to throw his belongings into a valise and departed.

The homesteader was pleased with the prospect of having the bed to himself but minutes later another stranger seeking a bed or half a bed was sent by the hotel clerk. The homesteader saw his hope failing but wasn't giving up and said: "I'm sorry I have to tell you but you'd better not sleep with me because I'm lousy."

But instead of taking the warning with alarm, the newcomer kept right on removing his clothing and preparing for bed, saying only: "Lousy? That's nothing to brag about; so am I." The homesteader, relating the story to Frank McGill, added; "And sure enough, he was."

McGill said the two men finally settled into the same bed and slept soundly.[7]

Harry Gunn's much-travelled revolver

Harry Gunn's old .45 Colt revolver had a story of unusual adventure. It had parts in at least two wars, one theft, one murder, was lost for 30 years and finally returned to its original owner, looking bright and fresh and ready for the next adventure. The story seemed too strange to be true.

Rancher Harry Gunn of Cowley was born in Ontario in 1879 and came west with his parents to homestead at Pincher Creek. From the homestead farm he enlisted for service with the Second Canadian Mounted Rifles, going to the Boer War. It was at this time that he was issued the .45 Colt revolver.

At war's end, he and others being discharged from the army were told they could keep their revolvers as souvenirs, unless, under circumstances of special need they were called back. At Montreal the returning men had their names engraved on their revolvers and Gunn's weapon was permanently identified: "Harry A. Gunn, Pincher Creek."

Came World War I and an emergency call did go out for the return of the revolvers. Gunn, by this time a prospering rancher at Cowley and a widely known polo player, returned his old Colt and heard no more about the object for the next 40 years. He didn't expect to hear any more, ever. But, strange to say, early in 1963, a resident of Southern Alberta received a letter from a party in Oregon, enquiring if by any chance he knew of a Harry A. Gunn at Pincher Creek, because a revolver bearing that name had appeared in a court case.

Well, just about everybody in Southern Alberta knew Harry Gunn who by this time was getting his mail at Cowley. The only information was that the weapon had been seized after an Oregon man was charged with shooting his wife. Now the police wanted to know as much as possible about the history of the revolver.

Presumably, the revolver had been stolen from army stores but where it spent the intervening years was unknown. In 1962, an Oregon man visited a secondhand store and there bought the weapon and, according to the police, used it to kill his wife. After the gun was used as an exhibit in the court case, the judge became interested in the engraved name and ordered that an attempt be made to locate the said Harry A. Gunn, Pincher Creek, and ascertain if he wished to have the revolver returned to him.

Somebody in the court knew a lady who had once lived at Pincher Creek and wrote to invite her help to locate the man whose name appeared on the revolver. The lady was glad to help and she reported Harry Gunn's Cowley address. The judge, as good as his word, tried to send the revolver by mail or express to Gunn but recent federal law prohibited the use of the mail or express for the carrying of such weapons across state or national boundaries. There was delay but, in the end, one of the judge's friends was travelling to Alberta and would carry the package and make delivery.

Late in 1963, the aging handgun was delivered to the man to whom it had been issued for war service 63 years earlier and he was delighted to have it back.[8]

Chapter 13

Tall tales

13

Paul Bunyan – superman of the logging camps

"That blighter, Paul Bunyan," said a recent immigrant to Manitoba, "makes me laugh immoderately. But to be honest with you, I don't believe half the lies I hear about him."

Paul, with the proportions of a giant and the strength of a Hercules, was the superman of settlement years. Almost everybody between the Atlantic and Pacific knew something about him but what they didn't know was if he lived in the flesh or in myth only.

But this air of uncertainty did not diminish his popularity. By 1952, there had been no fewer than 17 books published on Paul Bunyan in the United States. Lower Canada wanted to claim him as a French Canadian native son and, for the right to do so, there was support from the United States writer, James Stevens, who, in the introduction of his book, *Paul Bunyan*, relates from his own research that a giant woodsman, Paul Bunyan by name, followed Louis Papineau in the Rebellion of 1837 and returned to his own logging afterwards.[1] It seemed that Paul relocated in New Brunswick for a time and then moved westward. Wisconsin wanted to claim him; Minnesota and Oregon wanted to claim him.

Minnesota insisted upon a strong claim, contending that it was Paul who cleared the bush to make way for settlers in that state. The secret of his Minnesota success was in his use of two axes, one in each hand and used simultaneously. And if the Paul Bunyan stories this writer heard in boyhood years in Manitoba were any indication, Paul had been there, too. If Paul, with the help of his Big Blue Ox, Babe by name and born in the winter of the "Blue Snow," was in that part, it was doubtless he who ploughed the first furrows for the ditch that would carry the Red River, just as it was he who was credited with excavating the five big basins for the Great Lakes.

Nor were Manitobans going to overlook the theory that it was in Manitoba that Paul succeeded in breaking and driving a team of six rattlesnakes. No others tried it.

How big was Babe? There being no scale big enough to weigh him, the only indication of size was in Paul's measurement: "30 axe handles and a plug of tobacco from horn to horn."

Paul's achievements were lifelong. It was told that when he was two days old he sneezed and not only blew the covers off his cot but dislodged the roof poles of the family cabin. As a boy in his teens, he mastered what many other boys have tried since and failed, namely to blow the bedroom candle out and be in bed before it was dark.

Paul's appetite had to be big to serve his big body and his favourite food was pancakes. He invented something resembling a cement mixer to mix his pancake batter and was thought to have been responsible for popularizing pancakes, much as the once-famous Popeye the Sailor won kids to the consumption of spinach.

Still, his greatest fame was won in the lumberwoods where even the use of two axes, one in each hand, was not fast enough. So he invented a tree scythe based on the principle of the hay scythe.

When he became annoyed by the time being wasted in delivering his logs at a sawmill low on the river because of the numerous bends in the stream, he resolved to straighten the river. It should have appeared as an impossible task but, with Paul's ingenuity, it was simple. He fastened the heaviest logging chains he had around the river at its mouth and then hitched himself and Babe to the chains. With a mighty heave, and then another, something had to give and, sure enough, Paul and Babe pulled the kinks out of the river, leaving the streambed as straight as an irrigation ditch.

Talk about ingenuity! When the mosquitoes became so vicious that logging had to be curtailed, the great Paul looked for a solution. He caught an idea and, following it, he introduced numerous hives of honey bees, hoping they would interbreed with the mosquitoes and produce a race of insects not interested in human blood. Upon to a point the scheme seemed to be working but the great Paul couldn't expect to be a winner every time and as the Paul Bunyan scholars told it, when the hybrid insects matured they turned mean and, having inherited front end stringers from the mosquito parents and rear end stingers from the bee parents, they could sting from both ends at once – and did.

The reports of Paul Bunyan's escapades have been called lies and there is no point in disagreeing. But they were lies that misled nobody and hurt nobody. They made the woodlands ring with laughter – and laughter can be like good medicine.

Tales as tall as totem poles

Tall tales were inventions of the imagination created to aid relaxation and produce laughter and, being unlikely to hurt or embarrass or mislead anybody, didn't deserve to be regarded as lies or sins.

Although they rebounded to life in recent times, their entertainment value has been recognized for generations. The Paul Bunyan stories, outlandish enough to be funny and harmless enough to be respectable, were just exaggerated stories about commonplace happenings.

Like the once-popular farmspun, fashioned initially for waiting-room audiences at livery stables, tall tales were for everybody and did not exclude the academics and sophisticated in the community – if they chose to participate. The legendary Paul Bunyan would have been proud to claim many of the tall tales that have surfaced in recent years. A certain forestry story from Langley, BC, would have passed readily as a Paul Bunyan creation. It appeared in the "Straight From The Grass Roots" section of the *Country Guide* and was presented as a letter from Billy Gardiner of that place who was speaking of his brother, Rab:

> My brother, whom you may have heerd about, was one of the most power-ful men that ever hit the plains. He and I chopped cordwood one winter in the tamarack swamp southwest of Carberry, Man. It was a cool morning, forty-four below. Big Rab had forgotten his axe that morning until we were four miles from the shanty. Did he go back for it? Not Rab. He just started pulling the trees up by the roots, bumped them together to knock the dirt off and then broke them across his knee into cordwood lengths. I remember cutting one huge tamarack, a bit top heavy, which lodged against a tall spruce. Not having room to pull it clear, Rab borrowed my axe, grabbed it between his teeth, ran up the leaning tamarack and cut 'er loose. And then jumped clear, did you say? Not Rab. He wasn't feelin' away his time jumpin'. He went at that old tamarack on the way down with my axe and had it cut into stovewood lengths, split and neatly piled by the time it hit the ground.[2]

Not bad either as a performance or as a tall tale!

When Robert Gard was in Alberta in 1943 for the purpose of collecting the folklore of the area, one of the citizens who proved very helpful was Wardlaw's Dr. W. G. Anderson, medical doctor, politician, fox farmer, sheep rancher and raconteur. He greeted Gard with an effusion of farmspun, including an account of his alleged adventure in an Alberta storm. The blizzard blew up quickly and ferociously. The doctor's sheepherder was on his way from summer range with the big flock and Anderson was fearful the man would get caught without shelter. He resolved to ride out to meet the shepherd and help him bring the flock to the protection of a bluff or coulee. He dressed in his warmest clothes, slung his gun over his shoulder and saddled his best horse, Baldy. But before riding far, he knew he was lost in the blinding blizzard and his thoughts turned toward saving himself. He was becoming colder and colder, then weaker and weaker. What was he to do?

"Finally," said the doctor, "I shot Baldy, split him open, removed his abdominal organs and crawled inside. It was nice and warm there and I pulled the hide together and fell asleep." When he awakened, the storm had subsided and the doctor could hear wolves gnawing at Baldy's frozen flesh. Peering through the slit through which he had entered, Anderson could see the big animals. He admitted to being thoroughly frightened.

Almost instinctively, he reached out through the incision, grabbed two of the wolves by their tails and hung on to the startled animals. "They set out at a great rate with Baldy's frozen carcass and me bounding along behind them." Visibility by this time was favourable and the doctor found he could guide the team of wolves by their tails and he steered them right into his own farmyard, and then let the frantic animals go.

Having reached this point, Dr. Anderson said: "I started to yell like the dickens and one of my men came on the run and hacked me out."[3]

A tale known to have been crafted in Northern Saskatchewan concerned another big ox, one that was said to have been mothered by a Durham cow and sired by an Itinerant bull moose. The calf was big at birth with a big and extravagant appetite. The neighbours said it took three fresh cows and a dairyman's pump to keep the calf quiet. By one year of age, he was bigger than his mother and, at two years, he was too big to get through the stable door so the farm owner renovated the machine shed that had a door big enough to admit the threshing machine. At three years, the owner broke the big fellow to work in ox-harness and hitched him alone to a two-furrow plow. But that was not satisfactory because the big ox travelled so fast that he was throwing the furrow soil over the line fence into a neighbour's field and, with land worth $10 an acre, nobody could afford to lose so much good topsoil.

Still, the big Saskatchewan ox grew. The farm wife used his great spread of horns on which to hang out her Monday morning wash. The big fellow finally ended up at Prince Albert Fair.

Of those Westerners who contributed tall tales to "Straight From the Grass Roots" in the early 1940s, the name of I. N. Skidmore of Denholm, Sask., became most familiar to readers. His spring of yarns, it seemed, never ran dry. Herewith are two that served their purpose well:

> When I was a boy in Iowa, a man brought a sunflower seed from the dust bowl of Kansas and planted it in river bottom soil beside the Missouri River. He didn't step back quick enough. That sunflower sprouted and shot up his pant leg before he could get out of the way and, before he could cut himself loose, he was way up in the air. He started to slide for the ground but the sunflower grew up faster than he could slide down. A couple of neighbours did some fast work. They got a blanket and held it. By that time he was 90 feet in the air but he made it. The roots of that sunflower covered four acres when the frost killed it.[4]

And the other Skidmore tale was about a farm dog:

> When my father was farming in Iowa, beside the Missouri River, our Collie went down to the river to bathe. Coming out he got his hair full of that Missouri River mud and then trotted home through a field of ripe red clover. A lot of clover seed got into the mud on his coat and sprouted. From the crop of clover that grew on the dog's back, we pastured three cows all summer and had two rack loads of good clover hay left over. But we neglected to cut the aftermath and it grew so luxuriantly all over the dog that it smothered him to death.[5]

Chapter 14

Bob Edwards and the *EyeOpener*

14

Bob Edwards – paradoxical but great

Robert Chambers Edwards – commonly and widely known as Bob Edwards – was named in two separate Men's Canadian Club polls as Alberta's Prize Personality. Born in Edinburgh, he came to Wetaskiwin in 1895 and wasn't sure why he was there. Two years later, however, he was starting a weekly newspaper at that place, proposing to call it the *Wetaskiwin Bottling Works* but finally fixed upon the more conventional name, the *Wetaskiwin Free Lance*. It was the first paper to be published between Edmonton and Calgary and it remained for about two years, after which he tried newspapers in Leduc, Innisfail and South Edmonton before moving to High River where the *Eye Opener* name appeared.

He informed his readers that the paper would be worth five dollars per year but he was knocking off four dollars for irregularity. The paper would be printed, as he said, "semioccasionally," meaning it would come out when Bob had enough stuff to fill the columns and was sufficiently sober to perform the job.

When he seemed to have offended the Methodists he came to Calgary on the suggestion of his unfailing friend, Paddy Nolan, and *Eye Opener* became *Calgary Eye Opener*. Readership spread and circulation soared. About this time, Bob created the fictional character, Peter McGonigle, to be Bob's "straw man."

Bob was never easy to understand. He called himself a Conservative in politics but, in practice, he was a reformer. He "needled" the churchmen but, as long as he had money, he was the poor man's best friend. He was an alcoholic but, in the liquor plebiscite of 1915, he was one of the best supporters for the cause of the "Drys." He "roasted" the politicians but was persuaded to be a candidate in the provincial election of 1921 and without campaigning received the second biggest vote in the city of Calgary and sat in the legislature as an Independent. But Bob died before the second session.

On going to the legislature, Bob's friend, Reverend Robert Pearsob, who was also sitting as an Independent, asked Edwards for a promise that he would not take a drink of liquor for the full duration of the session and got it. Bob Edwards kept his promise and there is reason to believe he never took another drink in the months before his death.

Wit and wisdom from Bob Edwards

Cheer up! Happy New Year! All good people don't die young. Lots of them live to a ripe old age and die poor. [January 1, 1910]

By the time the average man is old enough to gratify his tastes, he hasn't any. [May 8, 1915]

Some people might as well be crazy for all the sense they have. [May 11, 1918]

Most people who are old enough to know better, wish they were young enough not to. [April 20, 1912]

Every man has his favourite bird; ours is the bat. [May 13, 1905]

Although the citizens of Calgary are not what you'd call violently insane, they still indulge in picnics to an alarming extent, eating sand and ants and doing other things which we admit are mildly idiotic. [April 2, 1913]

Some men spoil a good story by sticking to the truth. [January 25, 1919]

There isn't a woman alive so bad in arithmetic that she can't calculate how much her husband would save if he didn't smoke. [July 20, 1918]

The waterwagon is certainly a more dangerous vehicle than the automobile. At least more people fall off it. [August 25, 1906]

Nowadays it takes a regular bloody plutocrat to fill a drunkard's grave.

Some people are good because they find it cheaper than being wicked. [May 22, 1915]

There never was a man as great as the average dog thinks his master to be. [August 4, 1917]

The more tightwads we have at City Hall for the next few years, the safer we'll feel. By all means keep the tightwads in office and let the free spenders wait. [October 14, 1916]

A little learning is a dangerous thing but a lot of ignorance is just as bad. [August 20, 1921]

Bankruptcy is where you put your money in your hip pocket and let your creditor take your coat. [November 8, 1913]

To do right is easy when sin ceases to be a pleasure. [February 21, 1920]

What with whales at Edmonton, sharks at Calgary, lobsters at Okotoks and suckers everywhere else, Alberta bids fair to become an interesting aquarium of marine curiosities. [September 5, 1903]

If men could read women's minds, they'd take many more risks. [Summer Annual, 1920]

A woman's indifference has reached the limit when she no longer listens when her husband talks in his sleep. [May 22, 1915]

The public will pay more for laughing than for any other privilege. [May 11, 1918]

All the speculation in the world never raised a bushel of wheat. [February 10, 1912]

About the only people who don't quarrel over religion are the ones who don't have any. [July 17, 1920]

The *Eye Opener* Road Race

Bob Edwards was a drinking man and everybody knew it because Honest Bob told everything. He tried to quit the habit but without success until late in his life and, believing it was the "cross" he had to bear, he chose to laugh about it and give others the chance to laugh too. As he wrote humorously about his "bats," he may have given the impression of encouraging rather than discouraging the habit but such was not the case. Periodically, he spoke or wrote from his heart, confessing that, if he had the opportunity, he would use it to destroy the booze business rather than glorify it. His innermost convictions were made clear prior to the Provincial Liquor Plebiscite of 1915.

Bob believed that everybody had enemies, not necessarily alcoholic, and laughing at them was often a better policy than crying. With this thought in mind and the hope of salvaging something useful from every bad situation, he wrote the account of the *Eye Opener* Road Race, leaving readers wondering if it or anything resembling it ever happened.

The Eye Opener Road Race of 1906 was in the nature of a novelty and afforded intense amusement to the populace. Contestants started from the corner of First Street and Eighth Avenue, underneath our office in the Cameron Block, to the shot from a pistol fired, as now, by Captain Smart of the Fire Department. On this occasion there were fifteen starters, all of whom had agreed to abide by the rather unique conditions. At the crack of the pistol they were off in a bunch, with a contestant from High River slightly in the lead and the Olds entry close up.

Running west up the avenue, according to the terms of the race, the contestants raced up to the Royal Hotel, where each had to drink a glass of whisky at the bar, thence helter-skelter up the street to the Alberta, where a snort of dry gin was the next condition laid down; from there they flew around the corner to the Dominion to put away a schooner of beer, speeding on and on from bar to bar the whole length of Ninth Avenue, drinking horn after horn, no two alike. A corps of umpires followed the runners the whole length of the course. Rounding into Eighth Avenue, it was noticed that only three were left in the race, and these just barely managed to make the Queen's Hotel. Only one emerged ten minutes later to finish the race. He had just one block to go, and it was indeed fortunate for him that Eighth Avenue is a narrow thoroughfare, for he came along bumping against the buildings on either side and stotting from one side of the street to the other. This was the only thing that kept him on his feet. He was the Macleod entry and had been training for just such an event as this for years.[1]

Bob's account of the smelly cheese

It was Bob Edwards reporting and there is no evidence that he had taken an oath to "tell the truth, the whole truth and nothing but the truth." But, for what it was worth, this is the way he left the story for posterity:

Our worthy grocer, John Emerson, recently got a large consignment of cheese from the East. The cheeses that Mr. Emerson usually handles are the very best in the market but this happened to be rotten stuff with an awful smell. Of course he could not risk his enviable reputation as a merchant by trying to sell it and he began to think of how best to get rid of it. It would look bad to have it carted off to the nuisance ground and, what with one thing and another, the poor man was in quite a quandary.

A few days later, in came a travelling man. To him, Mr. Emerson unburdened his woes.

"Leave it to me," said the traveller.

Now, what do you suppose the travelling man did? He went down to Graham and Buscombe's undertaking parlour and bought the cheapest coffin they had. He had it brought around on a dray to the alley behind the store and filled it with the ill-smelling cheese. Then he drove the coffin down to the depot and had it conveyed into the baggage room, the 'remains' then being addressed to Simmens, the Liberal candidate at Lethbridge.

The baggage man approached with a countenance of becoming gravity. He at once began to sniff the air and cough. Taking out his handkerchief, he held it to his nose with pretence of blowing it, he being of a sympathetic nature and careful not to hurt the feelings of the bereaved.

"Is he a friend of yours and are you in charge of the body?" he asked.

"Yes," replied the travelling man. "He died out in the country a week ago and I wish to ship the remains south, COD."

"Well," said the kind-hearted baggage-man, coughing slightly, "there's one comfort: he's certainly in no trance."

When asked about the final outcome, Bob Edwards, according to his friends, said the liberals were accustomed to handling smelly situations but this one had cast an unpleasant odour over the party that lasted for many years in Alberta.[2]

A most extraordinary occurrence

Every city wanted a real estate boom and most cities managed to have one or more. Calgary had a hum-dinger that reached its peak of intensity in 1912. It gave the impression that most adults on the streets were either salesmen or speculators.

A Calgary man who was buying and selling was asked what he would take for a certain 7th Avenue lot he was known to have purchased a couple of days earlier, replied: "I don't own that property now. It's had three owners since I sold it and I don't know who has it now." It was the spirit of the boom.

As might have been expected, the mad scene of citizens gambling everything they had on the expectation of becoming real estate million-aires was sure to invite Bob Edwards and his satirical pen to action. One of the resulting sketches was described by Robert Gard as something "worthy of Aristophenes."[3]

This particular sketch, set in the surgery of a Calgary hospital in 1912, appeared in the *Eye Opener* of March 23, 1912. It was printed without a title although it may be permissible to use four words from the text, "A most extraordinary occurrence," as a title. The sketch in total follows:

A most extraordinary occurrence took place in one of Calgary's hospitals last Tuesday. It appears that a well-known man about town who had been suffering from decayed teeth, decided to have his upper row removed by a dentist and a plate substituted. Arrangements were made accordingly for an operation under chloroform, and in due course the dentist, a couple of doctors and the man with the bum teeth met in the operating [room] of the hospital. A French Canadian sister who could not talk English, though she understood it when spoken, was also present.

The victim was tastefully attired in a long nightie and sat jauntily on the edge of the operating table swinging his legs and watching the prepara-tions. The dentist produced a little case of steel instruments and created a pleasant diversion by pretending to extract a tooth from the sister's head. Finally one of the doctors said: "All set?" And being assured that every-thing was ready, added: "Well, old cockalorum, throw away that cigarette and stretch yourself out on the slab. That's right! By gum, you look just like a fellow I saw the other day laid out in the morgue. By the way, how's your heart?"

"Oh, cut that out, Doc! My heart's all right. Clap on the chloroform and get busy."

"Well, in any case, Dr. Slaughter will watch your heart while I do the chloroform act. Now let me get this dingus over your nose. Inhale gently and – Oh, I say Slaughter, did you ever sell those Elbow Park lots of yours?"

"No, McMurder, I have 'em yet. Scrunchem here has been trying to get them on an even trade for some lots on the corner of Seventh Avenue and fourteenth Street West, but I dunno, I dunno, that's pretty far out."

"Well," said Scrunchem, tartly, "I refused an offer of $20 000 for that Seventh Avenue stuff. If those Elbow Park lots were only a little nearer to the street car terminus they might be worth what you think they are, but they are away to hellan–"

"Say, Scrunchem, I'll tell you what I'll do with you. I'll bet you $50 my Elbow Park lots are not over two blocks from where the street car turns. I've a blueprint in my overcoat pocket down in the waiting room and I can show you in two minutes."

"All right. You're on. Fifty goes. Come on down stairs right now and show me. I'm from Missouri."

"And off went Dr. Slaughter and Dr. Scrunchem to settle their bet."

"Le Malade, il dort bien," said the sister, bending over the patient on the table.

"Wot's that?" said Slaughter. "Between you and me sister, I believe McMurder will lose that bet. I know where those lots are and they must be at least fifteen blocks from where the car turns. I don't see why Scrunchem doesn't tackle some of that south-east of the town. I could let him have a nice block not much over nine miles from the post off–"

"Mais, le malade!" cried the sister. "Pourguod ne faites-vous pas l'operation!"

"L'operation?" said the doctor, musingly. "I suppose she means the operation. By George, I came near forgetting this stiff on the table. I wonder if I have given him an overdose of chloroform? Lemme have a look?"

Dr. Slaughter put his ear down against the patient's heart and gave a relieved laugh.

"Well, sister, those other fellows will probably take some time going over that blueprint, so I'll just operate myself. Let's see. He's here to get his teeth taken out, and I'll just while away the time removing his appendix. McMurder and I can tell him afterwards that on examining his mouth we discovered that he had appendicitis and that an operation was absolutely necessary to save his life. That's $250 and will help some on a second payment."

Fumbling in his vest pocket, Dr. Slaughter produced a lancet and having duly ascertained the sharpness by plucking a hair off his head and carefully bisecting it, proceeded to prod around the victim's stomach to locate the appendix.

"Attendez, monsieur, attendez!" cried the sister in alarm. "C'est pour avoir ses dents arrachees que le malade est ici!"

"Oh, that's all right, sister. If he shows signs of coming to, just pour another bucket of chloroform over him."

"With that, Slaughter gave a magical flourish of his lancet and plunged it into the stomach of the unconscious victim."

"Now I come to think of it,' said Dr. Slaughter, thoughtfully, probing around with his forefinger in search of the appendix, 'McMurder did pick up some Elbow Park lots closer in quite recently. McMurder's pretty foxy. I'll bet these are the lots he meant when he went that fifty. I wonder what's become of this blighter's appendix? Oh, hullo, here you are you two! Well, who won?"

"McMurder brought home the bacon,' said Scrunchem. "I thought he meant those lots out near the bridge. I didn't know he had any closer in."

"That's all right," said McMurder, "but those close-in lots only go for cash. No trade or no 3, 6 and 9 stunts go with that stuff. It's gilt edged. Say, Slaughter, what on earth are you doing cutting up our patient like that for?"

"Oh, ha ha. I thought I'd take out his appendix as a slight token of my esteem. I need $250 anyway, to meet the second payment on my Altadore lots."

"But Slaughter, my dear fellow," cried McMurder, laughing heartily, "you've cut him open on the wrong side. It's the right side always, not the left."

"By jove, so it is!" said Slaughter, with a broad grin. "Do you know, I got to thinking about those Elbow Park lots and was not paying much attention. Oh well, let's sew him up and get on with the teeth."

"How long has he been under the chloroform?" said Scrunchem, taking up a pair of forceps and opening and shutting them with a series of ghastly clicks.

"About an hour, I fancy," said Slaughter, who was busy stitching up the gash in the unfortunate man's stomach.

"Well, I guess we better give him some more dope. I'll tell you what I'll do with you McMurder. I think I've got a buyer for my Seventh Avenue stuff and if he comes through I'll take a couple of those lots, though you're asking more than they are worth."

More than they are worth? Great Scott, man, you'll be able to double your money in six weeks. You will, for a fact. Say Slaughter, hurry up with those stitches. I want to take Scrunchem out and show him the lots, so that he can satisfy himself. Scrunchem, couldn't you be yanking out his teeth in the meantime?"

"Why sure," said Scrunchem, obligingly. "Just watch my smoke!"

Prying open the victim's mouth, Scrunchem inserted the forceps and jerked the teeth out with such astonishing rapidity that he kept one in the air all the time.

"Bet you a ten-spot, Slaughter, I'll have the teeth all out before you're done stitching."

"You're on," said Slaughter, without looking up.

Then ensued a most exciting race, Scrunchem keeping the air filled with flying teeth, while Slaughter stitched away for dear life. The gentle nurse stood by in horror, wringing her hands and crying: "Mon dieu! Mon Dieu!"

Finally, Scrunchem won by a tooth and Slaughter paid over his ten.

"Well, that settles that," remarked McMurder, putting on his coat and glancing casually at the patient on the table. "I guess you'll be able to set 'em up out of that ten, Scrunchem. We pass the Albion on our way to Elbow Park."

"Sure thing," said Scrunchem.

Half an hour later the patient awoke in a bed in a ward, feeling terribly rocky. The sister was sitting beside him with a rather anxious look on her face.

"Et comment vouz portez vous, Monsieur?"

"Pretty tough, sister. Pretty tough."

"Et votre bouche, sa fait mal?"

"I don't understand you, sister, but I've an awful pain in my stomach."

"Oh, cela se passera," said the sister, with a faint smile.

"Say sister, I feel a bit weak and would like a drop of whisky – not for boozological motives – strictly medicinal, strictly medicinal."

"Bien! Je comprends."

And away hurried the sister, returning in a few minutes with a freshly opened bottle of Seagram and a small glass. Pouring out a thimbleful, she gave it to the patient.

"Ah, that's the stuff!" said he, sinking back among the pillows. "Now, sister, I'm alright. Just you leave the bottle on that table, and when I need a small decoction, I can help myself."

The sister hesitated.

"Oh, that's all right sister. I only want it for medicinal purposes. You needn't be afraid."

"Eh, bien," cautioned the sister, "n'en prenez pas trop."

"Call again," said the patient, cheerfully, as the sister disappeared. The moment the door closed, Mr. Patient lost no time in pouring himself out a stiff hooker. Then he smacked his lips in deep satisfaction.

An hour or two later, one of the lay nurses, dressed in white, with a jaunty little cap perched on her curls, who happened to be walking briskly down the corridor, was not a little surprised to hear somebody carolling a beautiful ditty about a lady who wore rings on her fingers and bells on her toes. Pausing to locate the ward whence the warbling came, she gently opened the door of our patient's room and looked in. There he was, sitting up in bed with a glass in his hand, singing away for all he was worth. Catching sight of the nurse, he suddenly stopped and said: "You'll 'scushe me, nurse, but I was just trying out my mouth. I've no teeth – fact no teeth. I'm in ter'ble predic'ment, ter'ble predic'ment. Dentis' mushavbeen drunk, tried to pull teeth out of my stomach. I've no teeth there – never had any teeth there. Well, nurse, how are you coming anyhow? Purry lucky? Here's looking at you. Shay, nurse, would you like to hear the story of my life? Shay, you couldn't rushle me 'nother bottle, could you?"

"No," said the pretty nurse, disappearing into space.

"Well, I think I'll have a schnooze. A schnooze will do me good. Nothing like a good schnooze."[4]

The tribulations of Peter McGonigle

Peter McGonigle was one of the best known names in the West for many years, thanks to Bob Edwards. People in all walks of life talked about Peter, laughed at his misadventures, argued about his morals and speculated on the allegation that Peter, like Santa Claus, didn't really exist in the flesh.

His name appeared in the *Eye Opener* on August 22, 1903, when the Edwards paper was being published in High River. McGonigle was being introduced as the editor of the *Midnapore Gazette*, published at Midnapore, a few miles south of Calgary.

To remove any doubt about Peter's antecedents, Bob Edwards informed his readers that "P. J. McGonigle's father died peacefully in his bed. He had been suffering from tumours in his stomach, the complaint having been aggravated by his inordinate love of Burke's beer.... The old gentleman passed away full of years and tumours in '87, leaving a large family, of which Peter J. is the eldest, to mourn his loss. His further family history may be found in Burke's Beerage. It was probably the grandfather you were thinking of; he was hanged at Fort Walsh in '85."[5]

It was a time when editors had trouble making enough money to pay for their groceries and Peter felt compelled to diversify his sources of income, resorting at times to bootlegging and stealing horses or whisky or other essentials. He gained early notoriety when, with his usual thirst and no money, he visited a Calgary bar and whisked a full bottle of booze from a shelf and wrapped it deftly in a copy of the *Calgary Herald*. But bartender Fred Adams was watching and as Peter was striding toward the door, Adams ordered him to surrender his ill-gotten prize. Peter denied having the bottle. "But," roared Adams, "I see it right now rolled in the newspaper," whereupon Peter replied sternly: "My friend, you can't believe all you see in the newspapers."[6]

Being a man of many misfortunes, Peter had learned to live with them, as his unhappy adventure with an attractive young widow who sang in the church choir demonstrated. As the story appeared in the *Eye Opener*:

> P. J. McGonigle, the Midnapore journalist, is the most unfortunate of men. It appears that during the despondent stage following hard upon his last drunk, Mr. McGonigle got religion and joined the church. Having a voice far louder and more raucous than any of Mr. Brodeur's St. Lawrence foghorns, they put him into the choir and he distinguished himself the very first Sunday by nearly shattering the Rock of Ages into a thousand fragments. The trustees asked him to draw it mild, but since he has now been fired out of the church altogether, this makes no material difference.
>
> There happened to be a rather pretty widow who sang contralto and Peter warmed up to her in great shape. They sang out of the same hymn book and all that sort of thing. The other fellows naturally grew a bit jealous, though they did not seriously think that an ornery-looking slob like McGonigle would have much chance with the merry widow. However, the hot running made by the celebrated editor made them not a little uneasy.
>
> Now, it must be explained that on Mondays, Tuesdays and Wednesdays, when he didn't have to write stuff for the *Gazette*, McGonigle turned an honest penny by selling sewing machines. He decided one evening that to try and sell a machine to the widow would be an excellent excuse for calling. So, between eight and nine o'clock, accompanied by his faithful dog, he knocked at the front door of the lady's residence and, on being admitted, ordered the little dog to lie down on the porch outside and wait for him.
>
> While he was inside doing the polite, the dog sprang down from the porch to run after a passing rig and, during the five minutes that the dog was absent, Mr. McGonigle rose to say goodbye. He meandered down to the hotel to get a drink before the bar closed, then went home to bed, wondering lazily what had become of the dog.
>
> It seems that the dog, after chasing the rig for quite a distance, returned to the porch of the widow's cottage and lay down to wait for his master. He

was a very faithful animal and, between five and six o'clock the next morning, some Midnapore people who had to get up early to do their chores espied McGonigle's dog lying asleep at the widow's front door and drew their own conclusions.

Before 10 o'clock, it was the scandal of the town. In vain did McGonigle try to explain. In vain did the poor widow try to make the women-folk believe in her innocence. The minister called at the *Gazette* office and cancelled the editor's membership in his church. McGonigle threatened to write the whole lot of them up but inadvertently got drunk instead. In point of fact, there was no issue last week and it is not likely there will be another for a month as this drunk looks as if it will be a prolonged one.[7]

The Peter McGonigle banquet

It was late in 1906 and Peter McGonigle was in jail, paying for the crime of stealing a horse from the Bar U Ranch. But it wouldn't be for much longer because his term was almost up and his many fans among *Eye Opener* readers longed for his return to the paper's columns. Bob Edwards missed the great newsmaker too; he found writing about Peter's nefarious adventures to be much more enjoyable than reporting dull banquets and political meetings.

There had been a rash of monotonous banquets in which Bob recognized ostentation and for which he had neither time nor patience. He was not one to hide his disapprovals and he had an idea: he would borrow sponsorship from the Board of Trade and conduct and report a fictional banquet, a grand one honouring his superfictional hero, Peter McGonigle, on the occasion of his release from the Provincial Jail.[8]

As the *Eye Opener* reported the event – surely the highlight of the Calgary social season – even the menu had a rare distinctiveness and included "Herald and Albertan roasts, Commissioner style calf's head without brains, Muttonhead cutlets a la city council and boiled owl of aldermanic variety."

Invitations were said to have been sent to citizens of distinction everywhere in Canada. Naturally, not all could attend but many of those who could not be present wrote letters of regret. Mayor Emmerson occupied the Chair and read many of the letters, including those from Lord

Strathcona, Earl Grey, Premier Rutherford, Charlie Wagner, Joseph Seagram, Josh Calloway, W. Callahan, Col. G. C. Porter, W. F. Maclean, Joseph Fahy, Reverend John McDougall, Con Leary and others.

Joseph Seagram wrote:

> Dear Mr. Mayor: Though unable to be with you in the flesh, my spirit is no doubt with you in sufficient quantities. Wishing Mr. McGonigle all luck in his next venture.
> Yours truly,
> Joseph Seagram

There was special interest in the letter from Lord Strathcona:

> John Emerson, Esq., Mayor, Calgary –
> Dear Jack: You don't mind me calling you Jack, do you? I regret exceedingly that I shall be unable to attend the McGonigle banquet at Calgary, but believe me, my sympathies go out to your honoured guest. The name of Peter McGonigle will ever stand high in the roll of eminent confiscators. Once, long ago, I myself came near achieving distinction in that direction when I performed some dexterous financing with the Bank of Montreal's funds. In consequence, however, of CPR stocks going up instead of down, I wound up in the House of Lords instead of Stoney Mountain. Believe me, dear Jack,
> Yours truly,
> Strathcona

In due course, Mr. McGonigle rose to thank all present for their good wishes, saying that he was willing to let the dead past bury its dead. The horse in question had died shortly after he was parted from it. As a matter of fact, McGonigle said, he had been working for a dead horse for a number of years. And had it not been for the ignorance of his lawyer, he might have been acquitted, for the horse he stole was not a horse at all, but a mare. This point was entirely overlooked at the trial. It was a horse on him anyway. The speaker paid a high tribute to the hospitality of his Edmonton host, though he lamented that, in spite of the numbers of bars on his premises, there was nothing of an enlivening nature to drink.

The evening passed. The story appeared in the next issue of the *Eye Opener* and Calgarians and others laughed as they had done when reading the Bob Edwards paper many times before. But the story did not end there, not by any means. To anyone who did not know the story was fiction, it appeared like world news and the editor of the *Toronto Evening News* who happened to be the correspondent for a big daily paper published in London, cabled the story to the English paper. In England, where Lord Strathcona was living at the time, everybody knew something of the Earl and the London editor gave the story the prominence he believed it deserved. And so, Strathcona, when eating his breakfast toast and marmalade and tea at his English residence, caught sight of the story in his morning paper and, naturally, he was as shocked as he was surprised. He called the London editor for an explanation and received none. He then cabled the Mayor of Calgary and his nephew, Senator James Lougheed in Calgary, instructing the latter to lay charges against Edwards, McGonigle and the *Eye Opener*. Only with great difficulty was the Senator, who understood the situation, able to explain that Edwards was a humorist, that the banquet did not actually take place and McGonigle was nothing more than Bob Edwards' "straw man." The best thing for the Earl, the Senator advised, was to forget the whole story, just as Canadians would do.

Honest Bob's 1917 report on himself

Been broke − 300 times
Had money − 65 times
Praised by the public − 6 times
Asked to have a drink − 8 times
Refused a drink − 0 times
Missed weekly prayer meeting − 52 times
Been roasted − 524 times
Washed the office towel − 3 times
Missed meals − 0 times
Taken for a preacher − 4 times
Taken for a capitalist − 0 times
Found money − 0 times
Taken a bath − 6 times
Paid conscience money − 0 times
Got whipped − 10 times
Whipped the other fellow − 0 times
Cash on hand at beginning of year − $1.45
Cash on hand at end of year − 67 cents

More smelly cheese from the *Eye Opener*

"Ma sent me to pay a bill at the grocer's last Saturday. The boss behind
the counter made me a present of something wrapped in a piece of paper,
which he told me was a piece of Limburger cheese. When I got outside
the door I opened the paper. When I smelt what was inside, I felt tired.
I took it home and put it in the coal shed. In the morning I went to it again
– it was still there – nobody had taken it. I wondered what I could do with
it. Father and mother were getting ready to go to church. I put a piece in
the back pocket of father's pants and another piece in the lining of
mother's muff. I walked behind them when we started for church. It was
beginning to get warm. When we got in church, father looked anxious;
mother looked as if something had happened. After the first hymn,
mother told father not to sing again but to keep his mouth shut and
breathe through his nose.

"After the prayer, perspiration stood on father's face and the people in
the next pew to ours got up and went out. After the next hymn, father
whispered to mother he thought she had better go out and air herself.
After the second lesson some of the church wardens came around to see
if there were any stray dead rats in the church. Some people near our pew
now got up and went out, putting their handkerchiefs to their noses as
they went.

"The parson said they had better close the service and hold a meeting
outside to discuss the sanitary condition of the church. Father told mother
they had better go home one at a time. Mother told father to go the nearest
way home and disinfect himself before she got there. When they got home
they both went into the front room, but they did not speak for some time.
Mother spoke first and told father to put the cat out of the room, she
thought it was sick; it was sick before we could get it out. Mother turned
around and noticed that the canary was dead. Mother told father not to sit
near the fire, it made it worse. Father told mother to go and smother herself.
Mother told father she thought she was smothered already. Just then our
servant came in and asked if she would open the windows as the room was
very close. Father went upstairs and changed his clothes and had a hot
bath. Mother took father's clothes and offered them to a tramp who said:
'Thanks, kind lady, but they are a bit too high for me.' Mother threw them
over the back fence into the canal. Mother was summoned afterwards for
poisoning the fish. Mother went to bed. Father asked her if she had
fumigated. Just then someone sent father a note.

"Father came in to wish me good-night at 10 o'clock in the evening with the note in one hand and a razor-strop in the other. I got under the bed. The people next door thought we were beating carpets for our house. I gave my sister the rest of the limburger cheese. It was a pity to waste it."[9]

Bob Edwards' war against snobbery and affectation

Bob Edwards, like his fellow Scot, Robert Burns, hated class distinction and snobbery. Throughout his journalistic life, he used the *Eye Opener* to wage war against the pretension and sham so obvious in the society columns and notes carried by most prominent papers of the time.

The Edwards technique was to destroy those symbols of snobbishness by ridicule. The *Eye Opener*'s society column, intended solely to make people laugh at the silliness of all or nearly all the news items appearing in the space, was started in 1904, while the *Eye Opener* was still being published with the High River dateline.

The subtle Edwards plan, employing fictitious names and ridiculous situations, captured public imaginations and the *Eye Opener* society column became popular beyond anybody's wildest dreams. The laughter generated was the undoing of at least some of the conventional columns that had previously enjoyed wide readership.

Eye Opener "Society notes," presented over 20 years, numbered in the thousands; here are a few drawn at random:

Simon Cee, age 50 years and 13 days, died this week. Deceased was an ill-tempered man with an eye for the boodle. He came here in the night with another man's wife and joined the church at first chance. He owes us several dollars for papers, large bills to the grocers and butchers and you could hear him pray for six blocks…. He was buried in an asbestos lined coffin and his many friends threw palm-leaf fans in his grave, as he may need them. His tombstone will be a resting place for owls. [*Eye Opener Summer Annual*]

Miss Annabell De Petticoat gave a delightful recital at the Palliser Hotel one evening last week. Her interpretation of Beethoven's Moonshine Sonata was scholarly and remarkable for its technique. The charming artist remained perfectly sober until after the recital. She got excellent notices next day. [May 13, 1922]

Mrs. Alex Muggsy, one of our charming West End chatelaines, has notified her friends that her usual Friday musicale is called off for this week. Her husband, Old Man Muggsy, has been entertaining his own friends with a boozical for a change and is in an ugly mood. [February 21, 1920]

Mrs. P Buzzard-Chalomondeley, of 14th Avenue, astonished her friends last week by giving birth to quadruplets. The attending physicians said it reminded him of shelling peas. Mother and offspring well. [October 5, 1912]

Mrs. James McToddy of Mount Royal will not receive on Friday. She was run over by a truck on Thursday. [February 21, 1920]

John Moran of Sunnyside, who was killed last Wednesday by a Ford car, was a good fellow and deserved a more dignified death. There will be a sale of empty bottles at the Moran residence on Saturday afternoon at 2 o'clock to defray the funeral expenses. [September 1, 1917]

Mr. and Mrs. W. S. Stott, 11th Avenue West, had the mumps last week. A swell time was had. Mr. Stott will not be able to deliver his address at the Rotary Convention, much to the satisfaction of those who have heard him speak. [April 10, 1920]

Mr. and Mrs. Harry Binkley have returned from their trip to England where they went on their honeymoon. Mr. Binkley looks as though he had come through a threshing machine but reports a good time. He deplores the quality of the beer on the other side. The King begged to be remembered to the Canadian Rotarians and expressed best wishes for the convention at Calgary. During his stay in London, Mr. Binkley attended a function at court, being driven there in a patrol wagon. [Date lost]

A certain newspaperman got married

By 1917, Bob Edwards would have ranked with the best-known personalities in Canada. People who had never seen him face to face knew him as the founder and editor of the *Calgary Eye Opener*, a reformer, a humorist, an eccentric, a friend of the downtrodden and an alcoholic. He was also a bachelor and most people were saying: "He'll never marry." But the prognosticators should have known better than to speculate about this unpredictable fellow and in the *Eye Opener* of June 30, 1917, readers were attracted to his own report of his marriage to Kate Penman. But no names were mentioned, except that of Reverend Dr. Kerby who performed the union.

A certain newspaper man of Calgary got married the other day. He is pretty well known, especially to the old timers, and much sympathy has been expressed for the bride. On the eventful morning, he arose at seven o'clock, having spent a somewhat restless night, and donned a black suit which was laid out for him. After receiving the ministrations of his spirituous adviser, the condemned man partook of a hearty breakfast which consisted of ham and eggs, cookies and coffee, after which he smoked a cigar with apparent relish. To the last he stoutly maintained his innocence. At the appointed hour, the Reverend Dr. Kerby adjusted the noose and the distinguished criminal was launched into matrimony. The happy couple left by the afternoon train for Hooch where they will spend the honeymoon.[10]

Doctors McMurder and Slaughter again

"Dr. McMurder, holding a swollen face in both his hands, walked into Dr. Slaughter's office. 'Say Slaughter, can you draw a tooth?'

"'You bet I can, Mac. Got a toothache?'

"'I should say I have. This back tooth has been causing me untold agony for days. It comes on worst at night and even whisky does not seem to alleviate the pain.'

"'Have you tried brandy?'

"'Oh yes, lots of it but it doesn't do a bit of good. If you can draw teeth, I wish you'd get busy. I don't think I ever saw you draw a tooth.'

"'Why don't you go to a dentist? Doc Quirk will yank it out in a jiffy for you.'

"'No doubt. But there's no use my paying for a job like that when I can get it done by you for nothing.'

"'Oh, that's your little game, is it? Well, Mac, perhaps you recollect you buncoed me out of my commission for cutting off that man's leg last week. Believe me, I haven't forgotten that.'

"'Yes, I know. But you cut off the wrong leg and I had to take all the abuse from the man afterwards.'

"'But he paid in advance and you kept the money.'

"'Well, what of it? He is talking of bringing suit and I may have to cough it all up again. Then where will I get off at? Come on, Slaughter, be a good fellow and yank out the tooth.'

"'Not till you pay me my commission on the leg. It wasn't my fault that I lopped off the wrong one. You called me in to take off a leg and I came and took off a leg. You didn't specify which leg. Do you suppose I'm a mind reader?'

"'Great Scott, Slaughter, is there no heart in your bosom? I come here with my head swelled up so it looks like a jack-o'-lantern and you can hear above the city's traffic the dull rumbling of this blasted tooth yet, instead of getting busy, you sit there and yammer away about your commission. For God's sake, Slaughter, do something. If you haven't a forceps, I'll run down to the cellar and get a monkey wrench from the janitor.'

"'There is a new veterinary surgeon in town,' said Dr. Slaughter coldly, fishing a cigar out of his pocket and biting the end off it. 'He probably doesn't know your reputation yet and if you go to him he may be chump enough to attend to your tooth. All jackasses should go to a vet.'

"'This is the foulest insult I have ever had cast in my teeth,' cried poor McMurder, with one hand to his jaw. 'I'll get you some day. No man can insult me in such a way and live to tell the tale. What is the world coming to, anyway?'

"'I'll give you a drink out of my private bottle, Mac, but as for the tooth, business is business.'

"'I suppose,' shouted the enraged McMurder, 'you have forgotten when you came to this town. You were so poor that you had to shave yourself with a cheese knife and you used to go down to the Bow River twice a year to wash your shirt.'

"'Tut, tut!' put in Slaughter, pleasantly. 'Take this drink and stop shooting off your mouth.'

"'I won't. I saw your pitiful condition and thought I recognized excellent qualities in you. I believed that you would do some good if somebody gave you a helping hand, I neglected my own business and rustled around in your behalf until there was a trail of smoke behind me. For days together I stopped every man I met and asked him about his lungs or his liver and urged him to go to you and have them half soled.'

"'Oh, cut it out,' cried Slaughter, pouring himself out a drink.

"'That is the secret of your success, I made you. You owe everything to me. You remember that candidate for the House that you were betting against so heavily? And when he was putting up a devilish strong campaign, didn't I help you out by persuading him that he had appendicitis and was liable to drop dead during a speech? Didn't I haul him up to the hospital and cut him up and jolly him along until the election was over and he had lost his deposit, just to enable you to win your bet? Your ingratitude, Slaughter, is horrible. I wash my hands of you from this day forth.'

"'Well, well, Mac,' said Slaughter, mollified by his last drink. 'Let me have a look at the old tooth. Sit down in this chair.'

"'It's this one here,' said McMurder, with alacrity, jamming his finger half way down his throat.

"'Take your finger out – I can't see anything. Suffering snakes, but you have got an awful bunch of snags. Your mouth is full of caverns and tunnels. Why didn't you get a plumber? There's a painless blacksmith down the street.'

"'Hurry up, Slaughter, and get your forceps if you have a pair. Stay! Give me another drink.'

"Having thrown a stiff hooker under his belt, McMurder watched Slaughter like a cat. That eminent practitioner, after searching innumerable drawers, finally fished out a pair of somewhat rusty forceps and examined the prongs with professional interest.

"'I guess this will do the trick,' said Slaughter airily. 'Now then are you ready?'

"'Right you are!' said the other, leaning back and opening his mouth till there was no face in sight.

"Dr. Slaughter applied the forceps to the roots and put his knee into McMurder's chest. With a twist and a wrench he drew forth a fang that resembled the broken horn of a rhinoceros and held it triumphantly in the air. McMurder rose from the chair with tears in his eyes and grasped Slaughter by the hand.

"'Slaughter, old boy, that's worth a drink.'

"'I believe it is,' said Slaughter."[11]

Chapter 15

This is me!

Politics and conflict

15

The short-lived republic of Caledonia

It still comes as a surprise to most Canadians that there was a republic in the West – even though it was in name only. Actually, there were two, but the first one, called the Republic of Caledonia, is the subject of this sketch. The Republic of Caledonia was the brainchild of Thomas Spence who had been living at Fort Garry and growing steadily more impatient with the failure of the region to obtain some form of self-government. Coupled with demand for an elected government was a great store of ambition and egotism on Spence's side.

If the Imperial Government wouldn't grant Crown Colony status to Rupert's Land, Spence would start something on his own. The year 1867 found him living at Portage la Prairie, operating a store. The place was sufficiently isolated that a man like Spence could make his own laws and have a chance at getting away with it. Without formalities, Spence announced to the Portage people that they were now living in the new Republic of Caledonia of which he was President. His friend Findlay Ray would be Secretary.

Spence may have been naive but he was no fool and knew something about organization. He fixed and named boundaries, the United States boundary on the South, Rocky Mountains on the West, and Arctic Circle on the North and a poorly defined line between the Republic and Fort Garry on the East. He named members to his Council and, to furnish revenue for his government, he intended to collect customs duties on incoming goods.

He must have been doing something right because no serious constitutional trouble arose. Even his critics conceded that he was balancing the Republic's budget – nobody would lend Spence money and any surplus cash was spent on whisky for the president and his friends.

But, sooner or later, every autocrat makes a blunder that leads to his undoing. Spence was no exception. He should have known better than to pick a quarrel with a MacPherson. This man was a shoemaker at High Bluff and was accused of making treasonous remarks about the Republic. The president heard about it and ordered two of his cabinet ministers who were part-time constables to drive out through the snow and arrest the offender and bring him in to face trial. The constables, who were travelling with a team of horses and a jumper, found the shoemaker at home and in no mood to be arrested.

MacPherson resisted and there was a tussle in the snow. The two policemen, having fortified themselves with Republican whisky, were able to overpower MacPherson and soon they were all on their way to Portage la Prairie. But the trail passed the farm of John McLean, the first farmer on the Portage Plains, and he happened to be entering his gate when the police team drove by. McLean saw MacPherson and shouted: "Wha're they da'in' ta yu, MacPherson?"

"I'm under arrest for treason agin the Republic," came the reply, "an' I'm tae be tried this night at seven. Could ye be there in case I need yu?"

"Be there?" McLean said, "Indade I'll be there."

The evening court began as planned with President Spence sitting as judge and MacPherson as the prisoner. Cabinet members were sitting around the long table and two kerosene lamps furnished mediocre light. McLean was a few minutes late but he had several muscular friends with him. McLean paused in the doorway and, seeing Spence acting as both prosecutor and judge, challenged him in words that have come to us in a book written by a Portage La Prairie man and published in 1890: "Coom oot o' that, ye whited sepulchre: ye canna' be judge an' accuser, baith."[1]

Spence scowled in anger and commanded; "Arrest that man too. We'll try him next."

But McLean and his friends hadn't come to be arrested. One of them seized MacPherson by his coat and pulled him from the prisoner's dock, causing the table to be upset and the lamps to strike the floor. The room was plunged into darkness and a free-for-all resulted. In the end, McLean's men stood in triumph and the lamps were restored and lit. According to one story, the only person missing was the president who had apparently sought hiding. Whether that was so or not, the back of the Republic was broken and outsiders, hearing about the overthrow, were saying: "It served the President right; he should have known better than to pick a quarrel with a MacPherson and a McLean."

Nellie talked them down

Canadian males enjoyed the democratic right to vote long before it was shared with members of the other sex and offered strange reasons for perpetuating the inequity. Even the House of Commons heard that the dear ladies were "so pure and their roles in the homes were so essential that they should be prevented forever from wasting themselves by grovelling in the thin mud of politics."

But women in England and Canada were not prepared to be silenced by flattering words and were organizing to contend for their rights in the voting booth. England's women became militant and the world heard of Emmaline Pankhurst and her friends who delighted in smashing windows and harassing policemen. The Canadian struggle saw less violence but no less debate. Some of the best Canadian "tilting" matches were at Winnipeg where Nellie McClung and Manitoba's Premier, Sir Rodmond Roblin, were the leading "gladiators." Their first confrontation, as planned by the Political Equity League of which Dr. Mary Crawford was the president, was at the Provincial Legislature Building on January 27, 1914.

Four hundred impatient women and at least two inconspicuous men crowded into the galleries and onto the floor of the chamber. As president of the League, Dr. Crawford was the first speaker and, as if to make a public declaration of the support the women could expect from the Manitoba Grain Growers, the organization's secretary, Roderick McKenzie, spoke briefly.

The next speaker was Nellie McClung, the Ontario born girl who came with her family to make home on a Souris Valley homestead in 1873. Because there was no school nearby, Nellie didn't attend until she was 10 years old but six years later she was enrolled in the Manitoba Normal School, preparing for a teaching career. Now, as she addressed the premier, she was becoming well known as a campaigner for Temperance and women's rights, a prolific writer and a great orator. And her performance on this day, as judged by the press, "was a feature of the event, eloquent, logical and dramatic."[2]

Facing the premier, she said: "We are not here to ask for a reform or a gift or a favour but a right, not for mercy but for justice. Have we not the brains to think, the hands to work, the hearts to feel and lives to live? Do we not bear our part in citizenship? And, in addition, we pay the life tax on existence. No man can know as a woman does, the cost of a human life."[3]

Men have given of their best, she conceded, but men could not legislate for both men and women; they needed the help that only women could give. Then, with her gaze upon the premier, she said: "Sir Roblin, you're a great man; you and your cabinet have the power to grant or refuse our request…. It is your move."[4]

The premier replied, speaking bluntly but courteously. He congratulated Mrs. McClung on her presentation but did not hide the fact that he did not agree with her. If what he knew about the conduct of the suffragettes in England and the United States was an indication of what might happen in this country, he could not conscientiously support the principle. If the Mother of Parliaments can't find the confidence needed to extend the franchise over there, it would be foolhardy for a province like Manitoba to do it. Fearing that an extension of the franchise would be at the expense of home life, the premier said clearly that, if he were called upon to vote on the issue, he would have to be marked "opposed."

Sir Rodmond had been in office 13 years and may have believed he was politically secure as long as the men stood with him. But he was underestimating the new force. Two days after the meeting with the premier, Nellie McClung and her followers staged their famous Mock Parliament at the Walker Theatre in downtown Winnipeg and made the theatrical hit of the season. It was a clever satire depicting a day in the life of an all-female Manitoba legislature. Parliamentary rules were adopted and the debate was of a high order. Nellie McClung played the role of premier; Mrs. Francis Graham was the speaker and Dr. Mary Crawford, the minister of education. There was a suffragette minister for every portfolio and even the roles of sergeant-at-arms and the pages on the floor were filled by prominent women.

Three men in the cast appeared as a delegation, petitioning humbly for a legislative bill to extend voting rights to men in this women's society. The resolution was debated with humour and straight faces. In speaking against the resolution, Mrs. McClung, as premier, treated the question exactly as Premier Roblin had treated the request from the 400 women who visited the legislature building just two days earlier. She spoke with no trace of bitterness; she took Sir Rodmond's reply point by point and, borrowing his own logic and his own words, fashioned her argument against the resolution. Whereas Sir Rodmond had stated emphatically that "a woman's place is in the home," the Suffragette premier said that "a man's place is on the farm; he's not ready for political responsibility."

The vote was called and the resolution to extend voting rights to the men of Manitoba was soundly defeated, making it clear that men are not to be trusted with the vote. They are not yet ready for it.

Citizens comprising the big audience, predominantly women, loved every minute and howled for more. The show was repeated on the next night and then taken to various points in the rural areas. Change was in the air. Just one week after the meeting with Premier Roblin, Members of the Opposition in the Legislature introduced a motion calling for an amendment to the Manitoba Election Act that would allow Manitoba women to vote. Following a short time later was a promise from T. C. Norris, leader of the Opposition, that if and when his party was elected to power, the amendment to the Election Act would be one of the first orders of business.

Changes came quickly. The Roblin government was defeated in 1915 and, good as his word, the new premier took steps to make voting rights for women a reality. On January 27, 1916, exactly two years after the day on which Mrs. McClung and her "noble 400" faced the then premier, the new legislature gave third reading to the eagerly awaited Bill.

But, by this time, Wesley McClung was living in Edmonton where his work had taken him and his wife and family were with him. Naturally, Nellie McClung took up the challenge of voting rights for the women there and just a little later in the same year, similar legislation in Alberta and Saskatchewan gave voting rights to the women of those provinces. Nellie was elected to the legislature of Alberta in 1921 and was said to have been among the best speakers and best legislators in the house. She never quit.

In the years of farmspun stories and verses, there was one for Nellie:

Nellie was a lady, a mother and a wife,
But Nellie was a spitfire who filled strong men with fright.
She fought with words and common sense, and feats that made them frown,
They balked and bristled and sputtered with scorn,
But Nellie talked them down.

Intercity sniping

Towns and cities should strive to generate civic pride. They should encourage vigour and enterprise. Rivalry in moderation has appeared to carry some benefits but jealousies and slanders – both impediments to cooperation – have nothing to commend them except for a certain entertainment value. When Winnipeg and Brandon, or Regina and Moose Jaw, or Edmonton and Calgary took to fighting with slander, viewers knew they had a right to laugh.

Intercity squabbling is about as old as civilization and it is likely to endure about as long as sin. It has never been restricted by provincial or other boundaries and never governed by rules. As a fighting exercise, it would most nearly resemble the free-for-all.

The loudest outbursts in the new West came from Winnipeg after a treeless prairie site was chosen for Regina, the new capital of the North West Territories. The editor of the *Manitoba Free Press* held that "Whether Regina ever becomes capital or not, one thing is certain: it will never amount to anything more than a country village or town, for the simple reason that in neither its position nor it surroundings is there anything to give it the slightest commercial importance. Situated in the midst of a vast plain of inferior soil with hardly a tree to be seen as far as the eye can range, and with about enough water in the miserable little creek known as Pile of Bones to wash a sheep, it would scarcely make a respectable farm, to say nothing of being fixed upon as the site for the capital of a great province. The place has not a single natural advantage to commend it."[5]

Another Winnipeg paper took up the attack upon Regina, the *Winnipeg Times*, whose editor, without much backing for the statements, wrote: "Regina is collapsing. Pile of Bones Creek is frozen up and the solitary town well becomes erratic. The other day, at a meeting of the town commissioners, somebody said that, if a fire broke out, the town would be in grievous peril; whereupon another commissioner said that 'it would be cheaper to let the cursed place burn up than to buy water to put the fire out.'"[6]

At the same time, Regina was getting blasts of editorial buckshot from its near neighbour on its west side, Moose Jaw, inspired by jealousy. But through all this, Regina had its own newspaper, the *Leader*, and the biggest editorial "gun" of them all in the person of Nicholas Flood Davin, founder of the *Leader* and a brilliant orator and writer with Tipperary shamrock sprouting from his ears. He struck back with sarcasm and scorn, saying that all the mature and responsible editors were deserting Winnipeg and leaving the writing of editorials to the boys in the office and on the delivery routes. "Poor, Godforsaken, bankrupt Winnipeg," he was saying paternalistically. For the neighbour 40 miles to the West that he called "Loose Jaw," his treatment was no less genteel.

The bigger the city, the better the target for editorial attack. After taking a series of insults from Winnipeg editors, the editor of the *Brandon Sun* took aim at the area where the bigger city was particularly sensitive and vulnerable, namely, its deadly gumbo mud.

"The people of Winnipeg are at a loss to know what to do with Main Street," the Brandon editor wrote. "They have abandoned the notion of gravelling it, and block paving will cost more than they can stand. In its natural state it is becoming less and less endurable. The question: 'What will they do with it?' has driven all who have tackled it to distraction. The best thing they can do is to move out of the place. It was never intended as a site for a city. Let them move down to Stoney Mountain or, on promise of good behaviour, they may come to Brandon. This is the coming city of the North West, with or without them."[7]

Every town or city in the new provinces of Saskatchewan and Alberta in 1905 and '06 wanted to be a capital. Every editor was high in praise of his own community and equally high in condemnation of the qualifications of other contenders. The *Saskatoon Phoenix*, challenging Regina's right to be the new capital, declared: "What has Regina to offer? It is the coldest point known in Western Canada, lying in an unhealthy depression whose mud is proverbial. The government [of the Territories] has always disliked the capital location there. They have no buildings. Regina is not a railway divisional point; it is not in the wheat belt; it has no water facilities; it is adjacent to the sparsely settled alkali lands of Assiniboia and is not centrally situated, but at one corner of the new province, near the frontier."[8]

Edmonton was favoured by the Government of Canada by being named "provisional capital" of Alberta until a permanent capital was decided upon by the new Alberta legislature. Five points wanted the capital, Edmonton, Calgary, Red Deer, Banff and Blackfalds. Edmonton and Calgary were extremely eager and lobbied with determination. The *Lethbridge Herald* explained its town's nonentry this way: "Lethbridge is the only sane place in Alberta. All the rest are capital crazy. Everybody knows that Lethbridge could be the capital by snapping its fingers, but we don't want it. We are going to be the commercial capital, not the political capital."[9]

Red Deer wanted the capital appointment and with good reason believed it should be named: "Concerning the capital of the new Province of Alberta, the only solution which would be perfectly satisfactory to us would be that Red Deer be the capital. Of course there are a couple of other places such as Calgary and Edmonton that might not unnaturally expect to have their claims considered.... But instead of offending either, just appoint the capital at the beautiful little town of Red Deer, about half way between. It is centrally located, beautifully situated and already the foundations of a live young city have been laid."[10]

Calgary and Edmonton created most of the editorial "fireworks" during the capital campaign and, although Banff didn't have an editor to present its case and depreciate competing candidates, it did have a spokesman who brought some refreshingly original considerations to the capital question. This was the Banff message: "Although the times are peaceful and Canada desires peace, we ought to consider the possibility of war. If such an unhappy event should occur, what spot in the West could be so easily defended? A Capital on the prairies would always be exposed to the danger of easy capture while Banff could in a few weeks be turned into an impregnable fortress. By all means, Banff for the capital."

Edmonton was the winner. Calgary appeared like the main loser. And Calgary and Edmonton went right along in trading journalistic indignities.

Lincoln's jackass story

Now that Canadians have adopted a free trade arrangement with their American neighbours there should be a special effort to ensure a free exchange of humour and stories. It is one of the trade areas in which we should never quarrel.

Abraham Lincoln didn't create the story herewith to be related but he told it with glee so often that it became known as his. Moreover, Lincoln had a fine sense of honour and told a story well. And so, here is his "Jackass Story" as Americans have heard it many times and Canadians have not heard it very often:

> Once there was a King who hired him a prophet to prophet him his weather. And one day the King notioned to go fishing but the best fishing hole was nigh unto where his best girl lived. So he aimed to wear his best clothes and he called in his prophet and says: "Prophet, is it acoming on to rain?" And the prophet says: "No King, it haint acoming on to rain, not even a sizzle-sozzle."
>
> So the King, he got on his best clothes and he got his fishing tackle and he started down the road toward the fishing place and he met a farmer riding a jackass. And the farmer says, "King, if you haint aimin' to get your clothes wetted, you'd better turn back for hits acomin' on to rain, a real trash-mover and gully-washer."
>
> But the King drew himself up and he says: "Farmer, I hired me a high-wage prophet to prophet me my weather and he allows how it aint acoming on to rain, not even a frog-duster."

So the King he went afishing and it came on to rain, a real clod-mover and chunk-buster, and the King's clothes were wetted and they shrank on him, and the King's best girl, she seen him and laughed and the King was wroth and he went home and throwed out his high-wage prophet and called the farmer and says: "Farmer, I throwed out my high-wage prophet and I aim to hire you to prophet me my weather from now on."

But the farmer says: "King, I haint no prophet. All I done this evening was to look at my jackasses ears for when hits acoming onto rain, his ears lops down and the harder hits acoming onto rain, the lower his ears lops and this evening they were alayin and alopping." And the King says: "Farmer, you go home. I'll hire me the jackass." And the King did. And that's how it happened that the Jackasses have been holding down the best jobs in government at Washington and Ottawa ever since.

Political banter uncensored

Morning mist about as thick as gravy hung low in the North Saskatchewan River valley, a few miles above Rocky Mountain House, where paddlers and visitors were gathering and hoping for better visibility for the start of the Centennial Year Canoe Race, May 24, 1967. The 3283-mile race over an old fur trade route would finish at Expo '67 in Montreal. It was already promising to be a brilliant addition to the national program marking the 100th anniversary of Canadian Confederation.

Just minutes before the starting ceremonies were carried by national radio and television and the starters' guns would bark, sending the canoemen on their long voyage, the scene changed suddenly. As if by an order from Ottawa, the mist dissolved and the contestants became visible. Technicians were making last minute checks and dignitaries taking part in the starting ceremonies were asked to take their places on the platform at river's edge.

The mist having disappeared completely, the scene was made enchantingly lovely by tall spruce reaching skyward like church spires, campfire smoke twisting in curls to clear the trees, canoemen taking position on the clear mountain river and tourists, scholars, farmers, natives, young and old telling by their expressions that their pride was at the point of white heat.

As the official plan had been drawn, the first of three waves of contesting canoes would be started by the sound of an old gun to be fired by the Honourable Judy Lamarsh, federal minister in charge of the centennial year celebrations. The second wave would be started by the same gun in the hands of the lieutenant-governor of Alberta and the third of Honourable Alf Hooke, long-time minister in the Government of Alberta.

All was in readiness and the Hon. Miss Lamarsh was poised near the microphone with starting gun cocked and pointed skyward. The platform people were still not on the air – or so they thought – and they were finding it difficult to remain silent. The empty seconds seemed to invite some wisecracking. The lieutenant-governor who, perhaps, should have known better, said in a loud whisper: "When Liberal Judy Lamarsh is wielding a gun all cocked and ready, it should be enough to send all Conservatives to flight or into hiding."

Marcel Lambert who was the Conservative Member of Parliament for an Edmonton riding at the time and sitting nearby, answered: "No danger. Liberals aren't such straight shooters and Judy couldn't hit a barn door unless it was as big as a cathedral." To which the Honourable Judy was eager to make reply: "The Conservatives needn't have a worry because this old blunderbuss is pointed upwards toward Heaven and there'll sure never be a Conservative there."

At that point, the Master of Ceremonies was excitedly waving his arms to tell all those near the microphone to "shut up" because their words were being carried right across Canada.

There should have been some embarrassed dignitaries but, fortunately, the first gun was fired to send the first group of canoemen on its way, almost on time, and, strange to say, a few listeners wrote in to say how much they had enjoyed the early part of the program.

The politics of drought relief

"Apropos of the charges that relief distribution has been used for political purposes, we get this story from a former school teacher in Southeastern Saskatchewan. A teacher during the course of the lesson asked the pupil, 'Who gave the people the seed to plant?' The prompt answer was 'Jimmy Gardiner.' The question repeated to a second youngster brought forth the same answer. So the teacher tried again and the third pupil responded, 'God.' Whereupon, the boy who had replied first immediately broke in with, 'That's what you think, you little CCF-er.'"[11]

Chapter 16

Good neighbours

16

They carried Donald all the way

Donald Monroe was proud of his homestead farm in Western Saskatchewan. It had all the essentials – or almost all – good soil, attractive scenery and the best of neighbours. The thing he lacked was water but he was digging a well by hand and was down 30 feet and very much encouraged. When working alone, however, Donald made a miscalculation and fell to the bottom. He didn't lose consciousness but felt sure he had broken every bone in his body and would not emerge from the well alive.

By good fortune, his plight was discovered and, with much difficulty, he was raised and placed on a bed in his cabin. It was soon obvious he had a broken back, at least one broken leg and some unspecified fractures. He was in bad shape and terrible pain.

Neighbours hearing about the accident gathered at his place and asked the same troubling question: "What can we do for Donald?" The same comment was on every tongue: "There's no doctor this side of Coblenz, you know, and that's about 50 miles by trail – damned poor trail at that."

It was too much to expect that a doctor could be persuaded to make a 100 mile round trip by horse and buggy and probably take three days doing it. The doctor would have good reason to consider the possibility that, in taking the time for such a long trip, he might save Donald's life and lose the lives of two or three of the people depending upon him nearer Coblenz. Moreover, there was no telephone to permit consultation. The only hope, painful as it was sure to be, was to attempt to take Donald to the doctor and pray that he would be still alive at the end of a rough 50 mile ride.

"Even with the best we can do for Donald," said one of the sympathetic friends, "will mean nothing less than two days of awful suffering. He's got to be stretched out on a mattress and that calls for a wagon. He couldn't stretch out in a buggy. You have to wonder if he would survive the 50 miles of jolting he'd get from a wagon on our trails. But we have to do it that way; seems there's no other way."

"By golly, there is another way," another neighbour said with determination, "and we have to do it. We can carry him on a bed or mattress. We'll need 24 men working in teams, 12 men carrying him at a time. Can we get 24 men to set out at daylight tomorrow?"

Every man present raised his hand as a promise to start in the morning. One of the group said that, because fewer than 24 were present, he would personally reach more homesteaders to assure two full teams and another said he would get two teams of horses and wagons ready to carry bedding and food supplies for all who were travelling.

The plans were finalized quickly. One of the wives offered to sit at Donald's bedside through the night and accompany the men to Coblenz if they felt the need for a nursing volunteer.

Promptly at six o'clock the following morning, Donald's mattress was placed on a wooden frame and Donald on the mattress. The 24 men divided into two teams and the first team took position, gently lifted Donald's bedframe and strode away. The men stopped for lunch and believed they had the first 14 miles behind them. When they camped for the night, they were sure they had travelled half way and 25 difficult miles were behind.

The rest of the story was well told by a news item in the *Daily Phoenix*, Saskatoon:

> The first part of the trail was quite rough. The first day's march ended at Coleman's in [township] 33, [range] 20. Next morning the worst part of the trail was encountered, the crossing of Eagle Hill Creek, where the steep hills on both sides of the creek valley doubled the toil of the weary men.
>
> Mr. Monroe stood the trip fairly well with the help of opiates and on the second evening, shortly after eight o'clock, Coblenz was reached. Here a hard part of the trip remained, carrying the patient to the third floor of the hotel where a room had been arranged for him.
>
> Dr. Burrows, the Coblenz physician… assisted by Dr. Peterson of Saskatoon, and another doctor from Wilkie, performed the operation. A fragment of bone was removed from a broken vertebra, which relieved the pressure

on the spinal cord. The broken leg was set and the patient was then put in a plaster of paris cast and, after being under ether for two and a half hours, came out of the influence quite strongly.[1]

Cheerfully and thankfully, Donald's friends and good neighbours turned toward home. One of them, in answering a stranger's question, summed it all up: "We had to get him to Coblenz and we couldn't do it by train so we carried him."

Paint the other church too

The late Leishman McNeil liked to recall the time when his friend, Pat Burns, the self-made pioneer industrialist and millionaire – and devoted Roman Catholic – noticed that the little Catholic church at Midnapore was looking shabby and much in need of paint. That would never do, so he instructed two of his workmen to proceed to Midnapore and paint the church, "and do a good job."

Wishing to see how the painters were progressing, Burns drove out from Calgary. He liked to get out into the countryside by horse and buggy anyway. He was well pleased with the freshly painted appearance and congratulated his men.

But, on looking around, he noticed that the equally small Protestant church standing on the very next lot and a mere 100 feet away was suffering quite as much from lack of paint. The contrast with the new paint job on the Catholic church left the neighbouring church looking worse than ever. Burns gazed and whispered to his workmen: "When you're through here, go across and paint that one too and, to be sure, do just as good a job." The men did exactly as instructed and the big-hearted Pat Burns was pleased.

Neighbours helping neighbours

Some of the West's best stories were about rural people coming together to help one of their neighbours who had fallen upon serious misfortune – a fire, an attack of appendicitis at harvest time, an accident suffered in a four-horse runaway, a death in the family or something equally distressing. One typical act of neighbourhood compassion and co-operation in a Manitoba community survives as an oft-repeated legend, long after the actual names of the participants were lost.

It was in the spring when everybody was rushing with preparations for seeding. Farm machines were being reconditioned and lubricated; horses were being clipped to give them the same relief farm workers enjoyed when they abandoned their heavy woollen underwear, and seed grain was being cleaned and treated with bluestone. Everybody was in a hurry, a most awkward time for a family tragedy but troubles strike in their own good time.

A neighbour, an immigrant from the Ukraine with a wife and several small children, was rushed to the hospital with a ruptured appendix. The doctor said the fellow would be unable to do work of any kind for some weeks. Poor fellow, he was as worried about being unable to get his fields seeded as he was about his own health.

But his neighbours – most of whom didn't speak the sick man's Ukrainian language – knew that something had to be done to help him. The old party-line telephone began to tingle – two long rings for one home, one long and two short for another. And then the question: "What are we going to do about Mike's land? Can we all gather there with our ploughs, harrows and seed drills tomorrow morning and seed his farm first?"

Next morning at seven o'clock, the sick man's yard was full of four-horse teams and seeding machinery. Not one person in the entire district stayed home to do his own seeding. Quickly, the men of the community chose one of their members to be the boss for the day and then listened to him give the orders. In the hours that followed Mike's fields were ploughed, harrowed, seeded and harrowed again.

Just before noon, precisely according to plan, the farm women of the district, driving their own single horses and buggies, arrived with hot dinners that they spread out on the farmyard grass for what soon looked like a community feast. The faces of the men who had been working in the fields were covered with dust – same colour as the soil – but nobody cared. Canadians, immigrants, Protestants, Roman Catholics – all sitting together, eating ravenously, telling stories, laughing boisterously and enjoying the picnic.

Promptly, the workers returned to the fields but the expressions of concern and kindliness hadn't ended yet. At midafternoon a rented livery stable team and democrat arrived from the village. With it came the little Chinese fellow who operated the restaurant, bringing a load of sandwiches and tea for an afternoon lunch for everybody.

Nor was that all; a boy from grade six or seven came after school was dismissed for the day, anxious to get into the great neighbour act too. He carried a pail of cold drinking water and a tin cup and made sure that everybody wanting a drink got one. The lad, whether he thought of it or not, emerged as one of those who deserved to be counted among the heroes and heroines of that memorable day.

By six o'clock the neighbours, with their tired horses, their ploughs, harrows and seed drills, were on their way home, leaving behind a settler's farm unexpectedly transformed by cultivation and seeding. Mike's was the only farm for 10 miles around on which seeding had been completed. It was one more of Western Canada's comely demonstrations of brotherhood. Mike's wife cried for joy. Mike, well on his way to recovery, returned to the farm when the new crop of wheat was far enough along to allow the new rows to be counted easily.

Somebody declared that the day of the seeding bee was the community's proudest. No money changed hands – not a dollar – but the day's event generated a million dollars worth of good will, satisfaction and pride.

Samuel Larcombe's generous neighbours

When this writer was attending the International Live Stock Show at Chicago in 1925, one special pleasure was meeting Samuel Larcombe from Birtle, Manitoba, who at the age of 74 years was known as Manitoba's Grand Old Man of Agriculture and winner of the World Wheat Championship in 1917. Most Western Canadians had heard of Samuel Larcombe but not many had met this man of the soil.

When seen at Chicago, he was being pursued relentlessly by American press reporters who believed they had discovered the authentic English "John Bull." It wasn't much wonder that the reporters were following this chunky and jovial old man with muttonchop whiskers, all in the finest English tradition.

He was born in lovely old Devonshire, England, but life there was far from easy. At the age of eight years, instead of being at school, he was working on an English farm for a shilling a week. By good fortune, he made a trip to London but it left him restless, something that never left him until he was travelling to Manitoba with thoughts of free land dancing in his head. He arrived at Birtle later in 1889 and secured work on a local farm. A year later he rented a farm and then bought the land and became his own farmer.

His special interests were in plant selection and crop improvement and, being rather short in stature, he was often lost in the tall crops. It was when lost and using a flashlight that his gaze fell upon a single head of wheat that seemed to possess striking superiority. Carefully, he marked the plant and kept its seed separate. From it came the Sam Larcombe variety, Axminster.

In the years that followed, it was estimated that he won a total of not less than 3000 prizes for field crops. The climax, of course, was his winning of the world crown for wheat in 1917.

Ten years after the Chicago appearance, he was asked to identify the biggest thrills he had experienced in his life and he replied promptly as though he had rehearsed the answer: "Seeing London through the eyes of a boy who had never been far from home, winning the world championship for wheat, and seeing my friends and neighbours come to my rescue and build me a new house when we lost the first one in a fire."

The story of the house brought tears to his kindly old eyes. The fire was in 1929 and, without a proper firefighting service in the district, the dwelling was a total loss. The furniture, too, was gone. The Larcombes were destitute. But they had both rural and urban friends and, in true western spirit, they rallied to help. Lumber was delivered; cash was raised for immediate needs and, as if by a miracle, a new house appeared. And the furnishings needed for the new house appeared the same way, then new landscaping.

Friends in Winnipeg and Brandon wanted to have a part in the tribute to the great pioneer citizen. An official of the CPR presented a handsome easy chair; Lady Eaton, on behalf of the Eaton Company, contributed another comfortable chair; the Binscarth Agricultural Society donated a beautiful mantle clock; Honourable J. D. McGregor, the lieutenant-governor of Manitoba, came to Birtle to take part in the formal presentation of the new home and furnishings and Honourable R. A. Hoey, minister of education and acting premier of Manitoba, was on hand to declare the new house officially open and present Mr. Larcombe with an engraved gold key for the door.

Nothing was overlooked, it seemed, not even the renovation of the landscape, Mr. Patmore of Patmore Nurseries, Brandon, was present with a list of trees and shrubs recommended to improve the home's appearance and that would be supplied without charge for planting in the following spring.[2]

One of those in attendance at the presentation said: "The scene of the tribute to Sam Larcombe was such as is accorded few men. It was not a tribute to a Wheat King but rather a tribute to a lovable Manitoba gentleman."[3]

Good will and baled hay

Fire played all kinds of evil tricks on farm property, especially in the years when there was no organized firefighting service. Generally, it started without warning and, minutes later, its cruel work was completed or out of control. Nobody knew the grief of seeing a farm house or stable or a year's supply of feed going up in smoke as did the owner. None but those who had been through it could know the utter dejection and frustration felt by Emil and Muriel Turchyn of the Pierceland district of Northern Saskatchewan when a night fire of uncertain origin destroyed their extensive supply of stacked hay bales, without which they would be obliged to sell their 200 cattle, the source of their livelihood.

Earlier in 1975 they had worked hard to collect the needed hay. With 5000 bales – probably about 200 tons – in a long and tidy stack, they were proud of their achievement and had a nice feeling of security – until that August night when they were shocked at seeing their entire supply of hay enveloped in flames, past the point at which anything could be done to arrest the conflagration.

It was too late in the season to return to haying and hay could not be bought except at inflated prices. After considering all options dispassionately, Turchyn admitted that he would have to sell his cattle – and almost choked when he said it.

But the Turchyns had neighbours – good neighbours – and they were plotting something. They would hold a dance in the local hall but not an ordinary dance; it would be a benefit dance with all proceeds going to help the Turchyns. And, to make the dance more distinctive, the price of admission would be in terms of baled hay that could be left at the entrance or pledged for delivery later. Anybody who had no hay could pay for his admission with money to be used to buy hay.

The stock of committed hay became bigger and bigger and, with the pledges for hay to be delivered later, the Turchyn cattle were assured of winter hay reserves totalling 4500 bales. When the returns were announced, some of the local people laughed, some cried from the joy and satisfaction they felt. Everybody agreed that "the dance for hay" was the greatest event ever held in the old hall and the Turchyn cattle ate well all winter.

Chapter 17

Birds and animals

17

Kootenai Brown's grizzly

John George "Kootenai" Brown will be remembered as one of the most versatile individuals to have appeared on the western scene. He loved adventure, provided it had not been stripped of its risks and dangers. He was born in Ireland in 1839, served in the British army in India and, in 1861, sailed to Panama. Early in the next year, he was in Victoria, just in time for the Caribou gold rush.

In the years that followed, Brown was engaged in an unbelievable range of pursuits; he was a constable in a BC mining town, a hunting companion of Colonel George Custer, a pony express rider in the Western States, a dispatch rider for the US Army, a prisoner of war taken by Chief Sitting Bull, a Rocky Mountain guide, a scout in the rebellion trouble of 1885 and, finally, Superintendent of the new Waterton Lakes National Park. It made for a variety of frontier activities not likely to be surpassed. It wasn't surprising that he was at the centre of countless frontier stories although some people complained of difficulty in separating fact and fiction in Brown's stories.

One notable story of Brown's own telling is the subject of this sketch. It began when a grizzly bear cub, an orphan, was taken to Brown's cabin at the lakes. With the best of care, the bear grew rapidly and soon acted more like the proprietor than a pet. It proved to be a fast learner and the bear adopted Brown just as Brown adopted Little Casino, as the animal was known. They went everywhere in the foothills and mountains together. When almost full grown, the bear was taught to carry Brown's saddle with Brown in it. This led to more and more expeditions into the mountains, with Brown riding and Little Casino travelling at a single-foot gait.

Every morning, when Brown was ready for the trails, he would call or whistle and the bear would come bounding to the cabin door, like a well-trained dog, and the two would leave together, with Brown in the saddle.

It was a lovely relationship but possibly too good to last and one morning, when Brown called his bear, there was no response. He called again and whistled. Little Casino did not come. Brown was puzzled. Had the bear met with an accident? Had he chosen to return to his wild state? With a mingling of curiosity and anger, Brown set out on a mountain trail to see what he could learn. If he found that the bear had left deliberately, Little Casino would have to be disciplined. That could be dangerous because Brown had a terrible temper and nobody knew how the grizzly would react.

Brown walked all morning without seeing a bear but, just at the point of midday, he caught an unmistakable outline and marched directly toward it. It appeared that his grizzly had indeed run away. He called but Little Casino did not come to him and his anger mounted. He cursed as only Brown could, using words that would burn human ears. The bear stood like a marble statue and Brown, still swearing loud and long without repeating himself, jumped on the bear's back, like he had done lots of times, and cuffed the animal's head to turn it toward home, doing it all very roughly.

Away they went, making good time even though the bear was not as companionable as usual. Brown couldn't understand why he had to continue cuffing it bear on one side and then the other to keep it on the trail. Finally, the cabin came into view and to Brown's astonishment and shock – he couldn't believe his eyes – there at his cabin door waiting for his master was Brown's own bear, Little Casino. Brown lost no time in dismounting from the grizzly he had been riding and tried to drive it back toward the mountains.

Nobody could be sure but apparently Little Casino wasn't within hearing distance when Brown called him in the morning and, however improbable, Brown's friends chose to believe that it was Brown's withering language that had mesmerized the strange bear. And, for reasons that would never seem plausible without naming hypnotism, the strange grizzly did the unheard of thing and was too much fascinated by Brown's flow of angry words to think of attacking and devouring the strange creature with the nerve to ride it.

"Kootenai" Brown said it happened and nobody had the courage to dispute it.[1]

Angry elephants in British Columbia

British Columbia discovered long ago the magic mix of animal history and animal legend and then made sure that tantalizing aquatic monsters like Ogopogo residing in Okanagan Lake, Caddy of Cadboro Bay and the hairy and fearsome giant, Sasquatch, who stalks the lonely parts of the vast Interior, would survive. Then, as a topping for this melange of whimsy, the province displayed authentic animal stories with no less appeal and charm. The story of the big Thaddeus Harper cattle drive from the Caribou range to San Francisco is historical fact, just as the presence of genuine Old World camels brought in for use in freighting on rough trails of the Interior in the years of the Fraser River gold rush was factual. The same camels were later given their freedom in the BC wilds and enriched their own story by reappearing in unexpected places in intermountain country to make viewers doubt the reliability of their own eyes.

Stranger still was the story of the elephants – real and huge and angry – that bolted from their circus handlers at Cranbrook and headed for the wilds in 1926. A few people were injured; many were worried and most people were entertained although those of the Sells-Floto Circus who had to bear the responsibility were not amused.

The circus performing at Cranbrook was carrying 14 elephants and for some reason the big critters were in an ugly mood. They had tried to bolt to freedom during circus engagements at Edmonton and again at Calgary. At Cranbrook the revolt was more successful and seven of the big animals stampeded to freedom and headed for the wilderness.

Urgent messages were sent in telegrams to the company's head office in the United States: send an airplane to aid the search; send the best elephant authority in the business to direct operations.

The seven breakaway elephants vanished but, a few days later, three of them appeared in the garden of an Indian family living in the area. Marie, the woman of the home, was alone. She had never seen an elephant and wasn't sure if the animals in her yard were elephants. But she observed the animals' interest in apples that had fallen from a tree and fearlessly began throwing more apples to the visitors. The elephants were hungry and quickly forgot their anger. With Marie's help the three elephants, Cicero, Bessie and Virginia, were captured and taken back to the circus quarters. Marie was rewarded with $300.

The Cranbrook elephant stampede and hunt became international news. The *Calgary Herald,* being published about 400 kilometres away, reported daily. Elephants were the talk of the country and people in far parts were asking: "Where is Cranbrook?"

The next elephant to be captured was a female named Freda and then a young bull, Charlie-Ed, who evidently decided he had had enough rustling with a poor living in return and, when he caught sight of one of the trainers he recognized, he walked to meet him as if asking to be taken back to his circus home.

There were still two elephants to be accounted for, Tillie and Myrtle, both old females and both known to have short tempers. Tillie, however, was located and, being very hungry, yielded to an offer of good fresh food and was hobbled and brought back.[2] That left Myrtle, the recognized "man-killer," as the last to be located and recovered.

But Myrtle, when finally found, was in poor shape, hungry, fatigued and suffering from bullet wounds, presumably inflicted by somebody who shot in self protection. Myrtle was obviously sick but, being a big and very valuable elephant, the circus representatives were anxious to save her. The workers managed to administer a dose of morphine, hoping that they might load her on wheels and take her back to Cranbrook. But Myrtle was not to see Cranbrook again; she was found to be suffering from pneumonia and she died right beside the mountains where she had made her last stand.

It was a bad month for the circus proprietors who were reported to have estimated their losses at $50 000. But most people, in considering the lost revenue due to cancelled bookings and added expenses during the stay at Cranbrook, to say nothing of the inventory loss from the death of the best elephant, had expected the total to be far greater.

It was an unfortunate event but the "stampede" might have been more serious. As it was, a few people suffered broken bones and painful bruises but no lives were lost. The episode passed into history but for the people who witnessed the "stampede," 1926 was remembered as the "Year of the Elephant."

The turtle derby of Boissevain

Canadians have always loved horse races featuring every equine kind from Thoroughbreds carrying the blood of Man O' War to lowly school ponies expected to participate in at least one roadside race per week as kids drove home from school. For variety, race fans found fun in dog races, ox races, pig races and foot-races for human runners. But, surely, nobody expected to see turtle races until citizens of the town of Boissevain – north of the Turtle Mountains in Southern Manitoba – won a "tip of the western hat" and a modest "jackpot" with their National Turtle Derby, presented as an annual event.

This Boissevain classic may never be a threat to the social prestige of the Queen's Plate or the Kentucky Derby but, as members of the town's business community could report, the growing popularity of the turtle race festival, as proclaimed by the big mounted model of a turtle rearing as if in triumph on one of the main street approaches, was beyond doubt.

"But how in the name of Reptilia did this oddball derby get started?" tourists have asked again and again. It began as a bit of backyard fun behind a Boissevain store in 1972. A couple of local turtle owners were moved to conduct a race on a course of a few yards, strictly for their personal amusement. Nobody was thinking of a festival or carnival but an idea was born and the resulting Canadian Turtle Derby became an event of wide-spread interest.

The number of contestant entries grew and the contest rules were improved until townsmen could point to such advances as pari-mutuel betting facilities and what has been described as the "first and only electric starting gate for turtle races in the world," a donation from the Molson Company of Canada. And, if more were needed to give the Turtle Derby a big-time character, it set up its own Hall of Fame for outstanding contestants.

One of the first turtles of distinction carried the name Zorro, a name worthy of a marathoner with the stamina for a hard race of at least 100 yards.

The best racing "stables" were probably around Boissevain but derby entries came from far beyond. Of the 447 entries in 1983, 182 of them were from Boissevain and the immediate district, but there were 42 from Winnipeg, 37 from Deloraine, 10 from Souris and a few from each of many other Manitoba districts.

Enough racing turtles were entered from places outside of Manitoba to give the derby at least a modest claim to national and international standing. Thirty-nine entries were brought from North Dakota, a few from Minnesota, 29 from Saskatchewan, 11 from Alberta, 10 from British Columbia, nine from Ontario, three from Nova Scotia and one each from Quebec, New Brunswick, Prince Edward Island, Newfoundland and the Northwest Territories.

Unless visitors to Boissevain are prepared to assume the responsibilities of an owner and exhibitor of turtles, they would be well advised to avoid the turtle promoters and salesmen who have been found to be about as persuasive as insurance salesmen and itinerant evangelists.

In any case, the lowly slowpoke of the reptile clan has gained a place in racing that brought surprise to many spectators and perchance even to himself. If he had the stylish feathers to allow it, he might now be strutting like a peacock – in slow motion.

A bird without feathers

Many western place-names and most of the very attractive ones are native Indian in origin. Punnichy, the Cree name of a village in the Touchwood Hills area of Saskatchewan, slightly more than 100 miles southeast of Saskatoon, invites more questions concerning origin than almost any other.

When the Grand Trunk Pacific Railroad was being built across the West, rail officials responsible for choosing suitable names for villages and stations were in the district in question, enquiring for names of prominent pioneer settlers. The name mentioned most often was "Punnichy," a popular person whose conspicuous characteristic was an inability to grow whiskers on his face like most other men. This uncommon condition did not go unnoticed by the local Indians but, having no better word to describe it, they called the man "Punnichy," meaning in their language "bird without feathers." The railroad officials were impressed by both the name and the reasons for it and were quick to fix upon it for the new townsite.

Bill Martin's sensational sheep dogs

When travelling to an Eastern Canadian city to display the working skills of a trio of his famous Border Collie sheep dogs, William Martin was welcomed and warned by a hotel manager who said: "You'll understand that we don't allow dogs in our bedrooms but we have a nice room for you and the dogs can stay in the Kennel-room in the basement."

Martin was indignant and didn't hide his feelings. "These dogs are my best friends," he said, "and we'll be staying together or I'll no' be stopping."

The manager asked to be excused for a minute or two and when he returned he announced that the hotel rules would be relaxed for a few days and Mr. Martin and his dogs would not have to be separated. The near-outrage was forgotten and everybody was happy.

Bill Martin, who had become a familiar part of the Southwest – like the Cypress Hills – came as a Scottish immigrant from his home community of Hawick, in Roxburghshire, in 1902, bringing nothing more than a good herder's understanding of sheep and sheepdogs. In Scotland, he had been doing an adult's job of herding from the age of 13 years and he had no difficulty in obtaining similar work in Saskatchewan and Montana.

Bill's brother, Watt, came to join him and together they resolved to embark upon ranching on their own account as soon as their combined savings would make it possible. Their start was a modest one but they saw it grow quickly until they were able to count 50 000 sheep, 700 cattle, a few Pinto horses, undetermined native antelope and the inevitable few rattlesnakes.

By 1929 the Martins had become leaders in breeding and training sheepdogs and Bill made his first importation of a young female from Scotland and, at the same time, instructed his brother, John, who remained in Scotland, to maintain a constant search for a young dog with outstanding promise and, when he found and bought it, to keep it in Scotland for its early education. The search led to a pup with a surly disposition and powerful personality and registered in the International Sheep Dog Stud Book as "Scottie, 1108."

When brought to Saskatchewan in 1929, Scottie acted like a true individualist; he had no wish to play with the other young dogs; he wanted to get to work with a minimum of nonsense and wasted time. He'd accept petting and affection from Bill Martin but nobody else.

Scottie's skill in handling sheep gained fame and so did his unsociable disposition. He was a confirmed one-man dog. His loyalty was for Bill Martin alone and Scottie wanted nobody else interrupting his private life. When Martin shaved and dressed for travel, Scottie sulked until he knew that he was going too; it wasn't Scottie's desire for travel and adventure but rather his objection to being separated from the one man in his life.

Generally, however, when Martin travelled, so did Scottie. Together they travelled to Vancouver in 1931 where Scottie won the Sheepdog Trials, symbolic of the Canadian championship. In 1934 and '35, they went to Moose Jaw for the strongest Canadian competitions and again won the highest honours.

The invitation for them to perform as a special feature at the posh Canadian Royal Winter Fair in 1936 was in itself an honour and together they thrilled the thousands of visitors at the "Top-Hat" evening events. Scottie, Meg and Flash were the star performers, working with geese as well as sheep and doing it all faultlessly. The presence of geese would not worry the Martin dogs because, back on the ranch, puppies and older dogs, feeling the need to improve their skills, had often cut out a few members of the chicken or turkey flock and worked them over for practice.

For the appearance at the Royal Winter Fair at Toronto in 1946, Martin took Byng, Toots and Johnny – son, daughter and grandson respectively of Scottie – and presented them in a new format. By the customary technique, contestants worked singly with shepherd and dog entering at an end of the field. The sheep might be up to 400 yards away and the "outrun" or "gathering" brought them down the field and through a gap made with hurdles. The next feature was the "shedding" or the removal of a single marked sheep from the band and holding it apart. Finally, the sheep were penned. But, at the big fair of 1946, Martin multiplied the problem by using no hurdles and no marking posts.

As he entered the ring with three dogs, two of them immediately took up positions as "markers" and lay motionless while the third dog manoeuvred the protesting sheep between and around the canine markers to complete a "figure-eight." The dogs then changed positions so that each had its turn to perform and 10 000 cheering fans and endless bright lights failed to distract the amazing little dogs, working silently, taking signals from their master.

When somebody asked Bill Martin how he'd get along if he had no dogs, he laughed and answered: "Who'd be so daft as to keep sheep without good dogs? It would be worse than loading hay without a fork."

Dear old Scottie was a church goer

Scottie, a black and white Collie, was the "top dog" on the MacEwan farm in Saskatchewan. He was there for a dog's full lifetime, a life of usefulness and loyalty. If there is a home in Heaven for the humans with whom he lived, there must, in the name of justice with mercy, be one for him too.

He didn't have an official title but everybody who knew him called him the "farm foreman." He didn't milk cows, gather eggs or stook crops but he was always present, watching like a supervisor. He accompanied the buggy or wagon to town, went along with the horse teams when they were ploughing or seeding, and thought he had to be present when somebody went to bring the cows home at milking time. It was presumed that he could count because he was the first to show concern when a cow was missing from the milking herd, and then he was ready to help find her.

He insisted upon accompanying when another member of the family drove to town for groceries or repairs and when his friends travelled to church on Sundays. And, if the driver of the buggy or wagon was still in town at mealtime, he and Scottie would visit Sam Wing's restaurant where Scottie knew the boss and expected to see the tin plate kept expressly for him and piled high with choice bits of food.

It was generally agreed that Scottie liked music and often tried to join in the Sunday evening singsongs at the farm. Nobody said Scottie had the best singing voice in the family and nobody cared to be a loser by arguing that he had the worst. The only time his singing or howling – call it what you like – proved embarrassing to his friends was when he was left outside the church entrance to wait until the service ended and was inclined to join in the musical numbers rendered from within.

When Scottie insisted upon entering into the songs of praise from outside the church door, cynical friends said that he had acquired some Clan MacEwan parsimony and probably preferred to participate in the service from the outside where he would not be confronted by the Presbyterian collection plate.

Another church trait he did not hesitate to express was a dislike for long sermons and he was known to make noises resembling yawns and groans that could be heard throughout the little kirk and brought smiles of agreement to drowsy adherents.

But there came a Sunday when Scottie disappeared. Instead of being there, flailing the air with his enthusiastic tail, Scottie was not in sight. Members of his family waited for him to complete whatever took him away from the church and return. They called at Wing's restaurant and made a tour of the town but Scottie was nowhere to be seen. Had he been stolen or experienced an accident or just grown impatient and gone home alone? Hoping for the latter, the MacEwans hitched their horse and hurried toward the farm.

Home, however, produced nothing but further disappointment and it was reasoned that, unless Scottie had encountered some major misfortune, he would make his way home in his own good time. But the noble fellow didn't come home. A special trip was made to town to extend the search but there was still no trace of him. The sense of sorrow mounted.

Heavy rains and awful mud prevented church attendance for several Sundays but, on the fourth Sunday after Scottie's disappearance, the family horse and buggy went over the road to church and the reward was sweet. There at the church entrance was Scottie, waiting for his friends to come out of church if they were still there after four weeks or come to church if he had missed them earlier.

The canine demonstration was something to generate tears of joy. The dog leaped in the air, barked and made dusty footprints on good Sunday clothes – and he in turn was hugged. One of the MacEwan boys proposed walking the four miles home with Scottie but there was another proposal, to ignore church rules concerning dogs and take Scottie inside and hope he would lie quietly. It was agreed that if he made even the slightest attempt to sing, one of the boys would take him out forthwith.

But Scottie seemed to get the idea. He made a few silent yawns, just like some of the humans around him, and spent most of the church hour licking the hands and ankles of the people he was so happy to be with. Scottie's behaviour sitting at the feet of his friends was so good that the minister agreed that there was no serious reason why Scottie shouldn't be counted as an adherent with a legitimate claim upon the MacEwan pew.

An angry mother-in-law helped save the bison

Only a very few members of the late 19th century generation showed the desire and the will to do something positive to stem the terrible destruction of prairie bison.

Chief Sweetgrass of the Cree was one of the first to sound the alarm and call for protection of the wild herds. There was James McKay and Charles Alloway who went from Fort Garry to capture buffalo calves for rearing in captivity and had some success. After McKay's death in 1878 his herd, then numbering 13 head, was bought at an auction by Major Sam Bedson, warden of Stoney Mountain Penitentiary, paying the $1000 he had borrowed for the purpose from the man who was to become Lord Strathcona. Bedson, 10 years later, sold 83 head to "Buffalo" Jones of Kansas City and he in turn sold to Charles Allard and his partner, Michael Pablo of the Flathead Reserve in Montana.

Then there was the Indian tribesman who was equally at home on both sides of the International Boundary but whose family lived on the Flathead Reserve, Walking Coyote. Because of his alleged interest in other women on the reserve, his wife was critical and his mother-in-law was irate. The latter found numerous ways of making his life miserable and, when he could face her no longer, he fled north and pitched his tepee beside the Bow River.

It was a happy relief but, after a year or more of it, Walking Coyote was becoming lonesome for his own people and repented his lascivious ways and decided to return. His experience told him it would be a mistake to go back empty-handed; he'd need something with which to buy forgiveness from the old lady. Red roses and chocolates and mink capes had not been tested and he could think of nothing that would make better bribery than a gift of buffalo calves, especially since they were becoming scarce. But how was he to deliver such a gift?

Understanding the ways of animals, Walking Coyote shot some buffalo cows in milk and caught the motherless calves. He knew the young things needed milk and would likely die from starvation unless they got it. Resourceful fellow that he was, he traded his dry saddle horse for a mare nursing a foal that seemed old enough to wean. He weaned the foal, broke the mare to his saddle and kept her milking at least a small amount for each of the four best calves. Then, having taught the calves to take milk from his pail, they took to following him everywhere he went – just as they would follow a cow. The problem of delivery was solved.

There is no information about family reconciliation but, evidently, the calves flourished and then multiplied. Eleven years later, when these privately-owned buffalo numbered enough to justify making sales, 10 head were sold to Allard and Pablo who also bought more from the herd of Buffalo Jones. When Allard died in 1896, there were about 300 head in the Flathead herd, the biggest in the world.

Major changes lay ahead. The reserve was about to be opened for settlement and Pablo, anticipating the loss of his range, expressed an interest in selling his herd, which was growing bigger all the time. The United States government was consulted about buying it but showed only indifference.

Norman Luxton of Banff heard about the proposal to sell and consulted the Honourable Frank Oliver and, through him, the Government of Canada. Luxton described this as the last chance for Canada to acquire a big herd of the native animals. It was 1907 and the government acted quickly and bought the entire herd, 716 animals at $245 per head.

Moving this ferociously wild herd to new home ranges in Alberta should have been frightening and was. The unruly critters had to be rounded up and herded into loading corrals at the railroad and freight cars had to be reinforced. It took the best cowboys and the best horses and still there were accidents but the last of the herd bolted from the cars at Wainwright in 1910.

The first shipments delivered in Alberta went to Elk Island Park near Edmonton and that left 631 for Wainwright where the new buffalo park offered 197 sections of grazing land. By 1934, after 16 000 head had died or been slaughtered and 7000 had been sent north to Wood Buffalo

National Park, 6000 remained at Wainwright, the world's biggest herd and, doubtless, many of them traced to the orphan calves that were gifts to a mother-in-law. Unfortunately, the Wainwright herd was liquidated soon after the beginning of World War II but, by that time, the native race was assured of survival in other parts of Canada.

The hummingbirds remembered Priddis

Stories and messages are sometimes carried on small wings. Heather MacEwan Foran, a long-time observer, feeder and friend of wild birds and living at Priddis in the Alberta foothills, had reason to agree. Thousands of birds of many colours and kinds came daily to her kitchen window, the focus of her feeding operations.

Birds of one species, seen in flocks, may give the impression of being identical. But the person who feeds them daily soon discovers pronounced individualities, like children in a classroom. Some are timid while others are noticeably aggressive.

The birdlady at Priddis told of a certain downy woodpecker that grew to expect personalized attention whenever it came to the kitchen window – and generally got it. A redbreasted nuthatch, given the name Reuben, discovered the goodness of shelled walnuts and then left no doubt about his preference for the fresh ones offered to him from a woman's hand. Nuts that were not strictly fresh were brushed away with a disdainful flourish.

But the birds that generated the biggest thrills and the most admiration and laughter were the diminutive hummingbirds, both the rufous and ruby-throated varieties. Some amateur observers admitted mistaken identity on some occasions, thinking the tiny birds they saw were big moths or butterflies. Others, in a humorous mood, postulated that the "hummers" might have originated from a cross between sparrows and mosquitoes.

Be that as it may, the beautiful, belligerent and fast hummingbirds are paragons of courage and will tackle anything in the bird world, including eagles. They get plenty of combat experience from fighting among themselves. The females will accept the presence of their pugnacious mates until the chicks are hatched, then the "women," considering the "men" a dangerous menace, attack viciously and drive them far away. The unfortunate males may return but not until the children have "flown the nest."

However much their tiny proportions produce laughter, there is nothing but amazement for their performance. Their speed in flight is unbelievable; they can hover for long spells, fly backwards, sideways, upwards as well as forward. Their wingbeats have been counted at between 50 and 60-per second or more than 3000 per minute.

The hummingbirds were relatively late in establishing themselves as steady boarders at the Priddis feeding station in 1984, but what they learned they never forgot and the astounding demonstrations of instinct, intelligence or God-given guidance the next spring, when there was much speculation about the chance of the birds reappearing, left spectators pondering.

As the woman who directs that "friendship centre" for birds related it, she thought it unlikely that her hummingbirds, after flying far south to their winter habitat in Central America and returning on what seemed a 16 000 kilometre two-way trip, would find their way to the special feeders outside her kitchen window. Consequently, she made no haste in rehanging the feeders where they had been the previous year.

But, doubts notwithstanding, it happened on a morning in May, 1985, that a rufous hummingbird was seen hovering at the kitchen window, peering through the glass, obviously pleading. The bird and the message were unmistakable and the bird bottles were quickly filled and hung in place. Unquestionably, this was one of the birds that fed at the window in the previous year and, after travelling a distance equivalent to more than one-third of the circumference of the earth, had made its way back to the window it had not forgotten and was calling for its favourite sweet drink. The clever bird continued to hover at the scene while the bottle, its private fountain of sweetness, was being prepared and hung.

The amazing display was related to Mr. P. Winter of Viking, Alberta, who had a matching story from his experience with purple martins. Anxious to attract these birds, he constructed a martin house and installed it on a high pole. In due course, two pairs of martins discovered it, moved in and raised families.

Then, after the first nesting season, the house was taken down, cleaned and placed in storage for the winter. But the martins returned earlier than expected and the house wasn't up and ready. Mr. Winter was doing some springtime chores in his yard when his attention was drawn to a martin sitting on the high pole used for the nestbox. The bird was making a noise, obviously to get Mr. Winter's ear.

The urgent message was not lost. The martin house was brought out at once and made secure on the upright support. The two birds, just back from their winter home, watched with approving interest and moved in to establish their claim the minute the man's ladder was taken away. It proved again that the Deity's other children have something to tell arrogant humans who would like to think they have all the intelligence.

Chapter 18

Sentiment

18

The farm that wasn't for sale

Once upon a time there was a farmer who lived for most of his years on the same farm in Northern Saskatchewan but was becoming bored by the unchanging surroundings. The scenes that had once impressed him, became commonplace. The soil, some of which was the best in the world, was the only soil he had really known and he was taking it for granted. Even farm operations were appearing more and more like an eternity of sameness.

He longed for change, thinking it would bring release from monotony. He was simply tired of the old farm and was writing letters to Australia and Oregon, enquiring about opportunities there. Then, when unexpectedly invited by a real estate man to list the farm for sale, he replied impulsively: "Sure, list it."

The real estate agent visited the farm to make an assessment and write a formal listing. He then wrote a sale advertisement and, before placing the moderately complementary ad with the press, took it to the seller, asking him to check it for accuracy and give it his approval. Excited by the prospect of a transaction and a relocation elsewhere, the farmer smiled broadly, cleaned his glasses and began to read:

> For sale – one complete section of Carrot River Valley black loam, half in cultivation and with an unbroken 40-year record of crops without a failure. Ample water. Older buildings in good order and commanding excellent view of the pleasant valley.
>
> Five miles from a flourishing town, three miles from a grain elevator, convenient to schools, churches, hospitals and recreational facilities. Served by active agricultural society and federal experimental farm. A haven for good living. An ideal homesite for an aging proprietor and priceless heritage for children and grandchildren, where earthquakes, cyclones and floods are

practically unknown and nature and neighbours are kindly. Guaranteed to produce anything from agriculture's catalogue, including happy memories.

The tangibles are cheap at $500 per acre; the intangibles would be cheap at a million. Apply to Happy Acres Real Estate.

The owner, who thought he wanted to sell, gazed intently at the floor, then wiped a few tears from his eyes and blurted unsteadily: "I don't want to sell that farm. That's the farm I hoped to find in Australia. I'm sorry to have made work for you Mr. Realtor, but the farm is not for sale and won't be for sale as long as I'm around."

The Lord loveth a cheerful giver

"The offertory on the Sunday the Bishop of Saskatchewan spent at Assisippi included, besides money, the following articles which will be sold for the benefit of the mission: five mink skins, one fox skin, one towel, two yards of white cotton, seven bars of soap, one cake of scented soap, one plate, two ping mugs, a pipe with a few matches and a tin match box."[1]

"The young man who by mistake put a dog tag, No. 53, in the collection plate at the Presbyterian Church on Sunday evening, can obtain the same from the treasurer, W. Murphy, who will be happy to exchange it for the 25 cent piece evidently intended."[2]

"The gas went [out] on the churches at [recent] evening services and Holy Trinity, being unable to take up the collection, mourns the loss of about $40 or $45."[3]

Dancing with Mother Nature

"Most ladies, by their own admission, are at their best late in the day. There are exceptions and anyone who desires to dance with Mother Nature should make a date for early morning, preferably the first hour after sunrise. My solitary adventure on a recent morning confirmed the theory.

"There was a church-like stillness about the woods and along the shoreline, broken only by the distant drumming of a bush partridge and a domestic argument between two magpies. At that early hour, of course, it was a community without humans. The only domestic creature encountered was a multicoloured tom-cat staggering homeward under a load of mixed adventures at the end of a night out.

"Men's noisy and smelly motors were still silent. The surface of the pond was without a ripple and there was not enough breeze to tremble the leaves of the trembling aspen. It seemed that Nature was pausing for prayer in the midst of her best hour, or perhaps holding her breath from fear of what unseemly acts mankind might elect to perpetrate next.

"The grass was heavy with dew – receiving an early morning baptism – and a spider's web suspended between two twigs of dogwood was so laden with distilled moisture that it glistened in the early sun with crystal delicacy. With its exquisite quality, it might have enhanced the Crown jewels.

"And then the silence was broken with the abruptness of a firecracker, a distant barking of coyote pups, doubtlessly fighting over a morsel of food their mother brought to the den.

"Then a ripple on the pond, a beaver returning from an all-night work-shift, swimming toward home and towing a long branch of green poplar with the best of bark for breakfast. Sensing a strange figure on the shoreline, the provident fellow made a mighty splash with its big paddle-shaped tail and dived. The poplar branch was abandoned but not for long. Having cut it and hauled it a tiring distance, Old Beaver had no intention of letting it be lost and seconds later he surfaced to recover the makings for a meal and then continued on course to his home.

"Obviously, the hour marked the end of the night shift and the beginning of the day shift in Nature's workshop. The nocturnals, like the beaver and a weasel which disappeared into the recesses of a stone pile, were coming home; the diurnals or daytime workers, like a squirrel that studied me with curiosity more than alarm, were starting out. While I watched, mesmerized, the squirrel – that most skilful acrobat of the wilds – leaped from one tree to another and dashed to the top with more speed than I could have displayed by falling out of the same tree. I concluded that the squirrel's interest in me was not so much curiosity as sympathy for the big and conceited human lout that can't swim like a fish or run like a deer or climb trees without the aid of a ladder.

"Sure enough, the hour for change of shift comes early in the outdoors and, like the Changing of the Guard in London, it is well worth seeing.

"And for sweet music, there is nothing to surpass that of the early hour when robins seek the highest perch from which to deliver their inspired morning song. One robin in particular on that recent morning of adventure seemed almost frantic in determination to outclass a meadowlark and a redwing blackbird who were doing very well too.

"It is sad but true that people who refuse to stir at an early summer hour never see or smell or hear the best of Nature's day."[4]

Illustrations

Notes

Chapter 1

1. *Edmonton Journal*, December 30, 1965.

2. *Lethbridge News*, Lethbridge, May 7, 1890.

3. Canada, *Sessional Papers,* no. 9, 23, 1877.

4. McDougall, John, *On Western Trails in the Early Nineties* (Toronto: Wm. Briggs, 1911) p. 186.

5. Morris, Hon. Alexander, *The Treaties of Canada with the Indians* (Toronto: Bedfords and Clark, 1880) p. 272.

6. A Stoney Indian legend carried in *Alberta Folklore Quarterly* [Edmonton], March, 1946.

Chapter 2

1. Garrioch, Albert C., *A Hatchet Mark In Duplicate* (Toronto: Ryerson Press Ltd., 1929).

2. Pocaterra, George, *Calgary Herald,* November 13, 1961.

3. *Melfort Journal*, September 11, 1928.

Chapter 3

1. Deane, Capt. Burton, *Mounted Police Life In Canada.* (Toronto: Cassell and Co., 1916) p. 58.

2. *Lethbridge News*, September 12, 1888.

3. *Macleod Gazette*, September 26, 1889.

Chapter 4

1. *Macleod Gazette*, December 5, 1889.

2. *Country Guide*, August, 1943.

3. *Country Guide*, Winnipeg, August, 1945.

Chapter 5

1. *Edmonton Bulletin*, December 27, 1884.

2. *Macleod Gazette*, September 6, 1888.

3. *Calgary Herald*, October 18, 1957.

4. *Calgary Eye Opener*, August 3, 1912 (an advertisement, probably written by Bob Edwards).

Chapter 6

1. *Western Producer*, Saskatoon, April 27, 1961.

2. McArthur, Peter, *The Red Cow,* dated Ekfrid, Ontario, January, 1919.

3. *Regina Leader*, March 29, 1887.

4. Trotter, Beecham, *A Horseman in the West* (Toronto: Macmillan Co., 1925) p. 236.

5. MacEwan, Grant, *Hoofprints and Hitching Posts* (Saskatoon: Modern Press, 1964) p. 141.

Chapter 7

1. *Daily Free Press*, Winnipeg, October 12, 1876.

2. *Macleod Gazette*, January 13, 1905.

3. Told to Hon. James Gardiner when speaking at the convention banquet of the Western Livestock Union on December 8, 1937.

4. Turner, John Peter, *The North West Mounted Police, 1873 - 1893, vol. 1,* (Ottawa: King's Printer, 1950) p. 646.

Chapter 8

1. McDougall, Rev. John, *Saddle, Sled and Snowshoe* (Toronto: Wm. Briggs, 1896) p. 103.

Chapter 9

1. Told at High River, May 23, 1966.

2. *Edmonton Journal*, March 9, 1948.

3. Ibid. (story by Hal Pawson), September 7, 1948.

4. Ibid, September 9, 1948.

Chapter 10

1. *Calgary Herald*, July 9, 1884.

2. *Farm and Ranch Review*, Calgary, February 5, 1918.

3. Standish, Bertha, "Wit of the World," *Farm and Ranch Review*, Calgary, May 5, 1919.

Chapter 11

1. McDougall, John, *On Western Trails in the Early Seventies* (Toronto: Wm. Briggs, 1911) p. 224.

2. Ibid. p. 190.

3. *Macleod Gazette*, July 15, 1882.

4. Fort Macleod Historical Association, *Fort Macleod*, third edition, 1970.

5. *Lethbridge News* (advertisement), March 12, 1890.

6. Joseph Whitehead died at the age of 84 years in 1893. His grandson, Joseph B. Whitehead, became the owner and publisher of the *Brandon Sun* in 1903.

7. *Macleod Gazette*, February 16, 1886.

8. Ibid. April 11, 1885.

9. Ibid. November 12, 1899.

Chapter 12

1. "Straight from the Grass Roots," *Country Guide*, Winnipeg, November, 1943 (as told by a stranger in a small Manitoba town and reported by the editor).

2. *Moose Jaw Times*, January 11, 1884.

3. Based mainly on information obtained from Sam McGee's relatives and friends at Beiseker.

4. *Calgary Herald*, April 19, 1905.

5. Based, in part, on discussions with Mr. Slaney.

6. Centennial Committee of Carstairs, *Prairie Trails: A local history*, 1967.

7. McGill, F. A., "A Homesteader on the Prairie," *Western Producer* (magazine section), Saskatoon, February 2, 1950.

8. This account of the amazing chain of events in the story of Harry Gunn's service revolver was related to this writer by telephone from the Red Deer home of William Wylde, close friend to Harry Gunn, where the two pioneers were together, June 13, 1963. Mr. Gunn died in Calgary, February 17, 1968.

Chapter 13

1. Stevens, James, *Paul Bunyan* (New York: Garden City Publishers, 1925).

2. "Straight from the Grass Roots," *Country Guide*, Winnipeg, July, 1944.

3. Gard, Robert, ed., *Alberta Folklore Quarterly* [Edmonton], vol. 1, no. 1, March, 1945.

4. Skidmore, I. N., "Straight from the Grass Roots," *Country Guide*, Winnipeg, August, 1944.

5. Ibid. December, 1944.

Chapter 14

1. *Calgary Eye Opener*, December 25, 1920.

2. *Calgary Eye Opener,* October 3, 1908.

3. Gard, Robert, "Collecting Alberta Stories," *Canadian Cattlemen*, Calgary, June, 1949.

4. *Calgary Eye Opener*, March 23, 1912.

5. Ibid. September 5, 1908.

6. Ibid. January 18, 1908.

7. Ibid. May 2, 1908.

8. Ibid. October 6, 1906.

9. Ibid. December 7, 1918.

10. Ibid. June 30, 1917.

11. Ibid. May 4, 1912.

Chapter 15

1. Hill, Robert B., *Manitoba: A History of Its Early Settlement* (Toronto: William Briggs, 1890) p. 211.

2. *Manitoba Free Press*, Winnipeg, January 28, 1914.

3. *The Grain Growers' Guide*, Winnipeg, February 4, 1914.

4. *Manitoba Free Press*, January 28, 1914.

5. Ibid. September 1, 1882.

6. *Winnipeg Times*, November 16, 1883.

7. *Brandon Sun*, April 19, 1884.

8. *Saskatoon Phoenix*, as quoted in the *Calgary Herald*, July 10, 1905.

9. *Lethbridge Herald*, January 2, 1906.

10. *The Red Deer News*, February 7, 1905.

11. *Country Guide and Nor'West Farmer*, April 1, 1938.

Chapter 16

1. *The Daily Phoenix*, Saskatoon, May 22, 1909.

2. *Nor'West Farmer*, Winnipeg, p. 42, November 5, 1929.

3. MacEwan, Grant, *The Sod Busters* (Toronto: Thomas Nelson and Sons, 1937) p. 85.

Chapter 17

1. "Kootenai Brown and his bear, Little Casino," *Lethbridge Herald*, March 13, 1933.

2. *Calgary Daily Herald*, August 16, 1926.

Chapter 18

1. *Saskatchewan Herald*, Battleford, December 17, 1887.

2. *Minnedosa Tribune*, August 21, 1885.

3. *Morning Call*, Winnipeg, October 25, 1887.

4. MacEwan, Grant, "Dancing With Mother Nature," *Calgary Herald*, October 15, 1971.